MANDELA PARK

MANDELA PARK

ALAN WHELAN

Published by Inkstand Press

MANDELA PARK

An Inkstand Press book
First published in Great Britain in 2018
Copyright © Alan Whelan 2018
All rights reserved.

INKSTAND PRESS
Lancashire, Great Britain
Cape Town, South Africa

Cover design by Deeper Blue www.wearedeeper.blue
ISBN: 978-0-9572248-6-5

For their endless optimism,
to the good people of
Mandela Park / Imizamo Yethu.

I

The bell rang from the squat tower outside the whitewashed mission church as the congregation emerged into the blistering village square. A spirited small boy pulled on the bell rope more vigorously than was strictly necessary, but it signalled the end of the last service before Christmas, so he could be forgiven for trying to add to the festive atmosphere. His mother, Anna Schippers, bare-armed, petite but well-hipped, stood in the church doorway, smiling and blinking her way back into the light. She was smiling not just because it was Christmas Eve, but also because she had been looking forward to some time off work and having her family around her. It meant everything. To her left and right were four more children – her eldest wearing the outfit bought in Clanwilliam the previous weekend; the next, wearing the eldest's dress from last year, and so on down the line. The youngest, a glassy-eyed boy with a stripe of snot on his upper lip, was too young to worry about wearing his elder sister's dungarees; his mother would deal with that problem when he raised it. That she and Jakobus were the parents of the children there could be little doubt. Their golden colouring, coppery in the late morning sun, pinched lips and ski-slope noses meant that wherever they went and however old they became they would be forever identified as one of the Schippers clan: San blood, Cederberg raised.

Anna was beginning a week's leave from her two jobs: picking on the rooibos farm and cleaning at the lakeside holiday chalets on the Clanwilliam road. Jakobus, now talking to a neighbour across the square, was due four days leave from the shoe factory so, if the weather cooled, he would dig the piece of waste land at the side of the house and plant the seed potatoes they had been saving in a sack by the front door. The holidays would also give them a rare opportunity to cook for the extended family.

The last of the congregation left the church, save for the minister's wife who was still bustling in the aisles collecting discarded hymn books and straightening the pews. Minister Johannes shook the hand of the last congregant to leave and stepped under the archway entrance. For six months, since his arrival at the mission church, Anna had looked up to him the way a child looks up to an older brother. One day she would know what he knew, people would respect her the way she respected him, the secret of life would be revealed. Talk in the village was that he had travelled widely. Educated in Upington out towards the Botswana border then posted to a parish in Calvinia, he had lived a worthwhile life, something Anna, even if it was too late for her, hoped one day her children would experience. She felt lucky that Minister

Johannes had chosen Kouberg parish. He fuelled her imagination, something she never took for granted.

The minister stood in the shade of the church doorway next to Anna and surveyed the village square busy with boisterous children kicking up the dust.

'Ah, Kouberg,' he said, as if to no one in particular, 'all of life is here.'

As the only adult within earshot, she replied, 'And how wonderful it is. God knows, a mini paradise in the mountains.'

She put her hand to her mouth and looked up to him. 'I'm so sorry, minister, for using the Lord's name –'

'No need to apologise, my child, you may use God's name when no other will do. But you are correct, we must first find paradise on earth before we can follow the path to God in heaven.'

My child. He was no older than her yet she, a mother of five, felt as though she rested in the palm of his hand, as if one wrong action would prompt the squeeze of his fingers on her heart.

'God's love can be found in the lives of those we care for,' he said.

Anna stretched out her arms across the heads of the children before her. 'They say God is love, minister. If that is so, I have much to be thankful for.'

'Love is like the blossom of life,' he said, 'the most precious gift He gave us.'

The children ran off towards the Tra Tra river, leaving Anna alone with the minister. He glanced over his shoulder into the church where his wife was still scraping furniture and stacking books. He inclined his head towards Anna and, almost imperceptibly, lowered his voice.

'Life is for living. It is not God's will that we should deny ourselves the gifts that are all around us.'

'I try not to deny my family anything,' she said.

'But would you deny yourself if it stood in the way of happiness?'

'Of course not, minister.'

'We have known each other long enough for you to call me Johannes, Anna. We both have San blood rushing through our veins. We have much in common.'

He held a meaningful stare and his eyelids flickered as if to ask a question, but she wasn't sure what it was.

'If you are loved by someone,' he said, 'it is God's will that you should return that love.'

'I do, minister... Johannes.'

'Then if I were to say how much I loved someone in the village, how should they reply?'

'You mean your wife?'

'No, another. God has filled me with love, enough to share.'

'Did you not say in the sermon that there were many types of love? Those you act on and those you keep hidden.'

He glanced back into the church once more.

'It is the love I wish to act on that I am talking about, Anna.'

By now her children had scattered to the four corners of the square. He touched her upper arm.

'Minister—' she began.

'Anna, beautiful Anna.' He swallowed hard then licked his lips and seemed to settle his breathing. 'I have a deep thirst that must be quenched and should not be denied me.'

It was her turn to look back into the church. His wife was still busy wiping down pews. Instinctively Anna scanned the square for Jakobus, who was now sitting under a tree with their youngest on his knee. The conversation with the minister felt planned, so public yet so private; intimate even. The activity in the square spun around her like a carousel, blurred and confusing, while she, the only stationary thing, absorbed the moment.

'I must see to my children,' she said, taking half a step.

His hand slid to her forearm and lightly held it.

'Please come to the chapel when all is quiet,' he said. 'I feel God's will coursing through me. Do not deny me.'

He closed his eyes. She looked at the receding hairline at his temples and the dandruff on his shoulders. When he opened his eyes they were dead, but his wet lips were smiling.

'I can be useful to a family with children who need shoes and clothes, a husband who needs more work, and a wife who dreams of a better life.'

She relaxed her arm. 'Do you seek to buy me with gifts, minister?'

'I seek your reciprocal love.'

'What is that?'

'Don't hide your feelings, Anna, act on them.'

She stepped away, just out of his reach, and raised her eyes to his chin, which stopped the carousel.

'You assume I have feelings for someone other than the father of my children. To act on a love outside marriage is a sin.'

'Do you not have feelings for me?'

'As a minister, yes.'

'Then meet me... anywhere, anytime. I know what burns inside me, Anna.'

'And I know the difference between what is right and what is wrong.'

Five kilometres away, at the summit of the Kouberg Pass, riding on a donkey cart, Anna's uncle Soli and his wife Elani held a silence that had lasted for two hours. It was only interrupted by the routinely necessary, 'Hoy! Hoy!' They were both dressed in clothes appropriate for farming: he in overalls, she in thick trousers and a blue jacket; both wore heavy boots and a straw hat. So far away were their opposite gazes that, to any interested bystander, they might have looked as though they were travelling separately. In fact their thoughts were resting on the same distant city; so distant and so strange was it that neither could reliably imagine it. But they could both picture the young woman – their niece, Candice; Anna's sister – who took a mini-bus taxi there three years earlier, and whose opened letter lay guiltily in Soli's pocket.

The couple believed the information in the letter to be terrible and wished they would never arrive at the village, that the journey would continue until the news they were bearing would dwindle somehow, or that the Clanwilliam postmaster would overtake them on the donkey track and say it had all been a terrible mistake. While they remained on the cart the world remained as it was before their journey began, before Soli had been given the letter written in Candice's schooled hand. Before they learned that she was likely missing.

After tackling the slow, steep track down into the village, Soli and Elani hoy-hoyed the donkeys into the village square then roped them to a tree outside the schoolhouse. The Schippers children heard their arrival and ran over to pet the animals and put down two buckets of water quickly scooped from the river. Elani stepped down and patted each child in turn.

'Where's your ma?' she asked.

'Talking to Minister Johannes,' said little Marie.

'I cannot go inside the church,' said Soli, jumping down. 'Not with the news I have.'

Two children turned to each other with questioning looks and then climbed onto the cart.

'Stay here, children,' said Elani, and then, with Soli gripping her arm, set off towards the bell tower where she saw Anna leave the minister at the church door and make her way towards them.

'Merry Christmas, Elani. Merry Christmas, Soli,' she said. 'You out in this heat? It must be forty today. Come home for a cool drink.'

Anna turned towards the animals. 'The mountain passes are too much for these old donkeys,' she said, 'they must be retired.'

Elani managed one word before weeping. 'Anna –'

'What is it?' said Anna, with a gasp in her voice. 'What news do you bring?'

Soli handed Anna the envelope. 'There is a letter,' he said. 'The Clanwilliam postmaster read it to me; my name is next to yours.'

Anna noticed her uncle's sombre look and, slapping her hand against her mouth, fell back against the bell tower.

'Jesus have mercy, what is it?'

Anna lifted the flap of the envelope, but quickly closed it. 'We must bring this news home, whoever sends it. Come. Gather the children.'

Everyone returned to the Schippers' place on the east side of the square, opposite the church. There was barely room for everyone in the kitchen cum parlour, so the children remained at the doorway. The adults sat at the cedar wood table that Jakobus had made for Anna as a wedding present ten years before. Anna wiped the breakfast crumbs away and held the envelope by its corner. It was addressed to Anna, Soli and Elani Schippers, c/o Kouberg Shoe Factory, Kouberg, Cederberg. She upended the envelope and a note fell out. She read silently.

Sister Anna

It ails me to know that we have not spoken for many years. I believe that I will return one blessed day and bring happiness but I am a broken woman. Cape Town gave and Cape Town took away. If I wrote all the time it would not be good news so I kept my silence. I have written this letter for the girls Mandisa and Mosa who I have taken in when their mother Grace died with TB. The father drinks too much maize beer and is not good to the girls. Mandisa is growing very pretty. Mosa is no better than before. She needs much help it is true.

I have told Mandisa must send this sealed and stamped letter if I never return to our shack. The girls will be on their own because no one knows they live here. It has been my secret. Please God you will help them. Come to the Manhaton Salon in Mandela Park and ask for my shack.

Loving sister Candice

Jakobus paced the floor and could bear it no longer.

'What does it say?' he asked. 'I am in a torture!'

'Candice has finally written to us!' Anna said.

Next morning, Anna was up and dressed before Jakobus and the children woke. She grabbed a thick scarf and walked out of the village with barely enough light to see the outlines of things, then followed the donkey track towards the north side of the mountain where she would soon catch the first rays of the sun. The sandy earth was dewy and crunchy underfoot and her steamy breath gave out in bursts. Her movement disturbed a family of duikers, the doe standing to observe Anna step past the hollow where she had made a den for the night. Soon, faint shadows of the few remaining cedar trees formed on the ground and by the time she reached the stone wall they were made solid when the whole of the sun rose above the horizon.

Anna had a special affection for the cedar tree, its rarity now making a beautiful thing precious: the pale yellowish softwood, its pencil shavings smell and the way it took a fine polish that suited the gleaming doors on the old mission church. But the wood was too popular. Minister Johannes once told the story of the early white settlers who felled the trees and sold them by the wagonload for fence posts and telegraph poles to hold up the line between Piketberg and Calvinia, stretching 300 dusty kilometres. Although harvesting had long been banned, the cedar remained scarce in the Cederberg because the trees were slow growing. Anna had seen with her own eyes how the veld fires could spark the resin into flames and reduce a rare specimen to a cinder in a single day. It pained her to know that Jakobus would never again make a piece of furniture from his beloved *widdringtonia cedarbergensis.*

Anna stepped across a clear stream and scrambled up the shallow bank, holding on to a branch for balance, then strode out across open country towards the first summit. When she reached it, almost breathless, she stopped and looked back at Kouberg. The sun lit the mountain beyond the village and just caught the top of the bell tower outside the church; it would soon reach the sagging roof of the shoe factory and the migrant workers' dormitories. The geometric lines of shivering rooibos on the nearside of the village were still in shade.

Although she had never left the valley, Anna had always allowed herself to believe that the village had everything to make a life. There was a school, a post office, a church, even tourists visited occasionally, mostly to seek out the rock paintings drawn by her San ancestors and to gawp at the locals who spoke a jarring Afrikaans that people in the nearest town had difficulty understanding. Her five children were a source of joy, and she had everything she needed, didn't she? A husband who worked three days most weeks, children who needed her, and a church that nourished her spirit.

After yesterday's conversation with Minister Johannes in the church doorway she might have to reconsider the last of these, which occasionally prompted questions she had never voiced, and could not easily answer. That she and her family should follow the Bible as interpreted by German missionaries two centuries before seemed arbitrary. What if the village had never grown around the mission, one of ten Moravian stations in the mountains? What if the missionaries had not converted her docile ancestors? Would she not be saved, as she believed she was? Would she be no better than the rural San girls who painted their faces red and waited for a suitor to hunt an eland and present it to them?

Her musing on the topic was always confused because Anna recognised that she was likely an impure mix of Khoi-Khoi, San, Bantu and, quite possibly, white missionary. Since her earliest memories, during the time when everyone was first and foremost classified by skin colour, she and her family were told they were coloured. Coloured she had been ever since.

With her ancestors still on her mind, she leapt onto a fat rock, bent, picked up a flat stone the size of her hand and put it in her pocket. Whenever she thought of the naked men on the veld she thrilled herself anew that she carried their blood, their urges, their instincts.

Walking out on the flat top of the mountain felt like stepping onto a new planet. Before the road and the mission church were built, the San used the fantastically shaped rocks hereabouts to navigate by day; stars by night. Now she did the same, using the irregular rocks as markers as she quickly put another two kilometres of scrubby grass between her and home. Although for the past year she had resisted the yearning to return to her hidden spot, now that she had set out on the mountain path she could barely wait to reach it. It was a dark place, and this was a journey she could make only by herself, a pilgrimage to the place where she dug a hole on Christmas Day ten years earlier.

The experience she had come to revisit seemed so long ago it was as though someone else had lived it for her. Jakobus allowed her to keep her secret; they never spoke of it. When she thought her younger sister was old enough to hear the truth, she confided in Candice. But she was appalled and turned against her. She later used Anna's actions as an excuse to leave Kouberg for Cape Town. Anna regretted telling her the moment it was out of her mouth. She was looking for sympathy from Candice not blame. Perhaps her intriguing letter, three years in the waiting, was a confused cry for reconciliation.

The ground rose again. As dassies scampered into crevices, she followed the rough path that led around a rocky outcrop known as Bushman's View. She left the path and took the steepest route up to an overhang that resembled a giant hand, palm uppermost. She clambered under the rock, out of the sun, then zippered her fleece and caught a breath. On hands and knees she slid down into the cave, past clammy walls showing red figures holding spears in twos and threes and groups with bows and arrows hunting indistinct animals. The last rock painting showed a naked woman following another figure. Pursuing?

She continued deeper into the darkness and then pulled herself up onto a ledge that was faintly lit by a saucer of sunlight. The ledge was hers, undiscovered even by the occasional trophy hunter who visited the cave floor, and impossible to reach from the opening above.

Anna brushed away the dassie droppings and some loose dirt that covered a small raised area of packed earth. The sight of the mound, now sunken and no bigger than a shoebox, returned her to the moment she made it. She suddenly felt complete, as if she had come to finish a task she had set herself. Like a too-tight pair of shoes, she had carried around an ache for ten years, which told her she couldn't do anything bad ever again, any more than she could salt salt. This was her penance. She was wicked and that was that, until someone absolved her of her terrible wrong. But for that she would have to confess her sin.

Sometimes life had seemed to her like a series of collisions, accidents and flukes – meeting Jakobus at his stall at the

Clanwilliam fair, the miracle of her five healthy children, the chance offer of a job at the tourist chalets – or maybe that is what's called fate. But this tiny mound before her was no accident, it hid something she had created, with the help of Jakobus, and God, and the corrupt fruitfulness of her own body.

Anna was five kilometres from the nearest living person, yet she whispered, 'The day we die, a soft breeze will wipe away our footprints in the sand. When the wind dies down, who will tell the timelessness that once we walked this way?'

She got up off her knees and, crouching under the overhang, took off her red scarf and lay it over the little mound. Then she pulled the stone from her pocket and placed it on top.

Wet-eyed, and with a new sense of release, Anna headed back down the mountain towards Kouberg. The dawn had widened into a perfect summer's day. The prospect of the visit had haunted her three years past, the last time she was here. She knew she had to face it at some point, and face it alone, but now she wondered why she had waited so long. Perhaps the letter created a new perspective and helped her look through the telescope from the opposite end for a change. She would return again, and not wait so long next time. Her resolve fuelled her brisk walk home and spurred Anna to consider Candice's letter.

Soli and Elani seemed certain that the letter meant Candice was dead, but it did not say that, just that she had not returned to the shack and her cousins, Mandisa and Mosa.

'Of course, it did not say she is perished!' Uncle Soli had insisted after she read it to him. 'How could it? She wrote it! Read it once more, Anna.'

And she did. She read it six times and read it aloud to Jakobus six times more. The words allowed for both hope and despair. Perhaps Candice had moved on to another township. Cape Town was a city, and things happened in cities that were out of anyone's control. Or maybe she met a European and moved to a white neighbourhood. Unthinkable in the old days, such things occurred in the new South Africa. Cousin Grace perished from T.B. and Candice took in the two girls, that is all she knew. So? It is what she would have done. Anna remembered them when they were no more than babies: one, big-eyed and always laughing; the other, bent and tormented. But what could Anna do? It was Christmas Day. Christmas!

Anna stopped at an overlook and leaned with the crook of her elbow wrapped around a low branch of a cedar tree. She saw the whitewashed homes of the village now blazing in the hot sun and the first signs of life in the square in front of the church. Her eyes rested on her house, distinctive under thinning thatch that was coming off in tufts. She imagined the parlour alive to the sounds of Christmas morning.

Jakobus will know what to do.

The children spent a rowdy hour playing with their Christmas presents while Anna made them breakfast of porridge and tea. Jakobus knocked his pipe against the stove and looked on, silent, waiting for Anna to reheat some soup for them both. She guessed that he was thinking about the letter from Candice; she knew most of it by heart. Later, after the children, each clutching a slice of watermelon, had left the house, she slowly rinsed dishes under cold water at the sink. Jakobus sat at the table.

As if rejoining an unfinished conversation, she said, 'But what does she mean, *I have told Mandisa must send this letter if I do never return*? Why would she never return to the girls if she cares for them? Maybe she met someone and left for a better life. Would we blame her? Or perhaps there was a grievous accident. The crime is too terrible in the city and bad news may have paid a visit to her door. Young Mosa is surely now a handful, so perhaps Candice walked out!'

'A million possibilities,' said Jakobus. 'All are conceivable.'

'Candice has not contacted us or asked for our help in three years, Jakobus. And now this, this troublesome news that leaves too many questions to ignore.'

'True. There is a mystery.'

'And you know how hard it has been to say grace when there is someone missing from the table.'

He nodded and lowered his eyes.

'If she had wanted us to be part of her life she would have returned or written or called,' said Anna. 'Many things have changed, and anyway, it was always for her to return to the Cederberg, not for another Schippers to get lost in Cape Town.'

Jakobus stuffed tobacco into his pipe then sucked on it dry to test the draw. 'Whatever the reason for the letter, it is a call for help, is it not. If writing cannot be used to ask family for help, what is it for? Just scribbled lines on a page.'

'How do we discover the end of this story?' said Anna.

'Simple. If she does not return to the Cederberg, perhaps the Cederberg may go to her.' He left a pause then added with a tilt of his head, 'But don't go on the cart, Soli says one of the donkeys is lame.'

Anna turned and threw a tea towel at him. 'The cart would take a month!'

'You might make it by next Christmas!' he said, and smiled.

'Cape Town! But it is a hazardous journey for one who has never been,' she said. 'They say it takes most of the day by bus'.

'So go early tomorrow, Boxing Day. Hennie from the garage can take you to Clanwilliam and the shared taxis will run from there. Bring me back some koeksisters.'

'But the vegetables!' said Anna.

'I can work double. Solie will help.'

'And the money?'

'We have savings,' said Jakobus. 'Enough for your fare and a cheap bed in the township.'

'The children –'

'No more, my sweetness. You find problems quicker than I can solve them.'

'We must go to the ten o'clock service,' she said with urgency. 'I will feel more comforted for the journey.' She was picturing how she would not leave her husband's side at the church. 'O, that this has been visited on me at this time of year!'

Jakobus left a moment, then said, 'I believe you were at Bushman's View this morning. Your creeping was not so silent.'

Anna instinctively drew the curtains but did not turn from the window.

'So now visit another missing flake of your flesh and blood,' he said. 'If you can face the walk to Bushman's View, you can surely travel to the city.'

'I will.'

'Settled,' said Jakobus, lighting up. 'Merry Christmas.'

'Merry Christmas to you,' she replied, 'and to our absent family.'

||

Three years before Anna received the letter, on a blowy
January afternoon in Cape Town, her sister Candice stepped
off the mini-bus from Clanwilliam. A leering taxi tout at the
bus terminal laughed at her skirt billowing around her legs.

'The wind is called the Cape Doctor, lady,' he said in
English. 'It blows all the badness from the streets and keeps
us well.'

Then, as if in contradiction, a gust of wind gritty with sand
took her new hat across the street. A boy picked it up, placed
it on his head and walked off.

She blinked fiercely and let out a small 'O'.

'Welcome to Cape Town,' said the tout. 'You need a ride?'

'I seek Mandela Park township,' she said.

'Imizamo Yethu? You must take a cockroach along the
coast road.'

The tout enjoyed Candice's questioning look.

'A shared taxi, lady.'

He pointed to a white Toyota with a piece of cardboard wedged into the rear side window in place of glass and a caption scrawled on the back that read "Keep back! I learned to drive on my Playstation".

Candice confirmed the fare then took a seat next to a kindly looking woman carrying a set of cooking pots linked together with string. The younger woman set her bulging holdall on her lap.

'You just arrive in Cape Town?' asked the woman, in English.

'Yes, mama.'

'Look after your purse, girl. These touts will take what you have. Where do you go?'

'Mandela Park,' she said.

'That is what we called it when the squatters first arrived. Now they are trying to change the name to Imizamo Yethu. First time?'

'Yes, mama.'

'It is my language: isiXhosa. You say it Im-ee-za-mo Yeh-too. It means "Our struggle". Now it will be your struggle too.'

'I hope to find success.'

'We all do when we first arrive. Then comes the struggle.'

Candice gripped her bag a little tighter and followed the tired lines across the woman's face.

'I prefer the old name,' said the woman. 'Mandela Park. Hopeful. He promised a future for all of us. My time has come and gone, but maybe you will succeed and prove me wrong.'

The taxi hit a pothole and all the passengers jostled against one another.

'Where you from, daughter?'

'The Cederberg, six hours distant.'

'They come younger and younger every day,' said the woman, almost to herself.

'I am already nineteen,' said Candice, straightening. 'Just.'

The woman leaned back and looked Candice up and down, from her country beaded necklace to her white plastic shoes. She patted Candice's thigh. Candice believed the woman to say to herself 'Fresh meat' yet not loud enough to question it.

The taxi stopped at a traffic circle at the entrance to the township and everyone got out. Candice took her bag in both hands and stepped down into a flooded gutter. A man with a dirty smile leaving a spaza shop brushed his hand across the back of her skirt, then grabbed the flesh beneath. She skipped away and uttered a weak, 'Mama.' The woman from the taxi noticed the assault and yelled at the man in a language Candice did not understand.

Before her, streams of people, all of whom looked foreign, created a constantly moving collage, unreal as a carnival. Uphill and down people moved. There were dark-skinned men with square heads and jaws like sharks who swung their arms like loose ropes. On stiff heads women balanced oversized plastic bags, others carried filled jerrycans. Everything and everyone seemed dirty. She supposed it unkind to think the shacks grimy, but compared to her sister's cottage back in Kouberg the little homes seemed unstable and unfit for habitation. Even the gaudily painted cinder block buildings seemed strange and threatening. The people too had the exhausted look of those who had tried and given up.

Unlike the city she had imagined – one of well-heeled folk making their way on carefully swept pavements – people scuffed their way along unmade roads in flip-flops or plastic sandals. Some wore ripped sneakers with no laces; too many children were barefoot. Everywhere people had the look of exerting a huge effort. Perhaps that was why the new name translated as Our Struggle.

What before arrival, sight unseen, had seemed a place of possibilities, now appeared as a scene of obstacles, many as large as the mountain on which the township crept like mould on a curtain.

A thousand details of home, now vivid in their absence, crowded her thoughts. For the first time in her short life she was alone; alone in what looked like a squatter camp, no better than the life she had left behind.

Before nightfall she had found her older cousin, Grace, the first of the Schippers to leave the Cederberg for Cape Town. She had a hacking cough and was much thinner than Candice remembered; no doubt food was harder to come by in this shack town. Candice was pleased to see that, although Grace's two-roomed cinder-block house was small, it was more substantial and appeared better cared for than the shacks that surrounded it. It had a tile roof and the exterior walls and metal bars on the windows were half-heartedly painted orange.

She stepped into the main room which was full with family she had never met. Sitting on one of the three chairs at the table was Grace's husband, Errol. The light-skinned black man had a face of patchy stubble and wore black trousers rolled-up to the calf and a dirty white vest. On the battered sofa sat Grace's two daughters: Mandisa, a big-eyed eleven-year-old, and her younger sister Mosa, an afflicted girl with a lolling head, twisted legs and arms, and a harelip that made her look as if she was permanently snarling. Both girls were quiet and watchful: Mandisa for shyness, Mosa because she could not form one intelligible word in her mouth.

Against the wall there were two low cupboards with the doors removed. Placed precariously on one was an electric two-ring stove, the cable for which descended from where the overhead light should have been. The uneven walls were covered in Christmas wrapping paper, which created a swirling effect and made the room seem more crowded than it was. A torn curtain, held back by a short length of ribbon, acted as a door into the second room, which housed a double bed and a sink. A hand mirror was nailed to the wall. This would be home for the foreseeable future.

That sweltering night they ate chicken wings with pap and greens, then the two women sat at the table and enjoyed their new friendship. Errol sat opposite Candice while Mandisa fed Mosa, who was prone on the sofa with her head propped against a pillow. Candice noticed that more food was spilling down Mosa's chest than was going into her mouth, although no one seemed to think it worthy of comment. So off-putting was it that Candice turned her chair away and tried to concentrate on the girls' parents.

After the meal Errol stepped out for a breath of air and Grace opened a fresh two-litre bottle of Coca-Cola to toast Candice's arrival.

'We are blessed to have you, junior cousin,' said Grace.

Candice said, 'It is kind for you to bring me in, I will not forget it.'

'Why did you decide to come to the city?'

'I could no longer live under the same roof as sister Anna. We have love for each other, but some things I will not forgive. Even by family.'

'What is cousin Anna guilty of?' asked Grace.

'It is not for me to say; it is for God to judge.'

Candice had said more than she had intended. She shielded her thoughts by changing the subject.

'But your family is so wonderful – the girls, Errol.' Candice smothered a smile. 'Cousin, I did not know that you married a black man.'

'I have a man, that's what is important. If not him, I would not live in Mandela Park I would be in the coloured township at the harbour with the illegal fishermen and the drugs.'

'Cousin, I am curious. Why did they change the name of the township? My teachers always told me that Mandela was a great man, so why would anyone want to replace his name?'

'The older residents still use the old name but many newer people are disappointed. Madiba promised much but too many are still waiting for their share of the new South Africa. For them the promised land is always just out of reach.'

Errol rejoined them at the table.

'Whatever they call the township, it is still a squatter camp. A new name will not bring new houses or new jobs. Life is still a struggle.'

Grace cleared her throat noisily which turned into a short coughing fit. 'Excuse me, cousin,' she said, 'I cannot seem to shake this off.' She poured more Coke and took a large swallow.

Errol said, 'She coughs through the night and keeps me awake.'

'She doesn't want to hear it, Errol,' said Grace. Then to Candice, 'We will do what we can to help you get on your feet, cousin. The city has been kind to us, has it not, Errol?'

'Some may say,' he said, seeming to refer to an earlier conversation. He hitched up his trousers and turned his attention to Candice, adding, 'Others may say we have had enough misfortune and deserve some amusement in our lives.'

Grace smiled tightly. Errol then pushed his chair away from the table and reached for the cupboard on which stood two bottles of beer.

'I have much to be thankful for,' said Grace. 'I am blessed with a handsome man and a home of our own. It is true, Mosa is my burden, but we all have a cross to carry. The same God that sent me Mosa also sent me Mandisa, a gift, so we manage. As the church minister in Kouberg used to say,

"At every turn God reminds us that He is great and can give as He can take away".'

Errol put the top of a beer bottle between his teeth, lifted the cap and spat it into his lap, then sank a big mouthful, all the time keeping his gaze on Candice.

Grace said, 'But tell us more about you, Candice. What do you hope for in the Mother City? There are endless possibilities for such a sweet girl who wants to progress her life, is it not so, Errol?'

'Endless,' he said. 'If you don't want much in the township, you've got plenty.'

'Let me show,' said Candice, collusively.

She got up from the table and lifted her holdall onto the chair. She unzipped the bag and took out a pair of scissors, a set of plastic rollers, three wooden hair picks and a rat-tail comb, placing the items on the table as a street vendor might.

'Another barber in the township?' said Errol. 'We need one like we need another three-legged dog.'

'Errol! Why should Candice not be a stylist?' said Grace.

'There are many stylists here?' asked Candice.

'Of course,' said Grace, 'but always room for another who will work hard. You can... style?'

'Yes.'

'Black girls' curly hair?'

'I wish to learn. I have cared for friends' and my nieces' hair all my life. I have enough savings to see me through for a short while until I find a salon chair to rent. I hear they do it that way in Cape Town. Then maybe one day I can get a container salon of my own. I am a farm girl, cousin, I am not afraid of hard work and am prepared to do whatever it takes.'

'No doubt,' said Errol.

That night Mandisa and Mosa slept tangled up in the bed; Candice slept on the couch. Occasionally Mosa's head would slip off the pillow and she would struggle to breathe. Mandisa would then cradle her head, reset the pillow and settle her down.

Other young women in Candice's situation might have felt that by sleeping on a couch in a township they had taken a step down from the certainties of the family smallholding in Kouberg. But the strangeness of that first night gave her the feeling that she had taken the first step on a great adventure. Everything that happened to her from this day would be a staging post towards her new life. Even Mosa's throaty rasping could not distract her from that thought.

The following day, Saturday, Grace sat on the old couch outside the front door while Candice put everything she knew into styling her cousin's hair. She cut and gelled and combed her thin hair into an overly formal series of tight curls with a rigidly straight fringe.

When Candice had finished, Grace looked at herself in the mirror. 'Aiyee!' she yelped. 'Is it me! Must I go to the fish factory on Monday morning looking like Beyonce?'

Errol came out of the house at the sound of his wife.

'Cousin, it is the fashion,' said Candice. 'The other women will be amazed.'

'Or run for the other side of the mountain!' said Errol.

'Hush,' said Grace, 'she is doing her best.'

Then Candice styled Mandisa's wiry hair, which she found hard to control, but at least it brought a smile to her otherwise sombre expression. Mandisa then picked up Mosa and sat her on the couch. Candice was hesitant at first, but once she styled an old wig and placed it on the girl's dainty head, she could see that it brought her as much joy as it did to her sister.

Despite, or perhaps because of the crowded house, Mandisa seemed shy around the new visitor. She rarely volunteered conversation and spent most of her day watching over Mosa, wiping dribble from her clothes, lifting her about the house or carrying her outside to watch the neighbourhood children play in the dust. Their mother would often stroke Mosa's head of untidy bantu knots and tell Candice, 'Mandisa must be clever enough for two.' And it was true. Mandisa was not only pretty and timid; Candice could also sense an intelligence silently screaming from the girl's insides. Silent too was the afflicted Mosa. Camera-like, recording all.

That night, the family were woken by screams and the sounds of people running on the unmade road.

'Shack fire!' someone shouted.

Without conversation, Errol and Grace each lit a kerosene lamp then filled a bucket with water and ran towards the blaze four shacks over. They quickly returned and repeated the action.

'Keep Mosa in hand in case the fire comes this way,' said Grace.

Mandisa and Candice picked up the crippled girl and sat her near the open door in case they had to evacuate. Mosa grimaced at the flaring, yellowy sky. Candice then stood on the step and took in the neighbourhood in uproar. People ran towards a gushing standpipe carrying containers, buckets, bottles, basins, then threw water haphazardly at the flames. The wind swirled between simple homes and blew the smoke and flames towards more shacks on the far side, away from Grace's house.

Candice looked back at Mandisa, and said, 'Maybe I can help.'

She followed the crowd along a narrow path between shacks not much wider than her shoulders to the site of the blaze. She watched breathlessly as at least thirty people threw water on the smoking shacks, beat the flames with coats and blankets, or shovelled sand onto the burning timbers. Four homes were already destroyed, their corrugated roofs now buckled and smoking. A flaming electricity pole sent a pointer of burning orange into the sky as fire danced along the cables. Surrounding homes, packed close together, were either burning fiercely or beginning to catch. A Toyota taxi was ablaze. Neighbours comforted distraught women and children, their salvaged goods piled around them: two mattresses, a television, a small fridge, a child's bicycle, piles of clothing. Candice collected some water in a margarine tub and threw it on a smouldering dining table, which made her feel simultaneously useful and useless.

A siren filled the air, followed by the comforting red lights of a fire engine. It drove as close as it could, but the shacks were too tightly packed to gain access down the alley. The fire crew ran to the base of the fiercest blaze but the hose did not reach. They aimed the water at nearby shacks to douse them and prevent the fire spreading, but the water mostly ran uselessly down an open channel in the middle of the road.

'Another crew is coming!' shouted a uniformed man.

When the first crew left to unwind the second hose, unaffected homeowners, afraid that the fire might spread, stabbed holes in the hose and directed the shoots of water towards their own shacks. When the fire crew returned, they cursed the tenants before calling for yet another hose. And another. Soon, three fire engines were at the scene but the fire continued to eat through the neighbourhood on the south side.

Then an explosion erupted in front of Candice, sending timber, ceiling boards, corrugated tin sheeting, smoke and a blinding jet of flame into the air. A door landed at her feet.

'Propane canisters!' yelled an officer. 'Get back!'

Candice ducked into an empty lean-to until the thick smoke cleared. When she emerged she could see that the exploded shack left a gap in the row of structures through which she could now see the glinting lights from the grand houses across the valley. It took her momentarily out of the scene, as if looking at a painting for the first time. Then four more shacks that depended on the missing one for support collapsed.

It was five hours before the fire crews were sure the blaze was under control. By 4 a.m. everyone was walking ankle-deep in wet ashes and mud from the run-off. Two women with severe burns were taken to hospital.

Grace returned to the house with Candice to gather a few clothes, a blanket and some food to give to the people made homeless. When Errol returned, black with smuts and sweaty, Grace made tea and opened a packet of biscuits for breakfast. By some wonder of good fortune, their home was untouched, save for the choking smell of burnt plastic and wet timber: an odour Candice would come to recognise as the unmistakeable smell of human misery.

This was no time for words, just rooibos and a shared sense of relief. As the dawn whitened the window panes, Candice spoke first.

'That was madness.'

'It is common,' said Errol. 'It is the season. Maybe someone was cooking and turned over the coals. The shacks are so close together and can catch with little more than a hot breath.'

Candice asked, 'What happens to all those who lost their shacks?'

'The municipality will come with shack packs,' said Grace.

'What is a shack pack?'

'A pack of wood and corrugations, some plastic sheeting.'

Candice's face questioned her.

'To make a new shack!'

'It is too terrible.'

'In one week you will not know a fire was there. By this afternoon people will be fighting for their share of ground and start to rebuild. Many have sad stories but they will survive, there is always worse elsewhere.'

'Thank God for our safety,' said Candice.

'Today, with God's will, we were lucky, but our time may come,' said Grace. 'Our future is in the wind.'

III

For a week at least there was a new edginess on the streets. The township reacted to the fire as a body does to a lowered immune system, it struggled to fight off minor upsets and anxieties. Fist fights and arguments broke out over nothing.

Candice immediately began her search for work – in cinder-block salons run by flamboyantly dressed Zulu girls, in lean-to shacks where Congolese women plaited hair into fantastic shapes, and in gaudily painted containers where Xhosas sweated and sang along to music videos on scratchy TV screens. Nothing doing. She visited neighbourhoods with official designations like F Section, Site B and Mandela Road Boundary, known by locals as Graceland, Freedom Park and Galway Bay. She was alarmed when, seemingly at random, people shouted belligerently across the street to neighbours or strangers, and watched her go past as if wishing to begin a conversation. About what? she wondered. She couldn't gauge their intent; were they about to fight or hug? In between times the locals got teeth pulled and got high, bought secondhand cellphones and bartered for plastic sheeting, ate white bread and sugar sandwiches and drank *umqombothi* out of grubby ice cream tubs, met friends and ran from enemies. She saw weapons carried casually: short butterfly knives that folded out with the flick of a wrist, spring-loaded blades, kitchen knives, and long-bladed weapons more like machetes. One morning a man wearing overalls ran past her, chasing a barefoot boy not yet in his teens. She saw the glint of metal in his hand.

She asked a nearby street vendor, 'Is it common to have a knife?'

'Girl, every South African carries a blade.'

Despite the often fraught atmosphere on the street, she came to accept it as normal. Within a month, even though she returned to Grace's home every evening with nothing but other people's tales of township barbering, Candice had become infused with the excitement of possibilities; she could almost taste it. Hopefully something of the mystery and ambition of the township would rub off on her. She had nothing, but surely something was close. Outside the Amazing Grace spaza shop Candice saw a magazine pegged on a string with the headline "The Great African Melting Pot". She felt part of it. Six hours distant by road but a million kilometres away in every other sense, her home village now seemed backward. She surprised herself at how quickly she felt embarrassed about coming from the mountains, of not knowing how to deal with pushy taxi drivers and the men outside the shebeens and – although she would never admit it to another – of carrying the blood of the San. Compared to most in the township she was light-skinned and could not speak the dominant isiXhosa so people assumed she was just another Cape coloured who had lost her way, and she let that be. In fact she knew nothing about the coloured neighbourhood, which was on the opposite mountain across the valley, a place most local blacks viewed as off limits. She never ventured there. Whenever the Cederberg came up in conversation she referred to it laughingly as 'the platteland beyond the platteland', as if she could barely remember the details.

Although she rarely spoke anything but Afrikaans in the Cederberg, Candice's English was good, the result of a scholarship she won from a charity working to bring rural coloured children into the mainstream. In spite of being untrained for anything, it quickly became apparent that well-spoken English was a valuable asset. Encouraged by Grace – and her dwindling savings – Candice looked for work outside the township in the white-owned shops and restaurants in the valley, which might see her through until she was taken on at a beauty salon.

Wearing her best clothes, she found herself in an Italian restaurant called Antonio's in an upmarket neighbourhood of four-wheel-drives, garden sprinklers and pavement cafés. The restaurant was packed with diners, inside and out, and the door into the kitchen never stopped swinging.

Antonio, sweating and totting up figures out loud, was making up a bill at the till. He looked up.

Before she could say anything, he said, 'I hope you're looking for a job. We're bombed out.'

'If you will take me.'

'Sure, the customers will love you.'

A black waitress carrying a tray of pizzas paused at the till.

'Pretty thing, isn't she, Antonio?'

The waitress caught his eye and he smiled.

'You're hired,' he said. 'Grab a tray and clear that table.'

She surprised herself. She loved it. From the first full working day she felt more like the girl she wanted to become. The other waitress, velvet-skinned Beauty Nkosi who also loved to style hair, became a friend, and she looked forward to the days they worked the same shift.

'Keep Antonio sweet and your life will be fine,' was Beauty's advice.

The customers were mostly whites who thought little of paying the same for a bottle of wine as would see her through a week at home. And the amount of food dumped from the restaurant kitchen astounded her.

After a few weeks at Antonio's, a customer called her 'beguiling', and left a big tip. He was smiling at the time so she knew it to be a compliment, a new experience for her. The few intimate encounters she had had were with older men, and could hardly be called relationships, amounting to little more than childish experimentation. Growing up, she had drawn plenty of clumsy approaches from farm boys and enough jealousy from school friends to believe that others regarded her as pretty. There, it held her back. But in Cape Town, the soft, epicanthic folds of her eyes, full mouth and smooth, sandy-coloured skin seemed to open doors. And it didn't hurt that the avuncular Antonio treated her like a favourite niece. Her winsome looks ensured regular shifts at the restaurant and generous tips from tourists. She bought new clothes, the first she had worn for a single purpose – to look beautiful. This in turn brought her the attention, not all unwelcome, of dark-skinned Xhosa and Zulu men who seemed to be attracted by her delicate frame and high buttocks, which gave her the outline of a living rock painting. In short, she had the perfection of youth, a fleeting quality that would prove to be the surest hindrance to her success.

Once Candice could rely on regular wages from the restaurant, she paid her cousin a fair rent, more than Grace expected, and woke each morning with the solid feeling that her life had finally begun. Perversely, the reliable income also seemed to dull the dream that had brought her to Cape Town, namely her own salon. But all in good time, she told herself.

Months later, Grace asked, 'Do you wish one day to return to your sister? Forgive her her sins, whatever they may be?'

'Cousin, I have not the time to consider such a thing. Do you wish me to leave? Perhaps you have not the room.'

'That is not my worry. My concern is for your sister in the Cederberg.'

'But cousin, I came to escape the rooibos picking and the donkeys and the dust rising on the farm road. I will return when I have made my place in the world and have something to show, not before.'

After a year in the township, the phone calls to her sister stopped and even the texts between them seemed forced. Then her cellphone was stolen, with the numbers of everyone from her old life, and Candice accepted the bad luck as another big step towards freedom. If anything, it emboldened her because her mother, speaking the words of a great man she called Khulu, had always told her when things got tough, 'There is no easy road to freedom'. Her mother's own road had ended suddenly the year before and only after her death did Candice realise that hers was the strongest tie keeping her in the Cederberg. The Schippers will be proud of me one day, Candice thought. When I have something to show, I will invite them to see for themselves what a platteland child of the San can do in today's South Africa. We do not all have to push a broom and pick rooibos and pretend to have a good life.

Until then, the dream would remain in that less frequented part of her mind, as a ghost in an uninhabited house.

But Candice learned that in the new South Africa people fall as quickly as they rise.

One warm evening, eighteen months after her arrival, Errol came home from the shebeen and squeezed beside her on the front step.

He lit a cigarette. 'Hey, cousin. Where is the children's mother?'

'Grace is not yet returned from the clinic. She waits for hours to see the doctor.'

She stood up to go. 'I must see to the children.'

His eyes followed her.

'The world dances on a woman's hips,' he said. 'Your hips are keeping my world spinning.'

She stood in the doorway and looked at the top of his head. 'You would like to reduce the rent?' she asked.

He blew a slow stream of smoke and stroked her bare calf.

'Is possible. Perhaps for a private arrangement. Afternoons is quiet.'

She could have complied with his request for the agreeable comforts of family life, but she took his advance as the end of another chapter, a little push over the threshold that she had been unable to give herself. Candice immediately took matters into her own hands. She stopped a boy steering a pushcart on the street and told him to go into the house and bring out all her things and load them onto the cart. In front of neighbourhood women leaning on door jambs she walked beside the barrow boy to the home of Beauty Nkosi.

Beauty opened the door and looked at Candice's bags and bin liners piled up on the barrow. 'My lost lamb, come in.'

Candice soon discovered that one reason she was made so welcome was because her new friend was behind on the rent. Beauty begged her to pay off the debt or they would both soon be homeless. With all her savings now used up, money was instantly tight. Beauty accepted her own poverty; Candice resented hers. Even with extra shifts at the restaurant Candice had no cash left after paying her share of the rent and food, and a weekly visit to the hair salon, something she would never give up. Whenever cousin Grace came to mind, she begrudged the memory of her place at the table and missed the elegant Mandisa and the watchful Mosa. She briefly contemplated returning and accommodating the private arrangement with Errol. But after seeing him pissing in the open sewer outside the community centre one time, she knew she couldn't face it, and vowed to put the episode behind her.

And so the dream of the salon faded, pushed aside to make way for the more urgent tasks of housing and feeding herself. She took to eating at work. Antonio's strict rule against eating restaurant food forced her to take from the plates she carried to customers.

One evening she lifted a plate of penne carbonara from the pass intended for a German tourist. As she turned into the space between kitchen and restaurant, she plunged her hand into the plate and lifted some pasta messily into her mouth. When she raised her head she saw the customer standing over her. With a full mouth and sauce dribbling down her chin she stopped in her tracks. She couldn't get past him or return to the kitchen. She blinked fiercely.

'Toilet?' he asked.

Unable to speak, she pointed to the other door. He didn't move.

'Is that my food?'

Afraid to swallow, she nodded and wiped her lips with her free hand.

She waited in the space until the man came out of the toilet.

'I am so sorry,' she said.

'So am I.'

'Please do not tell Antonio. I need this job. I have no money. Take the food, I will not charge.'

'Take the food yourself. Looks like you need it more than me.'

He gathered his jacket from his seat and walked out. Candice waited ten minutes before alerting Antonio that the customer had left without paying – or eating.

It had come to this. Stealing food from Europeans. She was now a woman with a fading dream, and a woman without dreams is capable of anything.

Although the restaurant mainly served whites, one chilly spring evening Candice noticed a black customer sitting alone. He was a little older than her and had been in once before. The man was not tall but made his presence felt by slow, deliberate movements. He wore jeans and untied boots with lolling tongues, and a thick gold neck chain worn outside a branded sports shirt. Despite the warmth from the log fire, he kept his leather jacket on. His hair was styled in a grown-out buzz cut treated with oil, something she had only ever seen in magazines. White customers occasionally glanced at him the way people are aware of a feral dog. Previously, she recalled, he had arrived with a dark-skinned woman who wore more make-up than she had ever seen on anyone, even more than the white women on television. He sat with his back against the wall and kept his gaze on her, holding her in conversation every time she passed the table.

'What do you recommend, sister-sister?' he asked.

'We only make good food, make your choice,' she said, with forced indifference.

'Meat-meat will satisfy me this night,' he said, stroking the inside of her wrist.

Candice got the feeling he was there only for her.

In the kitchen she told Beauty, 'He's nice, but he says everything twice. Why is it so?'

'Candice, that brother knows what he wants. He has chosen his fruit-fruit from the tree-tree!'

They laughed so much the chef threw a cheese grater at them.

Before returning to the restaurant Candice checked her make-up and hair in the bathroom mirror as she mouthed the words, 'Sister-sister.'

When he had finished his penne with basil pesto and veal steak, the man took the napkin out from under his neck and ordered ice cream – 'You choose the flavour-flavour' – and made it last until the restaurant was almost empty.

When Candice came to wipe down the table, she initiated conversation for the first time.

'You appreciate good food.'

'To eat well is to live well,' he said.

'Did your ma tell you that?'

'No. Mama did not appreciate a quality meal. She ate too much the pap, like yours maybe,' he said. 'What is your name-name?'

'Candice.'

'You not a Xhosa,' he said, pinching his exposed forearm.

'No.'

'It pleases me that you are not. Xhosa girls disturb me. They are nothing but trouble, and expect too much.'

Candice took his denigration of his own kind as flattery of hers.

'What do they call you?' she asked.

'Zuko. Do you know why?'

'No.'

'Because that is my name. Don't forget it.'

She felt a blush coming on, one she thought would never fade. She was his.

Zuko left the restaurant with her new cellphone number. He called it before the night was over and waited for her at the entrance to the township to walk her home. He returned to Antonio's at closing time every night that week.

On her day off Zuko gave Candice money to style her hair at an expensive salon and then took her back to the restaurant.

'Order anything on the menu,' he said, 'serious.'

With meaningful glances between the two women, Beauty served them garlicky pork tenderloin and linguine in a fiery sauce that somehow tasted different compared to when Candice secretly dipped into it. That night she drank more alcohol than she had ever consumed; he sipped Cape brandy. She wondered what she had done to deserve such treatment. It was as if someone at random had offered her a deck and said, 'Pick a card,' and she had chosen the ace of hearts.

In the shared taxi back to the township, a little worse for drink, she said, 'This evening is the greatest moment of my life.'

'I am not all bad, as some say,' he said, implying this partial view of himself was a minority opinion.

'No one has ever spent so many rands on my belly!'

'You should never deprive yourself of good food,' he said.

'*Ja*, but those prices are hectic.'

'For sure, only poor people worry about money,' he said, putting his broad hand on her bare thigh. 'Do not be concerned about the price, human services will pay for it.'

She felt instantly close to Zuko, close enough to share her hopes for her future life in Cape Town. Later, in the sweaty darkness of his shack, she snuggled into his armpit and told him the reason she left the Cederberg, a terrible secret about her sister Anna, something she had not even divulged to cousin Grace. Knowledge that would surely bring her sister trouble if Zuko used it against her. In the morning she absolved herself of betraying the secret by reasoning that her sister and Zuko would never meet. But still she made him swear he would never repeat it.

Were Candice to look back on that night from some time in the near future, she would have seen that, while it may not have been the greatest moment of her life, it was certainly one of the high points of their relationship, which by this moment still existed in the margin between wanting to know the best about the object of her affection and refusing to know the worst. Those first days with him felt imbued with something special, as though their time together was somehow sacred.

The following month passed quickly. She moved into his shack – a structure more accidental than design that he called his 'bungalow' on account of it being divided into two rooms. Bungalow or not, the tin roof needed rocks and shrivelled pumpkins to hold it down next to a posse of squawking hadedas that had taken up residence. From inside they sounded like brazen burglars planning a robbery. When they flew off to feed elsewhere, the shack was alive with an uneasy creaking, like an aged tree in a high wind.

The main room was bare except for the kitchen area, which was centred around a two-ring hob fed by a propane gas bottle, and a half-size fridge. A bucket on the floor caught the drips from a tap sticking out of the wall. Electricity cables that powered the overhead light and TV ran out the window and fixed haphazardly to a connection box on a supply pole that also held up the streetlight. In the corner, three shelves were filled with a set of aluminium flat-bottom pots stacked neatly in size order, two heavy non-stick frying pans, a colander, strainer, cheese grater and, hanging on a neat row of protruding nails, a set of hand utensils. The second room had nothing but an unmade bed.

On her second visit, she said, 'Your kitchen is better than Antonio's.'

'My tools,' he said.

'Tools for food?'

'Why not? Tools are used to make things. Food is the greatest creation you can make.'

She knew he meant it.

'And my food is as good as Antonio's,' he said.

'A man cooking in the home? I am overcome.'

Now it was Zuko's turn to blush.

'I am from the Eastern Cape where I had enough of village food: fry everything twice and hope it does not kill you.'

'You are a strange man,' she said. 'Your shack has no curtains and yet you eat expensive.'

'*Ja*, blame my ma who would only eat pap and gravy. Only fit for babies and cripples.'

'Everyone eats it.'

'Everyone is not Zuko,' he said with annoyance. 'You think because I live in a squatter camp and drink in the shebeen I should eat shit? You think only whites eat well?'

Candice was surprised at how quickly his anger grew, like he was having an argument with himself.

'I appreciate good food also since I started work in Antonio's,' she said. 'I never saw Italian food before I came here.'

Nor drank red wine nor sat in the back of a taxi with a handsome man nor felt these freshly minted emotions, she might have added.

'Pasta is not difficult to cook,' he said. 'The secret is in the timing. Undercooked or overcooked it is disgusting, but perfect pasta makes a happy mouth. I will show you one day soon-soon. I like to cook when I am not alone.'

'We are two now,' she said. 'Is this a good time?'

Zuko rose to the bait. 'I will do it. Do not touch-touch the stove until I return. The propane and electricity are explosive,' he said seriously, then left the house.

He returned after an hour with two shopping bags of groceries. He laid out his tools and, with care, sautéed two fillet steaks, made a blue cheese sauce, prepared a mixed salad tossed in his own mustard vinaigrette, and boiled a whole butternut squash, which he served with some leftover chakalaka. By the time the food was on the table the shack seemed to sweat. He dished up and they balanced the plates on their laps with both the back window and front door open to get a little air through.

'You know the way to compliment a woman, Zuko,' she said, holding up a beaker of pineapple juice. 'I am blessed to find you.'

He met her glass with his beer bottle. 'You are found.'

Zuko cut the tenderest slice of beef from his own plate, picked it up with his greasy fingers and fed it into Candice's mouth.

'Wonderful,' she said, chewing on the too-large piece of meat and losing a little bloody juice down her lip.

He leant over and kissed the juice off her chin. He then covered her mouth with his and took the piece of meat from her tongue.

'Wonderful,' he said, mimicking her intonation, and swallowing the meat. 'Happy mouth.'

Except for the curiously well-equipped kitchen, Zuko's home had a temporary air that she put down to the absence of female influence. The shack exuded a kind of embedded scruffiness that appalled Candice's homemaking instincts, in which arena she was determined to make a difference. Soon, the floor was swept, the rug beaten, the front step scrubbed. She spent her days moving what little furniture he had into new positions, more to put her mark on the home than to improve the arrangement in any practical way. She brought her few possessions from Beauty's place in two oversized plastic holdalls. The clothes and her precious styling tools she placed in a bottom drawer; her books, bought in a sale at the Hout Bay library, the only reading material in Zuko's shack, she stacked neatly on top of the chest of drawers. The kitchen area she knew to leave untouched. She was surprised that he never complained about her reordering his furniture; she was never sure if he liked her changes or if he just didn't care enough to protest. Whatever the arrangement of his possessions, he remained ill at ease in his own house.

He happily handed over a fistful of rands to buy fresh linen for the double bed. She returned home with purple sheets, matching curtains and cushions and a framed photograph of Nelson Mandela, and from the last of her own money she bought him a tailored Madiba shirt patterned with a striking multicoloured swirl.

'Handsome!' she said, when he put it on, and hugged him.

'New sheets and a new woman to lie in them,' he said.

'Shall we try them now?' she said, indicating the empty bed.

Later, wearing his new shirt, he took her to the harbour where they ate hake and chips on the sea wall. His fish was grilled, hers deep-fried. To onlookers they looked like young lovers, happy, untroubled. She knew that being with a black man created a ripple in the township, but it was a new experience to be observed critically by what she saw as her own kind. Coloured fishermen unloading their catches threw comments at her in Afrikaans - '*Sy verkies swart oor gekleurde*' ... '*Gekleurde haan is nie groot genoeg vir jou?*' Candice could see that Zuko was disturbed by their interruption. He quickly turned belligerent.

'What do they say?'

The fishermen howled with ugly laughter and held their crotches.

'They want food,' Candice lied. 'They say they are hungry and want something to eat.'

'Do they mock you?'

'No, no.'

'Me?'

Candice tipped the last of her chips on the ground for some swooping gulls. 'Let's go. Take me to the lookout point above the bay.'

Zuko was reluctant to leave. He spat out a mouthful of food into the paper wrapping, then screwed it up and threw it on deck of the nearest fishing boat.

'Eat that.'

IV

For two months they lived a quiet, domesticated life. Through each small act together Candice felt herself taking leave of her youth. Being with Zuko was like sucking up all the things she thought were missing in her life: a place that felt like home; something to look forward to every night after work; a man to call her own. She savoured the intimacy of the nighttimes when she seemed to hold life between her thighs. It was as though a vacant corner in her life had been filled. Now, viewed through Zuko's eyes, the township was tameable. She began to see patterns in the kaleidoscope, the ebb and flow of people stepping in and out of shacks and ramshackle buildings now seemed meant to be. In place of dirt and squalor she saw a raw beauty and unquenchable hope, and returned her thoughts to the future and what it might hold. The dream of opening a container salon was surely more attainable with the right man behind her.

He took her to the open air restaurant at Chapman's Peak Hotel, an expensive place overlooking the wide sweep of the bay that served mostly tourists in idle poses of smug contentment. They sat facing each other: she in her best dress; he wearing his Madiba shirt.

'What are your dreams, Zuko?'

'To reach tomorrow,' he said, moving some overdone calamari around his plate.

'Serious?'

'There is nothing more serious.'

'I mean, do you have things you want to achieve?' she asked. 'Move out of the shack and into a house?'

'I am content. I built that shack. Why should I move?'

'Do you have a dream for a better job?'

He shook his head. 'But I could cook this food better with my eyes closed.'

'What do you work at, Zuko? You have never said.'

'It is not important. There is food on the table and a roof overhead, that is what matters. And now, whatever my job, I can share its rewards with another for the first time. Everything else is a blessing.'

This sounded like something he had never uttered.

'God tells us to count blessings every day, it is true, but some have dreams also,' she said. 'It is not a sin to want more. Do dreams not make the world turn?'

'Explain yourself.'

'I have a dream of my own. That is why I came to Cape Town.'

'You said you left because of your sister's wickedness.'

'Zuko, we must never speak of that. I told you because I had to tell someone, it was burning a hole in me.'

He shrugged.

'I came here to be a stylist, to open a container salon.'

'So do it.'

'*Ja*, it is so easy,' she said, reaching across the table to push his shoulder.

'What stops us opening a salon?' he said, smiling.

She felt like cheering. Slowly she said, 'Us?'

'Why can you not share your dream? We can open a container salon together.'

It was the first time Zuko had used the term "we" in relation to anything important. Candice almost felt giddy. She moved to the seat next to him and held his arm tightly.

'You mean it? We can do it together?'

'*Ja*.'

'We have a future together?'

'Be careful,' he said. 'The future comes disguised.'

She pulled on his arm. 'What does that mean?'

Zuko looked surprised. 'I must have heard it somewhere.'

'So can we find a container together?'

'Do you trust me?' he said, as if he had been storing the question.

'Like mother's milk.'

The following morning, if Candice had been asked, she would have said that it was the loveliest hour of the loveliest day.

She invited neighbours in for free stylings to practice what would soon be her new profession. She had only tried her styles on friends and family back in Kouberg, so now that she was styling 'for serious' she dragged a chair and table out onto the street in front of the shack, laid out her few styling tools and set a radio in the doorway to a dance station, loud enough to draw attention and create an illusion of busyness. She took a cracked mirror off the wall and hung it on a protruding nail on the side of the shack then nervously waited for her first client. By the end of the day she had seen three nonpaying customers who wanted a weave, a single twist and cornrows. She was learning as she went – especially the new treatments for tight, curly hair, which had a different texture to what she was used to – but nobody complained. That week she attempted straight backs, box braids in black and gold and red, added relaxers and colours, straightened and smoothed, wove single plaits, combos and even attempted dreadlocks. When two girls asked for knotless crochet braids and hair extensions she was stumped and had to admit she didn't know the first thing about them. But she would soon learn. Later that week she noticed a boy trying to sell a discarded pot of red paint door to door. She put it to good use. She soon had an old bed headboard leaning up against the shack adorned with a sign reading "Hair Affair - Barberliscious Styles". She was on her way.

She checked the prices of local salons and wrote up a price list that undercut them by five rands here, ten rands there. She had no seed cash to buy materials, colourings and sprays, so customers brought their own, an arrangement that suited everyone. The very smell of hair relaxer was intoxicating, her tools a daily call to arms. All spelled Freedom. Soon she was overwhelmed with custom, and people in shacks on all sides told her their neighbourhood had never been so busy. The man she was living with, they said, had never spoken to them. They didn't even know his name.

She wondered what Zuko really thought of their shared dream. She never saw him with other people – while he didn't seem to have any friends, he had no enemies either – so it was difficult to judge beyond his usual platitudes: 'Whatever you want' ... 'Fine-fine' ... 'No problem'. It appeared to her that, before her arrival, he had lived a disorganised life like many single township men. She hoped he preferred the new Zuko, the one who wore clean clothes, whose home was tidy and who shared his table and his bed with a San girl who, as imperceptibly as possible, had started rounding off his sharp edges. She was in love, and she was in love with the fact that he was in love with her.

The only part that didn't fit the idyll was his frequent evening and nighttime absences. She could never predict what time he would arrive home – many times he would be absent when she returned from Antonio's after midnight – or what he did while he was away. Whatever he did, while not exactly indulging expensive tastes, he seemed to spend cash as if certain it would never run out. 'Human services', as he called his work, allowed for a number of possibilities that burrowed deep within her. He had no apparent skills, his qualities being implied rather than defined. He spent most of the day close to home, mooching about while she plaited, braided and straightened hair, so perhaps he worked the evenings while she was waitressing. Whatever he did, she found herself profoundly satisfied that he was not a farm boy from the Cederberg. She wondered what her family and friends would say if they knew how quickly she had found her feet in Cape Town. The Cederberg mountains seemed to be faintly calling to her, but they were speaking in a language she was fast forgetting.

From Zuko's viewpoint, the moment was new. Candice was like the answer to a question he hadn't asked. For the first time he felt the joy of possession, and of being possessed, of living in a world that was occupied by another human presence. More than that, it was as if she had set in motion a chemical reaction around him, like adding eggs and sugar to warm milk. He trembled with an emotion that was new to him, or at least long forgotten. Even when Candice was out, the shack was no longer empty, despite the lights seeming to dim every time she left. The sight of her bare shoulder, the stroke of her delicate fingers and a waft of Noxzema body lotion were all thrilling. He was aware that he was undergoing something important, not alone as a single entity, but shared with another. Experiencing, not seeing, having something arc around him while he remained stationary, however much the opposite was true. The last time he was aware of such a feeling was as a child when he lay with cousin Maphule on the baked earth outside his mother's hut and gazed at the stars. Maphule described the feeling as vertigo. Now he knew what she meant, and it scared him.

If Zuko had been asked how he felt at this time, he would have said it suited him well enough. Others who were close to him, if there were such people, might have believed his new domestic harmony was what he had been missing, and that he simply looked happy. But like so much else that happened in his life, he put his new, unexpectedly agreeable situation down to blind luck. Much of his misfortune was due to random chance, why not account for the good things in the same way. What Zuko had not yet worked out was that domestic bliss was an end in itself for many people rather than a provisional condition permanently on the brink of collapse.

One wet afternoon a friend of Zuko's called Jesus came to the house and both spent time leaning like catalogue models up against a neighbouring shack. Candice had heard his name mentioned, but the way Zuko talked she had imagined someone deceitful, disturbing. From what she could see from the doorway, she thought he was neither. Jesus was tall and clean-shaven, with the cheeky manner of a naughty schoolboy. Now that she saw them together for the first time, by comparison Zuko seemed belligerent and insincere. They spoke in English so perhaps he was not Xhosa. Zulu? she wondered.

The house had no gutter so the rain fell in sheets from the tin roof. Jesus noticed her standing just inside the house and called her *obathanda* – dearest – which annoyed Zuko, and brought an irresistible smile to her lips.

Jesus said, 'It is raining – like the cats and the dogs, *obathanda*! But you remain dry inside your home sweet home!'

Zuko scowled and told her to go inside. Amid the rising stink of piss and garbage released by the rain the two men took shelter under the overhang of next door's shack and talked about an incident that had happened the previous night. Candice listened from inside her doorway, unseen.

'The plan was good, hey?' said Jesus. 'What a transaction!'

'You have some luck on your side.'

'There was no luck,' said Jesus. 'The better team won. What a good score, nearly five thousand rands. I have been watching him for a week. He walks that way every night from the store. It was a calculation.' He tapped his head. 'This is the new South Africa, we have to make a plan.'

'The man was afeared, is true,' said Zuko.

'You mean "frightened",' corrected Jesus.

'Whatever. Hit a man quick and hard and he will not get up. It could not be done without Jonno and Little Mabhuti, my good crew.'

'*Our* crew, Zuko. *Our* crew.'

'They were my crew before you fokken came to Mandela,' said Zuko.

'Leadership is the art of getting things done, my bruh.'

'More shit from books?'

'You may wish to acquaint yourself with a book,' said Jesus. 'It may calm you.'

'*Nyo kanyoko!*'

'You may curse me in your bastard isiXhosa all you like,' said Jesus, 'but only when you offend in isiZulu may I be vexed. In the meantime, English will answer our needs.'

'A book cannot tell me how to live *elokishini*.'

Jesus took a moment. The rain eased and dripped from the roof like a torn curtain of crystal beads.

He said, 'We can all live well enough in the township. Do we not make a good team? But we must recognise our talents. All for one and one is all: Little Mabhuti takes orders like a child, Jonno has a strong heart, you cut well with a knife, I make a good plan. If a plan is made we must stick to it.'

'If I see something I want, I will take it, with or without a plan,' said Zuko.

'But sometimes you must wait to choose the best time and the optimum situation,' Jesus said. 'Decide what you want in your mind, then go and get it. Buy yourself a pen and paper and make a plan, as I do.'

'Fuck your pen,' said Zuko. 'And fuck your situation. My way has worked for me and kept me alive. I have rands in my pocket today. Why should I not be rich-rich tomorrow?'

'Money does not grow wild in the bush, Zuko. No matter how much money you have, it is always a windfall to you,' said Jesus, shaking his head. 'Hah! You spend it as quickly as you get it. Me, I plan to save and retire when I am fifty; then the boys can work for me.'

Zuko snorted with exaggeration.

'You laugh, but with enough money behind you you can get people to do anything. Now that you have a beautiful girl in your bed you must save your money, bruh. Maybe tomorrow we will not score.'

'Maybe tomorrow we will be in jail. I cannot spend it in jail.'

The rain stopped. The earth steamed. Candice stepped quietly back into the shack and sat on the bed. Was this the same man she had lived with for two months? The man who made her feel so good and was going to help her find a container salon? She felt like she had been bitten by a dog she thought was house trained. And, like a dog, she never knew where he went each time he left the shack. Until now.

Zuko returned and sat on the bed next to her. He closed his eyes and fell back onto the mattress.

'Fokken Jesus,' he said.

'Is there a problem, Zuko?' she asked, as though to a child.

'Just kak going on.'

Her mouth was dry. She left a pause, hoping he would explain what she had just overheard.

'Is there anything I can do to make it right?' she said.

'*Ja*. Blow me, baby.'

He had never spoken to her so brutally, as if he was talking to somebody else. His thoughts seemed to be elsewhere, and she judged the time was not right to tackle him on his conversation with Jesus. She slipped off his jeans and did what she was told.

Zuko's thoughts were elsewhere. They were straddling the line between his newly tamed life with the girl whose head was now in his lap and what he might have called his real life, the uncertain one that paid for regular sirloin steaks and topped up his cellphone, the one he had so far been able to keep from Candice. The visit from Jesus had brought both sides into view simultaneously.

Zuko traditionally kept the lion's share of the crew's scores, but now that Jesus was organising more hits – and dividing the takings evenly between four – Zuko felt Jonno and Little Mabhuti were looking at him in a fresh light. Until recently he had always decided where and when they made a score, but last month everything changed. Jesus had come to the tavern with his notebook. That meant one thing: he had another fucking plan. Jesus led the crew up to the God is Good Evangelical Church on the south side of the township one Saturday evening. They crouched behind a large wild fig tree and waited for the singing to subside. They heard the pastor take the microphone and request contributions from the congregation: 'For the everlasting good of your church'... 'God is good and we have to show how much we appreciate him, my people'. There was a prolonged shuffle of feet and the unmistakeable tinkle of small change.

'Do you hear that, my brothers?' asked Jesus.

'I hear coins,' said Zuko. 'Not even enough to pay for mealies.'

'But what can you *not* hear?'

The crew scrummed down.

'The folding money that is going into the collection bag,' said Jesus with a grin.

Little Mabhuti and Jonno reacted as if it was a joke and shared a multi-gesture handshake.

'Do we storm the church and take it?' asked Zuko.

Jesus laughed incredulously. 'Don't talk kak. There are a hundred people inside. We wait our time.'

Soon the chapel doors opened, spilling light onto the roadway. Jesus moved the crew back beyond the spread of light and waited for the congregation to disperse. Gripping a small briefcase and an oversized Bible, the black-suited pastor walked to the side of the chapel and flipped open the boot to his battered car. Before he could place the briefcase inside, Zuko's knife was at his throat. The briefcase and Bible both fell to the ground. Little Mabhuti kicked the Bible away and opened the case.

'Score!' he said. 'Big score!'

Zuko pushed the pastor face down into the dirt.

'Sorry for your nice suit, Reverend, but we have needs also. Do not remember this as a robbery, but as a redistribution of wealth. It is what God would have wanted.'

Jonno and Little Mabhuti slapped each others' palms again.

'We take the car?' said Zuko.

'Do you drive it to your shack?' said Jesus with exasperation. 'Think, man. No, we have what we came for.'

On the circuitous route back to their neighbourhood Zuko counted the money, then Jesus counted it, a scrutiny that was well-received by the other two but one Zuko would never normally have allowed. Once the total was agreed, Jesus divided the score four ways.

When he boiled it all down, two things disturbed Zuko about Jesus. One was his book learning, which constantly reminded Zuko of his own lack, like a mirror reflecting a birthmark; the other was the recent, detectable shift of power within the crew towards Jesus, who always seemed to be planning his next move. Since the night they robbed the church takings, Jonno and Little Mabhuti had agreed to everything Jesus suggested. After each robbery that Jesus planned, Zuko could feel his grip on the crew loosen. Perversely, what troubled him more was that the takings had soared. Even allowing for the quarter share, Zuko earned as much as before, which even he had to admit was down to Jesus's sharp eye for detail. He planned the cleverest hijacks, stick-ups Zuko would never have attempted, and always new targets, far from their own quarter: cleaning out a taxi driver's takings last thing at night; jumping exhausted vendors returning from the market; waiting for whites to reverse out of their garages in the morning before the central locking kicked in. The robberies – what Jesus called 'transactions' – were clean, often without the need of a knife. How long Zuko could lead his crew under these new circumstances was becoming increasingly uncertain.

His method relied on instinct, like an untrained gun dog on a shoot. He would threaten random targets into emptying their pockets, and give a warning slash with his blade if they took too long about it. A little blood always focused the mind. At those times surely they shared the guilt for the knife in the ribs. Why didn't they just turn out their pockets? Too many resisted or dug their hands inside their jackets. They raised the stakes, and always ended up chopped. In frustration, he even cut cooperative people if the score was disappointing, such as early morning beach joggers who ran with little cash and old cellphones worth next to nothing.

One thing stayed with Zuko after Jesus left his shack, stepping through the flooded potholes: if Jonno and Little Mabhuti lately seemed to be drifting away from him, he needed to find a new way to make regular money, outside of his involvement with the crew. He wasn't yet sure what form that might take, but most of the neighbourhood's cash at some point was passed hand to hand at the Lucky Strike tavern, so that was a likely place to look.

V

The following morning, while Zuko was still sleeping, Candice took a taxi to the expensive grocery store in the valley to buy dinner: ribs in braai sauce, a carton of prepared butternut squash and a packet of potato dauphinoise. After the disturbing scene yesterday with Jesus, she wanted to fill their lives with some domestic certainty.

The sun shone with a new intensity; for once she didn't even mind the sickly smell wafting up from the fishmeal factory at the harbour.

The noise of her return at midday woke Zuko and he came to the stove as she was unpacking the shopping.

'Why all the trouble?' he said.

'No trouble.'

'I don't eat that package shit,' said Zuko. 'Real food only. Do you not listen?'

'It might depend on the occasion,' said Candice.

'What-what?'

'My birthday. Today.'

'Serious?'

'I am twenty-one years,' said Candice, reaching for him.

Zuko lightened up.

'We will celebrate tonight at the Lucky Strike,' he said. 'I have been waiting-waiting for the right time to take you. Put on a dress.'

Candice expected the Lucky Strike to be a stylish club in the valley, one that mixed colourful, sweetened drinks and served food like paintings on a plate as she had seen in magazines. Afterwards, perhaps they would end the night on a dimly lit dance floor. But the Lucky Strike was not a club in the valley, it was a corner shebeen at the bottom of the township set back from the tarred road, barely more solid than the shacks that surrounded it. Inside, the airless space was filled with pulsating music and the unclean air of burnt boerewors and a full urinal. In place of fragrant people sipping cocktails were sweating men necking beer from bottles; there were no tapas, only grilled liver and chicken wings brought in from Mama Rosie's kerbside braai. Bare bulbs of various colours stuck out of walls at shoulder height giving faceless drinkers strangely animated silhouettes.

She noticed a clear division in the shebeen: men either crouched on the bloody margin of torn red plastic seating that edged the semi-dark room or sat balanced on upturned crates. The few women in the place, gaudily lit by a red glow emanating from behind the bar, were perched on high stools like specimens in a museum. Everybody knew Zuko, who seemed more relaxed here than in his own home, as if the Lucky Strike were his natural element. He sat Candice down at a table with Jesus and two other friends she had not met before: a simple-minded man with a nervous tic called Little Mabhuti, and Jonno, a sweating drunk with carious teeth who leered from beneath a trilby. She wondered if he ever washed. Zuko called for service. The shebeen owner, a middle-aged woman called Lucky Lulama, had a deep voice and matching cleavage. Her curly Afro wig did not sit straight on her head, and she had to keep pushing the fringe out of her eyes.

'This is Candice, my dearest one,' said Zuko. 'We celebrate her birthday and two years in the township. Bring beers for all at the table, gogo, our shebeen queen.'

Lucky Lulama scanned the crew sitting at the table. 'For Jesus, Mary and Joseph also, neh?'

Zuko laughed. 'Even for them. Can you not see it is a special occasion?'

'Pineapple juice for me, mama,' said Candice.

'It cannot be,' said Zuko. 'Lucky Lulama, bring her a real drink. She is from the Cederberg; they are gentle souls in the veld.'

'Lord save us.'

Lucky Lulama headed towards the bar under a banner that read "A Merry Heart is Good Medicine". Zuko turned to huddle with his friends, which gave Candice a chance to observe more closely the people in the tavern. The men were mostly poorly dressed, but the girls on stools had made an effort with lipstick and false eyelashes, silky skirts and heels, sitting erect as if waiting for someone to paint their portrait. She wondered if she should go and make friends with the one closest, an attractive, big-eyed girl wearing an orange two-piece outfit and a tiara wedged into her hair extensions. Then a man, who Candice took to be the girl's boyfriend, walked up to the bar and put his arm around her shoulder. They talked for less than a minute before the girl slipped off the stool and nodded goodbye to Lucky Lulama. The girl patted the man on the back and they left the shebeen arm in arm.

At that moment Candice became aware that Little Mabhuti and Jonno were staring at her after every pause in their conversation. They disturbed her, Little Mabhuti flinching and Jonno leering wet-lipped, sharing multi-gesture handshakes after each private joke. Jonno, who was petting a beautiful blonde dog not much more than a puppy, began an incoherent conversation with her; so much so that she moved her seat away and took a large drink of pineapple juice which, unnoticed by her, had been spiked with something alcoholic. She watched Little Mabhuti make regular visits to a girl he called one-eyed Sara; Jonno took money from a fleshy girl called Esihle. Now that Zuko and his three companions were drinking heavily she sensed a bond tightening between them, less like friends, more like accomplices. The music got louder as new bodies crowded the dark shebeen. She became a little alarmed by the constant comings and goings, which made her feel like a spectator. When, an hour later, she was sure that she saw the same girl leave arm in arm with a different man, she told Zuko she wanted to leave.

'Be real, baby. We in a tavern. We leave when the drinking is done.'

Later, at home, despite Zuko's drunkenness, Candice tackled him about the Lucky Strike.

'Those women... are friends of yours?'

'Some.'

'And the men? Where are their wives?'

'Doing what wives do,' he said. 'At home. They begged their men for children, now they must raise them.'

'I know there must be such places in the township, Zuko, but do not bring me there again. The men, they look at me as if I was just another girl.'

Zuko swayed and loosened his belt. 'But you are, my sweetness, you are.'

In the smoky haze of the shebeen he had seemed more like the other customers than the man she knew at home. He had treated her like she *was* just another girl. The only difference was that she sat at a table with him rather than on a bar stool.

'And Jesus?' she said.

'Don't talk about that fokker to me,' he said, angrily wiping a slow-moving lizard off the table.

'I overheard you talk about money this afternoon – on the step. And other activities.'

'What about money?' he yelled. 'Who pays for this house? Who bought that dress?'

She raised her voice. 'I bought this dress! I work for my money. But I think not everyone in this house works a job.'

'So what if other people's money pays for what I have. Not everyone had an easy home and good schooling. I have survived where others have been tramped into the dirt.

There are enough foreigners in the township who are taking their share, so why not me.'

Zuko waved her away and, sleepy-eyed, reached for a Heineken.

During the course of just one evening, Candice felt like they had run out of road.

'There are names for men like you,' she spat.

'Call me what you like-like,' he said, flipping the top off the beer.

She accurately guessed a reading of his thoughts.

'*Tsotsi*! Gangster!'

He stood up, dropped the bottle and whipped the back of his hand across her face. She fell on the bed.

'And what do you call *izifebe* who live with *tsotsis*?'

He staggered a little then collapsed into a chair with his trousers at his ankles. Within a minute he was wheezily snoring.

In time Candice would realise that this was the moment she should have left him, simply picked up her bag and walked out the door. Beauty, despite lately taking up with Zuko's partner in crime, Jesus, would have taken her back. But who knows the workings of the human mind when the human heart is in turmoil – the belief that something is possible despite all contrary evidence. And she still yearned for her salon. Somehow, despite having worked almost a year at the restaurant, she had not been able to save any money. She seemed to spend more on home-making than on home-building. It would eventually become evident to her that the home she was making was Zuko's, not hers, or even theirs. But for now, unable to spread out her thoughts, as an unfurled fan might reveal a hidden picture, they assaulted her one by one. She was unprepared for what she had learned about Zuko in the past twenty-four hours: the robberies with Jesus, the way he ordered her to service him, the girls at the shebeen, and the hostile character he adopted while drinking. As for his companions, Jonno and Little Mabhuti seemed capable of anything.

She went to bed that night with the idea that she would make a big decision the following day. Daylight would bring a little clarity. But morning has a habit of forgetting the fury and insults of the night before. The next day Zuko was sober, contrite and affectionate, in equal balance to the drunken, nasty and revealing scene some hours before. Then he played an ace.

Unprompted, he said, 'I know where is a container salon we can rent for you.'

Candice's world shifted on the night she discovered Zuko's means of income, when she decided to stop pretending that 'human services' was some legitimate form of employment. Now that he had nothing to hide from her, Zuko seemed to revert to an earlier self, a character she did not recognise. It was as if an unbidden pact had been signed between them, one that left her on the losing side. The house was once again his, and her place in it felt temporary. The promise of the container salon came to nothing, and yet it remained the tightest bond she had with him.

She could feel him taking greater control of what she did and when she did it. He questioned her about her time at Antonio's and who she was with. He brought one of the neighbourhood girls to the shack, seemingly to take Candice in hand.

'Show her how to dress for real,' he said. 'I wish for a township chick, not a farm girl.'

She was given revealing clothes that would be regarded as unseemly in the Cederberg. Suddenly she was all bare legs and shoulders, and every time she looked in the mirror she seemed to grow more curves. Before they went out he would say 'a little make-up would not hurt', and at the Lucky Strike he added large hits of vodka to her pineapple juice. 'You cannot expect me to drink alone,' Zuko would say, and order her another.

He told her to stop working at the restaurant and always be available to him. On the walk home from the shebeen – three or four times a week now – he encouraged her to share his dagga. Her descent was swift. Within two months she had reached the point where she couldn't make a single decision that mattered. Finally, she didn't even know her own name.

'Candy,' he said, one evening with her face in his lap, 'you are more like Candy to me.'

The path of her life had taken a strange course. She felt that her time in Mandela Park accounted for all the formative years between childhood and what passed for maturity. She knew little else. Candy was now fully reliant on Zuko as her provider and the image of her salon remained as a figment of her mind. It was the moment Zuko had been waiting for.

'In time, the container will be found, no doubt,' he said. 'But to make a salon is not cheap-cheap. It requires work, it requires to be nice. Your hands must wash my hands.'

In the months since accepting the new name as her own, Candy often tried to pinpoint the moment that she believed being with a strange man was worth the promise of her own salon. But looking back to this time it seemed like she was stuck in a revolving door, neither with a past nor a life that lay ahead, just the constant smack of savage, present moments.

One sticky night at the Lucky Strike Zuko pulled a ziplock bag from his pocket and asked her to choose a pink tablet.

'What is it?'

'It will stop you having a hangover from the vodka,' he said.

'Not for me.'

'Take it.'

'If it is medication it must come from a pharmacy.'

'It is fine-fine. Look,' he said, popping one into his mouth. 'I feel better already, heh heh.'

She took one and held it up to a bare lightbulb. It was slightly grainy and had an impression of a heart described on one side. She bit the edge off it.

'See? Fine-fine,' he said, 'no problems with the pink pills.'

She popped the rest into her mouth and swallowed it with a swig of whatever was in her glass.

A few minutes later they were joined by a round-faced man, a regular visitor to the bar who often made short transactions in dim corners. He wore three gold rings with a matching heavy bracelet and a collared jacket, which, like Zuko, he always wore no matter how steamy the weather. The men slapped palms then shook hands and ended by clicking fingers before the man dragged up a crate next to Candy and called for a Johnnie Walker.

'Sister, I have watched you from afar and you are so beauteous,' he said. 'Like a film star.'

She sat a little straighter and brushed down her dress, then turned to Zuko for guidance. His face relaxed into its newly adopted picture of animal repose, both content and vulpine.

'Sorry for my English,' said the man. 'My father was poor Tsongan king with many children, who could not afford good schooling for me. I am one of thirteen, but perhaps is lucky for you.'

Candy forced a rare smile.

'So that would make you a prince?' she asked.

'Yes, call me Prince. Fresh Prince of Limpopo!'

Zuko said little, but Candy noticed the two men talking with their eyes every time she took a sip of vodka and lemonade. Rather than curing the future hangover, the combination of alcohol and the pink pill had the opposite effect. She felt hot and the room spun a little faster even as she felt a wave of joy break over her. The man bought more drinks, doubles. Everything he said was designed to make her laugh, often touching her arm with his fat fingers for emphasis. It certainly made a change from the unsettling

Jonno and the tics and twitches of Little Mabhuti. Zuko was a changed man, not his usual jealous or indifferent self, and seemed to encourage her to befriend the man from the north. Zuko left the shebeen to urinate in the open sewer outside, but did not return.

The man said, 'Your boy has disappeared. I am blessed to spend some time alone with you.'

'You are fresh prince, true,' she said, now released from Zuko's gaze.

He laughed long and loud, showing beautiful white teeth.

'Yes, Fresh Prince! He not only left me his woman, he also left me the key to heaven.'

He held up the distinctive brass key to the padlock on Zuko's shack door. Lucky Lulama appeared at the table with two more large drinks.

She paused next to Candy. 'All is fine, neh?' she asked.

'Fine-fine,' answered the man without looking up, then handed her a big tip.

He turned to Candy. 'One more drink and we go to paradise.'

It seemed undignified to drink quickly, but the moment demanded it and she gulped it down. She had come to enjoy the sensation of alcohol hitting her system, which often brought on a flashback to her first wine-fuelled date with Zuko at Antonio's: a memory simultaneously recalled and disregarded.

She followed Prince out of the shebeen and into a black BMW parked on a slip of waste ground. He tipped two teenage guards holding knobkerries, then drove her home. It was not the worst experience of her life, in spite of his sour smell. In some ways he was more attentive than Zuko was lately. The man left and she wiped his sweat off her belly, then sat blindly watching TV, weighing up what she had done. What had she done? Nothing that God would hold against her, surely. And if God disapproved, she was comforted by the 200 dirty rands rolled up on the bedside cabinet. What troubled her just as much as the stickiness between her legs, was the deceit. Before this night she would never have pretended an emotion, yet it had come easier than she would have believed, and she wondered if it had something to do with the pink pill.

One man was as well as another, so when the following week Zuko told her that someone at the bar would like to be alone with her, she knew what was expected. She took another pink tablet and it was over so quickly her drink was still cold when she returned. She was a natural, Zuko told her; easy as stringing beads; easy as taking a pill. Soon it was a regular thing.

Lucky Lulama took her aside for a woman to woman conversation. She told Candy that now was the time to take another path if she had any doubts about the course Zuko had evidently laid out for her.

'Mama,' Candy said, swaying a little, 'I am blessed for your concern, but do not worry for me. I have a dream that will come true with Zuko's help. For now the money is welcome.'

Lucky Lulama bought another bar stool.

Older bar girls who showed signs of too many nights spent at the Lucky Strike resented the younger, light-skinned competition. Candy took to flattery to keep them on side: 'No, but you still look so beautiful, Esihle,' she would say, 'and men, they like the big girls.' She even told one-eyed Sara, 'But you have pretty hair, and your face is a picture, it is true, my sister.' The scene in the bar every evening seemed unnatural, was unnatural, to her. It was as if they were all taking part in a play – the girls, the men, Lucky Lulama – but she was the only one without a script.

To save Candy time taking men home and back again, Zuko threw a mattress into the empty shack behind the tavern. Afterwards, she brought him the money and he stuffed a few rands into her purse.

What he didn't give her was the hair salon he had promised. Whenever she brought it up, he would say, 'Human services will pay for it, in good time.' It especially hurt that Jesus had recently cleared out some Brazzaville barbers from a shipping container close to the Lucky Strike and in their place had set up shop for Beauty Nkosi, who by now had also stopped waitressing at Antonio's. The day a sign-writer painted the words "Beauty Girl Salon" across the side of the unsteady container was the day her friend began living Candy's imagined life.

Meanwhile her situation after dark at the shebeen escalated from gentle persuasion to expectation to insistence that she perform on demand. Daytimes she spent resentfully killing time at Beauty's container salon; nighttimes she spent loathing her bar stool. Within six months, without realising it, she was dressing indecently and layering make-up like the other girls. She had given up on her appearance in all areas except the one that would attract a man after dark. The girl who arrived in Mandela Park with the plastic beads was no more; she had been blown away by the southeaster with the other grains of sand, occasionally a blink in someone's eye, but nothing more.

Following a busy night at the shebeen, long after it had become commonplace, Candy returned home in the early hours to find a teenage girl sitting on the step wearing her new dressing gown. Candy could hear the splashing of water inside. Her pulse raced and she tightened the grip on her handbag.

'Where is your manners, child?' Candy said.

'Haw! Manners for what?' said the girl, stubbing out a cigarette.

'Respect to your older sister. This is my house, my man. I know a bitch on heat when I smell one.'

'Jags! He has pressed me good tonight!' she said.

Candy swung her handbag and caught the side of the girl's face, knocking her blonde wig into the dirt. The girl recovered, scrambled to her bare feet and took a swing at Candy, but missed.

'*Ja*, it was an operation!' goaded the girl. 'He was lekker, you Afrikaans speaking pig!'

Candy jumped on her, pummelling the girl's face left and right. They both fell into her painted barber sign and split it in two. Zuko came to the door wearing a towel. He moved to separate them but hesitated, folded his arms and leaned on the open door.

A neighbour pushing a bicycle stopped on the street. 'The girls are dancing tonight, heh-heh. In the moonlight!'

Candy pulled the dressing gown off the girl and threw it around her own shoulders.

Naked and gulping for breath, the girl appealed to Zuko. 'Who is this gammie minstrel?'

'This is my Candy. Sweet-sweet Candy.'

'Proudly San, to you,' said Candy.

The neighbour laughed. 'And your Candy knows how to fight for her man.'

'I fight for what is mine,' she said, kicking the girl's wig into the open sewer.

The naked girl, full of pain, howled, then grabbed a towel off a washing line and ran.

Zuko put his arms around Candy's shoulders and led her to bed. The adrenalin surge that helped her fight in the street was not yet spent, and continued in his bed. Sex with Zuko, no matter how savage, was the one moment she could fool herself into believing they had a future together no matter how much he made her feel like nailed prey.

Candy fought many times in the coming months. The routine of late nights and the presence of fresh country girls in Zuko's orbit stoked her contempt. It seemed that everything around her now was hostile. Even Zuko's once endearing habit of repeating random words irritated her as a child might with a permanent snuffle. As he cared less about Candy's reaction to other girls, more distance opened up between them, giving her time to calculate what was at stake: the salon; her joyful return to the Cederberg; happiness. The space where her future and hope resided was fast being eroded, and left her a woman with ever diminishing resources.

The fights with Zuko became fuelled less by sexual energy, more by vexation. It made for a heady brew. He would fly into a fury if they ran out of milk. A simple 'No, it is my woman's time,' when Candy was due at the Lucky Strike, would send him into a rage. Occasionally she was cheated into fleeting moments of well-being, but deep down she knew she was kidding herself. She sometimes got the better of him in arguments, little victories that returned to her a sense of identity and some sort of control, a feeling that, in her quiet moments, she knew she had completely lost. Not like something stolen, a necklace taken and missed in the morning, more like water slowly trickling through palsied fingers. If she looked closely she would see the fire was out and the grate was full of ashes.

Soon she was troubled by a feeling that she was less winning the fights than he was giving up on them. By now he had no secrets left, she knew everything she wanted to know about the *tsotsi* who had taken her in. There was no more promise in him. They both knew it. The space between them, once so special, had become a lie; a lie in every meal, every morning, noon and night, a lie in every bulging backpack he brought home, and in every crumpled 200-rand note.

Finally one afternoon a loud, big-hipped girl from Khayelitsha showed up at the door with a knobkerrie under her arm. Behind her on the street her belligerent brother was unloading a cart loaded with stuffed bin bags and a mirrored dressing table. Candy treated her arrival as inevitable, although it made it no easier to accept. By the time Zuko, high and drunk, came home with the remains of a big score in his pocket, the woman had moved in.

'Is she to remain?' Candy asked. 'It is unthinkable.'

'Am I not a man to be respected?' he slurred, holding the back of a chair for support as his eyes seemed to spin. 'You know what they say at the Lucky Strike? You are too much upkeep.'

'Who are you to pass judgment?'

'I am Zuko. That's my name, don't forget it.'

The new girl shrugged and put a large pan of water on the stove for Zuko's supper. Candy grabbed the pan and ran at him. She swung it and hit him on the shoulder, spilling the contents over both of them. He made a fist and seemed to muster everything he had, then punched her in the chest. Candy went down like the twist of a screw and was out cold from the blow. She felt herself being picked up and thrown outside, her body hitting the ground with a dull thump to the accompaniment of shrieking neighbourhood women and small children. The girl from Khayelitsha took the cue and quickly scooped up what looked like Candy's haphazard collection of clothes and threw them after her.

'Am I not a man in my own house, with a woman of my choice?' roared Zuko, before slamming the door.

Candy gathered what belongings she could find in the dark and spent the night at Beauty's house, pouring out her ruined life. By chance, among the ragtag assortment of

Candy's clothes, Zuko's new girl had thrown out his Madiba shirt. She took it to bed with her.

The following day she found a simple shack in a shapeless, temporary neighbourhood on the sandy edge of the township and spent what money she had on a mattress and a padlock for the shaky door. The area of newly erected structures assembled from scrofulous iron sheeting and recycled wood felt like the raw beginnings of something profane. Or the end. She cared little for the rented shack she now called home; it was just another place she was destined to be unhappy. Now enveloped by the indifference of the world, she sat in the bare shack feeling like a childless orphan: no future, distant past. That night a storm broke over Hout Bay. Wearing the Madiba shirt, she took to her bed and wrapped herself in a single sheet. She breathed in the darkness and listened to the rain like peace falling, as if washing away her sins, past, present and future.

Although the move out of Zuko's shack seemed to push her return to the Cederberg ever further into the future, at least now she was able to spend daytimes as she wished. She was tempted to get her sister's number from cousin Grace and call home to hear the familiar accents of childhood, but she didn't trust herself not to burst out the wretchedness of her life. The thought of all the lies she would have to tell exhausted her. She would save her family from the truth, and they would be better for it. Still, she lived with a nagging guilt that she acted cruelly towards her sister when she revealed her sin, especially since Candy had committed so many of her own.

She now regretted burning her bridges when she left Antonio's restaurant without giving notice, so by the end of the week when she was reduced to begging for breakfast, she returned to the Lucky Strike and waited for Zuko to show up.

He could not hide his surprise at her return.

Levelly he said, 'No more the fighting. You come at night after sundown, your life will be tranquil, and none of the other men will bother you.'

They reached an arrangement that kept them close yet not tied together, like a divorced couple who kept in touch for the sake of the children. In Candy's case she wanted somehow to prolong the warm glow of their – what would she call it? Relationship. Arrangement. Transaction. A more insightful person would have recognised that Zuko had made her the woman she had become, and was also the obstacle to her moving on with her life. But her shrinking world seemed to cut her off at the exits – what would she do without him? He had been like a rock between her and the world.

She drank to keep the old glow alight, not vodka and lemonade now but cheap beer and anything a trick would buy her to anaesthetise herself against the evening shift. As other girls flitted about his light, Zuko seemed both amused and puzzled, and yet happy, that she showed up at the Lucky Strike most evenings now that she was, effectively, free to leave. She did not want him to know why she spent nights at the tavern as if working under a spell, customers taunting her with the joy of life. She accepted a rate she would be paid for each customer, then watched him scuff out of the shebeen like three wasted years.

Within two months she stopped going to Beauty's salon to learn the new styles and only visited in the early evening, for company, before going to her bar stool at the tavern. The other girls recognised her predicament. They were now more than fellow bar girls, they were sisters. And like them, with no savings and carrying around a history of defeat, she was ready to admit her mistakes and hope the future was worth waiting for.

On a sweltering night two weeks before Christmas, the crew left the Lucky Strike and splashed their faces in turn at the standpipe. Jonno's mongrel, now a matted-haired cur, was tethered to his belt by a length of string. They were out of cash, having pooled what money they had on beer and pap with gravy. Zuko had eaten nothing. Street lights were either burned out or used for target practice in this part of the township, which made it good hunting ground, despite what Jesus said about kakking on your own doorstep. Zuko needed real food, but he needed cash more.

'I have an idea for a score,' said Jesus. 'Tomorrow, my bruhs. Patience is virtuous.'

'Why wait,' said Zuko. 'My pocket and my belly are empty and I must fill them both.'

'What do you plan?' asked Jesus.

'No plan. That is why the Shell station on Main Road is open twenty-four hours, so we can take it.'

'Go home, Zuko. You smoke too much dagga.'

'Little Mabhuti, are you in?' asked Zuko.

'*Ja.*'

'Jonno?'

'For real,' he said, petting the dog.

'Leave the animal,' said Zuko.

'He is pocket luck,' insisted Jonno.

'Jesus, are you coming with my crew?'

'You crazy. You walk in the station and just ask for money? There is armed security.'

'Security will be sleeping. And there are four of us – too much for a fat fuck. Would *you* take us all on?' Zuko smiled. 'Hoods up, my bruhs.'

The crew, including a reluctant Jesus, made their way out of the township. On the way they passed a man wearing a black suit and holding a Bible who Zuko recognised but couldn't place. The man looked at each of the crew in turn then retreated inside a red-painted shack. With heads bowed, the crew walked in single file on the undeveloped side of Main Road that bordered waste ground. As they came parallel to the Shell station they all looked up, their faces partially lit by the station's neon lights and the occasional oncoming traffic. A uniformed guard was slouched in a chair near the pumps. An attendant wearing a felt hat adorned with plastic reindeer antlers was pumping diesel into a Range Rover.

'Two will take security, the others go inside,' said Zuko. 'The forecourt brother will run, no doubt.'

'You have a blade, Jonno?' asked Zuko.

'*Ja.*'

'We will take the guard,' said Zuko, 'Jesus and Little Mabhuti, you pussies take the till.'

Jonno tethered the dog to a tree. When the forecourt was empty of cars, Jesus and Little Mabhuti pulled their hoods down over their eyes then crossed the road and entered the station shop. Once Zuko could see them browsing, he walked across the forecourt. From the far side of the station Jonno threw a comment at the pump attendant, which caught the guard's attention, then Zuko stepped up and grabbed his neck from behind and floored him. He took the Glock from the guard's holster and held the gun to his temple.

'It takes only my finger to end your life, bruh,' said Zuko. 'Be cool.'

The pump attendant ran down the road, as expected. Zuko then turned his attention to the station shop where he could see Little Mabhuti holding his knife at shoulder height and the cashier crouching behind the counter.

'Move, bruh!' shouted Zuko.

Little Mabhuti then leapt over the counter, took out a short crowbar from his jeans and levered it into the till drawer. Jesus kept his foot on the door in case the cashier had managed to switch on the automatic lock.

Outside, Zuko ripped off the crackling walkie-talkie from the guard's uniform and threw it across the forecourt.

'Move, my bruh,' shouted Zuko once more through the glass to Little Mabhuti. 'Fokken mompie!'

Jonno joined Zuko.

Zuko said, 'Keep him still, I go inside for the money.'

Zuko left Jonno with his foot on the guard's neck, then pushed Jesus out of the way at the door and jumped up onto the shop counter. At that moment Little Mabhuti prised open the till and notes and coins fell to the floor. They both stuffed the paper money into their pockets and ran. As they reached the station door they heard a shot. Instinctively the three men dropped to the floor and peered out towards the pumps.

'Kak! The guard has another weapon,' said Jesus.

Jonno's dog, which must have worked its way free from its tether, was now splayed out on the forecourt with its stomach heaving and blood pumping from where its left eye should have been. Jonno was running in the opposite direction into the darkened road. The guard got to his feet and fired his handgun at the men coming out of the station. Three shots struck the station windows before Zuko fired back and caught the guard in the shoulder, exploding a piece of body armour and spinning him around. He fell heavily face down and his gun skittered towards the pumps. Zuko reached the weapon before the guard, then kicked him full in the face before running with Jesus and Little Mabhuti into the veld.

Two nights later Zuko pushed open the door to the Lucky Strike. He waited for his eyes to get accustomed to the new light before making out Lucky Lulama wiping down a tabletop and, closer, the silhouettes of his crew drinking at the corner table.

'Where is she, bruh?' he asked. 'That bitch, Candy.'

He slammed the door behind him into its flimsy frame, but it rebounded open into a table, toppling a glass to the floor.

Before the men had time to answer, Lucky Lulama stepped into the rectangle of sunlight.

'Zuko, it is early yet. Too early, neh.'

'Have you seen her?' he said.

'She has not arrived. Look, the time.'

She waved towards the Castle Beer clock that showed 6.30 p.m., then moved towards the bar.

Zuko cursed, then called, 'Beer, gogo.'

He counted coins into his palm, then upended them on the bar. 'My last,' he said with an effort.

'*Ja*, a cold one. Is good. Is too hot, Zuko,' said Lucky Lulama, placing a Black Label through the grill. 'If you were a white, the sun would melt your balls today.'

She laughed as she threw the coins into the till. 'And you would turn the colour of my tomatoes! Aiyee!'

Before picking up the beer, Zuko used his forefingers to wipe the sweat from both eyelids and flick it on the floor. He eased off his jacket and sat on the only upright bar stool with the bottle between his legs and leant an elbow next to a handwritten sign: "Leave your guns at home this Xmas – your caring management". He looked over at the three silhouettes, which formed into Jesus, Jonno and Little Mabhuti. He would have to face them about the messy score at the Shell station.

'What's up, chana?' Jesus called from the corner. 'Poverty has struck?'

Zuko ignored him, and asked, 'Where are the girls-girls?'

'The Beauty Girl Salon, man,' said Jesus. 'It's cool. Chill.'

'I fokken chill when I chill. Don't wise me, man.'

Jonno kept quiet, but he looked on edge.

'Well, boys,' said Jesus with thick sarcasm, 'do we take an Esso station today? What do you say? They have all of Hout Bay SAPS on duty, but Zuko says we can take them.'

Little Mabhuti twitched heavily then started to laugh, but quickly killed it when he saw Jonno's reaction, who looked as if he had words in his mouth he could spit.

'Fok you,' said Zuko.

'My fokken dog, yo!' cried Jonno. 'For one thousand rands only I lose my friend.'

'If that's your only friend —'

'That's one more than you have Zuko, so fuck yourself.'

'Fuck you! Who takes a dog on a score?' said Zuko.

'We should not have taken the Shell, is all,' said Jonno. 'The dog got loose and attacked the guard to protect me, but he took another gun from his jacket. You have no plan, you fuck!'

'You have no brains.'

'And now, within two days we are already poor men,' said Jesus, palms up like some corner philosopher. 'Just like our kind: making the worst of what we have.'

He put his elbows on his knees. 'Let the sleeping dog lie. Is cool! We living in paradise.'

He smiled solemnly and stroked Little Mabhuti's palm.

'Eish! The promised land!' he said. Then, pathetically, 'With one less dog in Mandela Park.'

Little Mabhuti broke the mood and shouted, 'More cool chillin' beer, gogo!'

Zuko kept his eyes on Jesus and took a swig from his bottle before checking his cellphone. He pushed a number, put the phone to his ear and through clenched teeth, hissed, 'Fokken voicemail, man.'

Lucky Lulama swept up the sand from the floor that had blown in behind Zuko then threw the full pan out the door and pushed it closed, returning the drinkers to ghosts in the twilight. She brought three cold Castles to the corner table and held her arm outstretched. 'The money, neh.'

'Always the money, gogo,' said Little Mabhuti, his shoulder jerking.

'If you look hard you will find somebody's rands in your pocket,' she said.

Lucky Lulama left the table with a fifty-rand note, then Zuko dragged up his stool.

'This is our problem. Not too much the money.'

'Not enough money,' said Jesus, avoiding Zuko's eyes.

Zuko let that one go.

'Fokken rands is the problem,' he said. 'We need more-more.'

'*Ja!*' shouted Little Mabhuti.

'The girls, man. What to do?' said Zuko. 'Charge more expensive?'

'Increase the prices,' said Jesus.

Zuko swung the bottle with agitation between finger and thumb. 'What must we do?' he asked.

Little Mabhuti took a swig and washed the lager around his mouth. The cords in his neck stretched involuntarily for a few seconds before he was able to speak.

'Not charge more,' he said, 'work more longer. Three stukkies each night is for three of us, okay, but Lucky Strike is open now, where is the girls? Men want to fuck at all hours.'

'I like, I like,' said Zuko. 'Is possible.'

'It certainly is feasible,' said Jesus.

Zuko, eyes blazing, swigged his beer deeply.

'So the girls must be here,' said Zuko. 'Now-now. Fokken kak.'

'All in good time,' said Jesus, opening his palms. 'They say woman's time is not man's time. Especially your bar girls.'

'More book learning?' said Zuko, slamming his bottle onto the table.

'You can find all the world's wonders and failings in the pages of a book, Zuko, even characters like you.'

Little Mabhuti gurgled with laughter and lost some beer down his chin as his head twitched so severely it almost rested on his shoulder.

Zuko had had enough. He shrugged into his jacket then headed for the door and up the hill to the Beauty Girl. Because of the incline, the container was held up at one end by cement blocks, which were perishing under the weight. The salon rocked whenever anyone made a sudden move. Underneath the open end, precariously, lay a sleeping dog. Zuko stepped into the shade of the container and placed one foot on a discarded car seat, exposing his ankle and a glint of steel. He looked inside. Candy and one-eyed Sara were sitting in chairs bedecked with what looked like last year's tinsel in front of two tapless sinks as Beauty and new stylist

Patience set their hair in cornrows. They sang along to a rap version of a Christmas carol playing on the TV.

Two girls wasting their time and the crew's money. Nearly sundown and they do nothing.

Candy acknowledged Zuko's presence with a dismissive hand. 'Coming,' she called.

He said nothing. The bloom of female compliance had long been replaced by challenge and rebellion. She then looked directly at him. He didn't blink.

'I may not leave with my hair like this,' she said.

One more word.

'Is time enough,' she said, returning her attention to her mirror image. 'You will have to wait.'

Zuko pulled himself up into the container, rocking it like a fairground attraction. He snatched a pair of scissors and with his other hand grabbed Candy by the hair and slammed her face into the mirror, cracking it. He pushed the closed scissors up against her cheek like a finger in a pillow. The other girls screamed, but Candy knew to keep quiet.

'You have time enough now?' he said. 'Time enough to waste? My time?'

Blood oozed from her eyebrow and smeared the broken glass in which he could see his fractured reflection. The chairs were pushed over and Patience and one-eyed Sara retreated far inside the container.

Beauty pulled on Candy's T-shirt. 'My God, Zuko, please!'

'This does not concern you,' he said.

Candy's hair, half plaited and half frizz, was coming out in his fingers. Zuko kicked the chairs away and the other two girls ran from the container. Beauty stayed in the corner. He pulled tighter as Candy struggled, but with every wrench she lost more hair.

'Be merciful!' yelled Beauty. 'She will go to work.'

He barely heard her. He caught sight of himself in the mirror and smashed the scissors into the cracked glass. Candy's eyes were clenched and tears were forming in the creases.

He pulled her face to his, chins touching. 'Look at me. *Look at me*!'

She complied.

'Pay no heed, my Candy, and what can happen?'

She whimpered and pleaded with her eyes. As a trickle of blood made its way down her cheek, Zuko eased his grip to watch its flow. He bared his teeth and lost a globule of spittle from his lower lip, which made Candy flinch. He stuck out his fat tongue and licked the stripe of blood from her face. He released her hair, pulled up his jacket sleeve then grabbed a large shard of the broken mirror and dragged it down his bare arm. A reflex made him pump his fist and a twenty-centimetre line of red formed on his skin as he held the bloody glass before him. 'My arm, your face.'

When Zuko saw the blood dribble into his palm he stabbed the shard into the seat of a chair and jumped into the road, leaving the container rocking from side to side. Jesus was there with the two women who had fled. A small crowd who had left their shacks to witness the scene were being addressed by a familiar besuited man holding a Bible.

Jesus looked in at Candy who was on the floor holding her head and weeping.

He said, 'Is too much. Your girl must work, but suffering we do not need. And my fokken salon, man.'

Then he repeated Zuko's words back at him. '"Work the day and the night"? "Charge more expensive"? How? Look at her. For all our desires, we must be reasonable.'

Zuko looked back at the aftermath of the brawl, which had not only created a scene of destruction inside the container but also shifted the cement blocks on which it rested. Candy was holding a towel over her eye as Beauty helped her to her feet. Zuko put his foot up on the car seat and placed his bloodied hand on his ankle. The crowd, including Jesus, caught the significance of the move and quickly stepped back.

Zuko held out his wounded arm, allowing the blood to drip into the dry earth.

'*You* be reasonable.'

Then he spat at Jesus's feet and headed towards the Lucky Strike.

VI

Two days later Candy helped Beauty wipe off spots of her own dried blood from the mirror.

'Careful, my sister, it will cut you,' said Beauty. Her form was kaleidoscoped around the starfish-shaped crack. Candy dropped the cloth and slumped in a chair.

'Let me see your eye,' said Beauty.

She peeled off the bloodied dressing. 'I will find another,' she said, and jumped out of the container, leaving it gently swaying.

Left alone, Candy's mind followed the dialogue of the dubbed South American drama on the TV. A girl discovered she was adopted and an old man denied being the father. Someone else's ambitions were being thwarted while their mother planned a murder. Candy was not the only one with a troubled life.

A few minutes later Beauty returned with a clean bandage. 'Lucky Lulama is a good woman,' she said. 'The cut will now heal first-class. You must stay out of Zuko's way.'

'I try,' said Candy, 'but if his pocket is empty it is I who must fill it. For months I have been filling it. Now he thinks nothing of beating me in public. I am hurt, I am in disgrace. Everybody knows it.'

'Zuko is all aggravation for you,' said Beauty, 'but sister, you say you now style hair in a salon on the top of the mountain, so why do you remain at the Lucky Strike?'

'I have needs for extra money,' said Candy with deliberate vagueness.

She chose not to share her adopted burden. Beauty was the one friendship she did not want tarnished with the secret troubles of her life. She would solve the problem on her own; it was hers alone, and gave her a reason each day to return to the shack on the edge of the township. It was true, she could earn extra money cleaning or caring for the children of rich white families if she put her mind to it, despite the competition from all the Malawian girls handing out photocopied CVs at the Suikerbosse traffic lights. But something drew her back to the Lucky Strike night after night: the bar girls who had become friends; Lucky Lulama's easy welcome; the rude sounds and dirty smells of the tavern, now as familiar as her own body odour. The treadmill of her routine kept her unaware of how small and soiled her life had become. What was once brutal and shocking was now the nearest thing she had to a family. Home.

Beauty sat in the empty chair beside her. 'I have never said, but I know what you are going through. When I was very young I spent my evenings on a shebeen bar stool. It is true. I have felt numb and sore and sorrowful at the same time, so I feel what you feel. But there are other ways to earn money.'

'Never!' said a voice from the roadway. 'It is the way.'

Zuko was standing on the first step. For once he was not wearing his leather jacket. He must have made a recent score because he was wearing fresh clothing: new All Star trainers, black jeans and a paisley short-sleeved shirt with contrasting collar, which showed off the self-inflicted wound on his forearm like a trophy.

'Shave-shave, sister,' he said.

'I will fetch the water,' said Beauty.

'Candy will shave me,' he said.

As Beauty left the container Zuko grabbed her arm. 'You talk too much,' he said. 'It is for me to say when Candy must leave, not for you.' He gave her arm an ugly twist. 'I hope you are understanding.'

With undisguised disgust, she said, 'Remember, Zuko, Jesus is my boy,' then pulled her arm away and jumped into the road.

Zuko stepped up into the salon. When it stopped rocking he picked up the cut-throat razor and held it at eye level. He purposely nicked the end of his little finger before handing it to Candy. 'Use it wisely, girlfriend.'

He sat in front of the shattered mirror and smiled at his distorted image while they both waited for the water.

Adjusting his oversized collar, he said, 'You like the new shirt?'

'A man must dress the part,' she said, counting the number of images reflected back at her.

'But it is not my favourite,' he said. 'You remember the shirt you bought me?'

'Mmm.'

'I cannot find it.'

'And?'

'It disappeared when you left,' he said.

'Maybe you left it in another girl's bed.'

He examined Candy's divided image.

'Always the last word,' he said.

When Beauty returned and filled the sink, Zuko closed his eyes, leaned his head back and Candy lathered his face. She squirted methylated spirit on the blade and went to work.

He said, 'Enough blood has been spilled, my Candy. Be easy on my cheek.'

She took this not as a warning but as a challenge, and a flaunting demonstration of his power over her.

Even with a blade at his neck, have I not the will to set myself free.

The scene was interrupted by Jesus carrying a large wall mirror.

When Beauty noticed him, she called, 'Heavens above! You are a wonderful man.'

He lifted the mirror into the container and jumped up beside it, sloshing the water in the sink with his action.

'It is better to give than receive,' he said. 'It was left at the dump and I gave ten rands to the pickers. A stylist cannot be a stylist without a mirror. It is not as big as the smashed glass but it will be sufficient.'

With eyes still closed, Zuko said, 'Accidents happen.'

Jesus ignored his comment. 'I will find bricks to wedge under the container. It rolls like a boat on the ocean.'

Beauty lifted her chin and pointed her face at the ceiling. 'Good God, I love this man.'

As Candy lathered Zuko's face for a second, closer shave, Jesus leaned over and picked up the razor. Smiling, he put a finger to his lips then dragged the blade across Zuko's cheek. Jesus rinsed off the lather in the sink then prepared for a wide arc beginning low on his neck. Zuko opened his eyes. He flinched and tried to grab Jesus's hand but succeeded only in pushing the blade across his own skin, scoring a cut into his neck that quickly released a spill of blood.

'You will kill me?' screamed Zuko.

'I am shaving, bruh!' said Jesus, pulling back.

'Yo mama!' cried Zuko, pushing a towel to his neck.

Candy and Beauty both swallowed hard and stared at Jesus. He held the razor aloft and they watched the mixture of shaving foam and blood drip from the end of the blade.

'Chill, man,' said Jesus. 'You cut yourself. Again.'

'This will not be forgotten,' said Zuko, looking from Candy to Jesus and back again. He jumped out of the container and was gone.

Candy turned to Jesus. 'I had the razor in my hand, yet you cut him. I have often thought about it. Next time one of us must finish the chore.'

The following evening the crew were in a tight knot in a dark corner of the Lucky Strike packed with the usual Friday night crowd. Zuko, showing a large plaster on his neck, sat on a reversed chair with his forearms resting on the back. Jesus sat with his back to the wall facing the door with Little Mabhuti and Jonno on either side. Nobody mentioned the plaster until Jesus took out a blade to cut into a mango and warned the crew to keep Zuko away from all sharp objects. Zuko said nothing.

Jesus had a plan to hit a new tourist viewpoint on Chapman's Peak Drive.

Above the sound of Brenda Fassie booming out of the cupboard-sized speaker next to the bar, he said, 'It is their own fault if they wait too long after sunset. We will be waiting too, for easy pick. This is Cape Town, not England with their bobbies. The tourists will go home with a souvenir memory; we go home with their money and cameras.'

'*Ja!*' said Little Mabhuti, clinking bottles with Jonno.

'We go tomorrow night!' said Zuko.

'No,' said Jesus. 'Good things come to those who do the waiting.'

Before Jesus could continue, Zuko pressed. 'I say we go tomorrow. Money is short-short. We have the manpower and the time is right.'

'Zuko... ' Jesus waited until Zuko's eyes settled on him. 'We go when the evening is clear and the sunset is colourful. Then they will all have their cameras and videos up on the outlook.' He spoke slowly as though teaching a child. 'We do not want what happened to Jonno and his dog.'

Little Mabhuti's eyes blinked rapidly at Zuko, who was aware that he had to make a decision. Jesus's logic made sense, but so too did Zuko's desire to adopt the hit as his own and quickly refill his pockets. The immediate decision was taken out of his hands when Beauty announced her arrival at the door with a laugh loud enough to be heard in the valley. She was wearing a spiky wig, micro mini dress and kitten heels. Jesus's face lit up.

'It is a marvel!' he shouted above the music. 'Tina Turner is in the township tonight. Better than all the rest!'

'*Yebo*!' called Lucky Lulama, as she changed the CD in the machine. 'Shake your moneymaker!'

Tina Turner pumped out of the speakers and the tavern roared. Beauty gripped her thighs with painted fingernails and shimmied across the floor on the soles of her sandals. When she reached the bar girls she hitched up her dress even further. '*Give me everything I need.*'

The girls got up and, on cue, sang as one: '*Simply the best!*'

Everyone in the Lucky Strike sang along to the music while the girls strutted around, singing and shaking and jiggling at all the tables to the delight of men who were now only thinking about one thing. All but Zuko, who was still considering his decision over the next hit. When the shebeen quietened down Jonno and Little Mabhuti would want to know where they stood.

This Tina Turner nonsense reminded Zuko of how Jesus still made time for Beauty, putting a hand on her shoulder when she washed laundry at the pump, helping her turn chicken pieces on the braai outside the salon. 'Beauty is worth living for,' he would say, 'What would life be without a little Beauty in it?' It always made her laugh. Even before he set up the salon for her, when she spent evenings at the

Lucky Strike with the neighbourhood men, Jesus had found a way to make their bond special, as if they knew something no one else knew. It seemed that Zuko was practising while Jesus was composing, he was preparing for life while Jesus was living it.

Love. The idea of it enraged him. Everything about Jesus grated on him now: his white teeth, the clean Nikes, even the things he didn't say had the power to rile him. Zuko would have preferred to make peace if only Jesus would accept his place as his junior, but whenever they met, Zuko was quickly angered and a silent quarrel filled the air. And while the plaster remained on his neck, he wanted Jesus to know that he was seething.

Finally, Beauty made her way to the crew's table, wafting in their direction a stirabout of perfume, sweat and sex.

Jesus got up and shouted, 'What would life be without a little Beauty in it?'

She gave a comic grimace, then turned her back and shook her rear end. 'Do you call this little?'

The girls collapsed in laughter and the men roared.

'It is a Beauty-full world,' said Jesus, leaning over the table and clasping her buttocks. 'Paradise by the handful!'

Zuko stood up, threw his half-drunk bottle of beer into the corner and stormed out.

He walked to the corner and lit up. The roar from the Lucky Strike sounded like the rumble of a distant ship, the cacophony occasionally escaping as customers came and went. He heard heels clip-clop down Mandela Road, then abruptly stop. He turned. Candy, late for work as usual, was stopped by two men, no doubt potential customers from the shebeen. She was out of Zuko's earshot but seemed to be protesting something. One man swung a tight arm around her shoulder and grabbed her breast. Zuko quickly slipped between two shacks and took a narrow cut-through parallel to the road. Silently he emerged behind the two men.

One said, 'But sister, why go to the tavern? Come to our place for a private party. We have sounds and beer.'

The other added, 'And two black mambas to make you feel good.'

Candy tried to shrug the man off and moved to step away, but he covered her mouth with his hand; the other pushed her into an abandoned shack where she fell to the dirt floor, losing her shoes.

Zuko, knife in hand, stepped up to the edge of the doorway. Before he made a move he checked to see if either had a weapon to hand. The two men were facing away from him and he could see their blades tucked into the back of their waistbands. One man, with his trousers at his ankles, was already lying on top of Candy who was struggling to free herself, the other was kneeling and untying his belt.

'You will open your legs for us, *nyukazi*, whether you get paid or not.'

Candy whimpered.

With both hands gripping the handle of the raised knife Zuko stepped into the shack and buried the blade in the kneeling man's shoulder, who slumped to the ground. Zuko retrieved the knife from his flesh as the other man looked up at the bloody blade.

He got to his knees, and pleaded, 'No, man, it's just a bit of fun. No harm done.'

'This is my woman,' said Zuko. 'Now and always.'

The man stood up, his glistening, erect cock wagging in the half-light. Before he could pull up his trousers Zuko swung the knife downwards and cleanly lopped off the quivering organ.

Disregarding the man's screams of pain Zuko picked up Candy's discarded shoes, grabbed her hand and they both ran. They got as far as the next streetlight before Candy broke down in gulps of tears. Zuko held her. He inhaled the familiar smell and was hit by a wave of yearning. What he longed for and what he believed was lost was before him. He just needed to make the decision to take it back.

'Zuko?' she said, eyes swimming and full of a hundred questions.

All he said was, 'That's my name.'

VII

Once she had gathered herself, Zuko hailed a taxi and sent Candy home. A part of him wanted to be with her, spend the night inhaling her smell and wake to hear her making milky coffees. His instinctive act of rescue rekindled something he had pretended didn't exist since he threw her out of the shack.

The attack on Candy seemed to compound something that was troubling him about the evening at the Lucky Strike. The cloying closeness of Jesus and Beauty, two infuriatingly happy people, retrieved a space in his mind that he had rarely entered as an adult. He allowed himself to believe that he was always this way, the version he wore like a cloak, and that his past remained exactly there. Now, walking in the darkness back to his shack, he couldn't stay out of the place. From this distance his younger self seemed as foreign as the immigrants streaming into Mandela every day. Without willing it he was returned to boyhood when he was expected to do things for his mother that no child should ever have to do. When his older sisters and aunts were away, which was most of the time, he would have to help his mother up from the mattress onto the pot, wipe her, then swing her back onto the bed before doing his best to dress her. With her good hand, her left, she styled her own hair with a wooden comb as she balanced a mirror on her raised knees. He was small for nine, so occasionally Zuko misstepped and his mother lost her footing, landing heavily on the floor. There were times when he had to change her monthly rags and wash the dirty ones in the bucket by the chicken pen. It tortured him to know his mother was bleeding, and thought she would use up all her blood and shrivel like a mielie left too long in the sun. But she continued on, calling for her pillow to be rearranged, for food, for a flannel, for the pot, for the hand mirror in her bedside cabinet. There was no time for school.

'I am helpless, Zuko,' his mother would say. 'If I need-need you during the day, can I call for you at the schoolhouse? Of course I cannot.'

'But school, Mama, school!'

'Who brought you, my last child, my late gift-gift, into this world? Only God and your mother! God and your mother! And who will take you out? Only God. But he will only receive you in that golden place if you honour the one who bore you here and now! Respect me now and remember me when I'm gone-gone.' She reached for the cabinet. 'Hand me my mirror.'

'You look fine, Ma.'

'Not for me! Look for yourself. What do you see?'

Zuko held the mirror to his face.

'Is that a boy who would dishonour his mother?' she asked. 'Or a fine soul who will care for his flesh and blood, no matter what-what?'

'Ma, I would not dishonour you as long as you live.'

'Hayi! Is true-true. Now reset my pillow.'

After seeing to her each morning Zuko would bubble up a saucepan of mielie pap. By accident he discovered that he preferred his breakfast pap with milk, margarine or sugar, but it was rare that they had more than one extra ingredient to hand. They would eat nothing during the day, save for the occasional mango brought by a village well-wisher and weekly bread that he picked up from the kiosk shop down the hill. In the early evening before the light faded he would bring her tea in a jar then cut up the leftover breakfast pap and fry it, often with no gravy. Chakalaka was a rare treat.

'Cousin Maphule says she had meat, Mama.'

'Meat, is it? When God provides meat we shall eat meat. In the meantime, pap and tea will deliver us from hunger.'

One time Zuko added sliced banana to the breakfast pap, which sweetened the porridge and gave it a sugary aroma, but his mother quickly pushed his food experiment aside. Despite his mother's protestations his portion tasted delicious. The next day once more he cooked pap plain for her, but left his portion on the heat and added banana, sugar and butter. From that day, when the ingredients came to hand, he taught himself a new recipe. His food creations were not always successful – and barely edible, on occasion – but in time his cooking improved and mealtimes created a private world in which he was both teacher and pupil.

Each morning Zuko stood at the door and watched the village children walk down the hill to school. He waited for them all to pass before hanging out the laundry, then later gathered it in before their return after two o'clock. He knew that his junior cousin Maphule felt bad because he was missing out on the things she took for granted, so she would bring magazines written in English that showed photographs from what she called the outside world. They mostly showed smiling people reclining on comfortable settees in large houses.

One sluggish summer day Maphule brought him a history book with a picture of Table Mountain on the cover. It was a gift he treasured because he lived on top of a hill and he could imagine himself sitting on the edge of the mountain in Cape Town swinging his legs and turning the pages. Maphule was now years ahead of him. Sitting on the baked earth in the shade outside the hut she told him about school, enough to both make him gasp with astonishment and bring him to tears of longing. Zuko's mother called from within the hut, but he refused to answer. He picked up a bowl of beans leftover from the previous evening and handed it to Maphule.

She took a handful, raised it to her mouth and whispered, 'Do you manage your ma, Zuko?'

'Fine-fine,' he said.

'While I sit in the schoolhouse, I think of you caring for her,' she said. 'It is too much for a boy who is not yet a man.'

She kissed the book and handed it to him before skipping home. He searched the book for letters of the alphabet he recognised, finally discovering the letter Z, but mostly the words lurked in the shadows as if waiting to ambush him. Meanwhile he enjoyed the pictures and, with care, wrote his name in capital letters on the first page. He thumbed the pages and inhaled the waft. It was a smell he would never forget.

When the village children his age moved on to secondary school, Zuko was keener than ever to join them.

'What? You will leave me now?' yelled his mother. 'The only one who knows how to help me, who knows all my intimates. He wants to abandon me. Abandon me!'

'But the school, Mama. The other children are beyond me. I will be in a low class if I do not return soon.'

'Do you think I asked God to be like this? Do you think I asked him to transport the cart into the ditch? Your sisters are married and gone, so until God gives me the power to walk, you must honour your mother. Honour me now and remember me when I'm gone, but never abandon me.'

There were times when members of the extended family visited and told him he was a wonderful boy and how proud his mother was. But they didn't stay long, sometimes a few days, and always promised to return soon. They usually left clutching an item taken from the kitchen, a knife or a frying pan. 'She cannot use this now,' they would say. 'There are others who have needs also. Worry not, it will stay in the family.'

He was reduced to cooking food with no more than a potjie and stirrer, a flat pan and a teapot. He made a cooking fire outside in summer; in winter he burned sticks precariously close to his mother's bed, occasionally singeing the edge of the sheet. They ate off enamelled tin plates with their fingers.

One time a white from an NGO in East London arrived. Zuko thought she was more orange than white, and told her. She said it was because she was from a place called Scotland where it was so cold that everyone turned ginger. The woman with a million freckles made him laugh and said she was there to 'assess the situation and recommend a course of action'. Unfortunately that action involved moving his mother to a clinic in town. Zuko could have saved her the trouble if she'd only asked him at the outset what his mother's response to that suggestion was likely to be.

As the orange woman left the house, his mother shouted, 'More people die in the clinic than in the village! Come with a coffin next time if you want to kill me! God have mercy, this woman wants to kill me! And me in my own bed!'

The NGO sent a carton of sanitary towels and a sack of mielie meal and Zuko never heard from her again.

As the years passed, Zuko found it easier to move his mother about the room, but he didn't fully appreciate that while he was getting stronger her condition was getting worse. Where once she could shuffle to the near side of the room, he now had to either pick her up and place her before the wash basin or bathe her in bed like an infant.

On his fourteenth birthday his mother arranged for someone in the village to buy him a white shirt, his first pair of long trousers and a secondhand pair of shoes.

'It has been five years since my accident on the mountain pass, so you have earned your clothing,' she said. 'I do not deny you anything, do I?'

He carefully put on the clothes, the material seeming to stroke his skin. So big were the shoes, he could leave the laces tied and still slip them on. His mother handed him the mirror.

'My boy-man is growing,' she said, and laughed.

'Yes, Ma,' he told his image.

'But you will always be my child, until the end-end. You will never abandon me.'

He spent the rest of the day doing his chores while trying not to put creases in his trousers. That night he carefully folded his new clothes and stacked them on the floor next to his bed – shoes then trousers then shirt – where he could see them from the pillow.

The following day, after seeing to his mother, Zuko took the mirror and breathed heavily on it. He wiped it with his sleeve and was excited to see the reflection of Maphule coming to the door. She had not forgotten his birthday after all. From her pockets she produced some nearly ripe tomatoes and two chicken wings. She also brought him another book, one with a picture of the new president on the cover, an old man who looked tired. She said it was too exciting because, unlike all the previous presidents, he spoke their language, isiXhosa.

'This is a new text book,' Maphule said, 'to replace the old history.'

He took it and sat in the shade against the mud wall of the hut with his knees up.

'Read it to me,' he said.

'For shame,' she said. 'That's for babies.'

'Read it. Please, Maphule.'

She read him the first page. The book told the story of how the Hollanders discovered the Cape of Good Hope and built a city there. Then, after wars with the English, the Boers ran the country and kept the Africans down. It said that there was now a president for all the people and the future was hopeful.

'We must now see history from all sides, black and white and coloured,' Maphule said. 'Our teacher says that we all have history in our hands because the future comes disguised.'

'What does that mean?'

'I am not sure, Zuko, but the teacher said that if we want something we must grab it. In the new South Africa we make our own future. It is our time and nothing must hold us back. Ma says that if I studied hard I could be the first of our clan to go to university.'

She kissed the face on the book cover and handed it to him. After he fed and settled his mother, Zuko stirred up the pot of pap with chicken and tomatoes and leftover greens and Maphule and he shared the meal in undisturbed silence like a ritual. Then they lay side by side on the hard red earth until the first point of light shone.

'The evening star, Maphule.'

'It is not a star, Zuko.'

'What is it?'

'The planet Venus.'

'How do you know?'

'Stars twinkle; planets don't.'

Zuko concentrated on the point of light.

'Are there people there like us?'

'There is nobody like you, Zuko.'

'Or you.'

They talked of childish wishes, boys and girls they liked, their parents, things they could never say face to face. It was like sharing thoughts with the night air.

The outlines of the mountains faded and the sky was soon filled with white specks.

'Are you making shapes with the constellations, too?' she asked.

'Yes.'

Without knowing her thoughts, he was thrilled that they were both likely making the same patterns in the stars.

She pointed. 'Do you see the three bright stars in a row?'

'Yes, I see them every night.'

'Orion's Belt.'

He tried to trace the outline of a figure wearing the belt.

'Who is Orion?'

'Orion the hunter.'

'What is he hunting, Maphule?'

'I don't know. Maybe the question is not what, but who.'

Even the stars were hunting; something or someone. Through Maphule's eyes the world seemed different. It *was* different. She noticed things and used words to describe them in a way that he could never hope to match.

'Can you feel the vertigo?' she asked.

'I feel like I am lost,' he said. 'The stars, they move every time I blink.'

'The stars are not moving, Zuko, we are.'

'How can we move without doing anything?'

'That's vertigo.'

After his cousin went home, Zuko retrieved his other book from under the bed and returned to his place outside on the dry earth with his back against the mud wall. He cradled them both until his mother was asleep, then took to his cot. That night, before their time, the rains came. In the chilly, damp morning, Zuko got his mother up and made her pap as usual. After he got her off the pot and back into bed, he stood at the door and watched the children walk to school as last night's downpour rose in steam off the road. He took a bowl of laundry outside but stopped when he noticed he had left the two books out in the rain. His eyes watered, and he recalled the feeling from last night. He felt lost. He squatted on his haunches and tried to peel apart the sodden pages while passing children looked on as they made their way down the hill. He brought the ruined books inside and lay them at the foot of his mother's bed. He changed into his new clothes then took the pillow from behind her head and, placing it over her face, pressed with all his weight and held it there until he stopped crying.

VIII

The evening following the attack by the two men on Candy, Zuko sat on the oil drum outside the Lucky Strike. It had been a warm day, hotter than usual for mid December. The last of the copper sun was about to dip behind the mountain opposite as the dust settled and everyone in Mandela Park took a breath. The choir in the community centre down the hill was singing a familiar Christmas tune; it sounded like half the township was in there. Lucky Lulama closed the shebeen and walked down to join the congregation. Whites, mostly middle-aged women, were parking up on the rough ground beside the community centre and taking boxes and stuffed bags in Christmas wrapping to the side door. The man who ran the neighbourhood kitchen was trying to organise everyone but he was soon overwhelmed by the number of donations. The cars didn't stay long. After being thanked, the whites reversed into the unmade road by the spaza and were soon gone. Once the sun had fully set behind the mountain, a white Mercedes remained. Slowly, with a gangster lean, Zuko went over for a closer look. Full leather, sun roof, hands-free phone kit.

A voice behind him said, 'You touch it, you're dead.'

Zuko stepped away. A white man more than twice his age was smiling. When Zuko saw the man limp heavily, he leaned back on the car.

'This is not a place for a crippled white after dark,' said Zuko.

'Insulting me, and I've only just arrived.'

'Well, now go.'

'Relax. It's Christmas,' said the white man. 'What happened to you? Been in the wars?'

Zuko raised his hand to the peeling plaster on his neck. 'Accident, sho. Shaving can be perilous with a sharp razor.'

'That depends who's wielding the razor.'

Zuko acknowledged the man's accurate assumption about his injury.

'You have my sympathy,' said the white, 'crime is taking over our beautiful, if divided, community in Hout Bay.'

The man then deftly lifted his walking stick into the air and pointed the carved brass end at Zuko.

'Talking of beautiful things, I've been told you're the man to see about a girl.'

'You dig-dig black chicks?'

'Why else would I come to this shit hole?'

Zuko smiled. 'You bold, man.'

A customer with a stick and a white Mercedes thinks he's shopping at the mall.

'It is too early for the girl-girls,' said Zuko. 'Even the Lucky Strike is closed.'

'I could make it worth your while,' said the white, 'if you can source for me the specimen I desire, so to speak.'

'What-what?'

'Young, light-skinned. One that speaks English, for a change.'

Zuko looked into the man's eyes, the only blue ones in the township, probably.

'What is your number?' asked Zuko. 'I will call when I have located her.'

'Don't worry about my number. Just get the girl and I'll see you right. I'll wait.'

'Okay, baas. My Candy will be good-good price.'

'Aren't they always.'

Zuko pushed a number on his cellphone and the two men leaned side by side against the white car in the growing darkness. Twenty minutes later they watched Candy get out of a shared taxi wearing heels, jeans, a sparkly top, and an unruly wig that couldn't quite hide the cut on her eyebrow. The white man's eyes widened, showing his approval, and he thrust some notes into Zuko's palm. Candy grasped the man's free hand and led him, leaning awkwardly on his stick, behind the Lucky Strike. As Candy unhooked the shack's door latch Zuko thumbed another number on his cellphone.

The buildings and shacks of the township receded into the night and one or two dim streetlights came on. Apart from two drunk old men on a bench sharing a container of *umqombothi*, the street was empty. Nothing was happening except the joyous sound of the choir in the community centre.

Jesus arrived first.

'Whose car? What is to be done, Zuko?' he asked.

'Tonight we score. The car belongs to a rich white, behind with Candy. He is ours.'

'In our own neighbourhood?'

'He is rich.'

'He came here? He is police, I know it,' said Jesus. 'He packs a gat and will cap you.'

'No, he does not carry a gun. He is a cripple and walks with a stick.'

'Then why did you call me? You take him.'

'I called Little Mabhuti and Jonno but they have not arrived.'

Jesus said nothing.

'You have a knife?' asked Zuko.

'The whole crew for a cripple behind the Lucky Strike?' said Jesus tapping his temple. 'For once, my bruh, think. Use your brain, man.'

'Fuck you. I am not your bruh. You don't want to, you fuck off now.'

'Fuck this,' spat Jesus. 'The heat is too hot for this shit, I am leaving the kitchen.'

'Go fuck your mother,' said Zuko.

'No, I will fuck *your* mother – when you are in jail,' said Jesus, stepping away.

'Watch for me,' said Zuko.

He crept down the side of the Lucky Strike and listened at the shack door. He heard low voices, then a gurgle of girlish laughter. He looked back. Jesus remained in the space between two shacks.

'Watch for me!' said Zuko once more in an urgent whisper.

Then he pulled out a combat knife from his boot, kicked at the door and burst in. The naked man rolled onto his back as Candy screamed and curled up in the corner.

'Money, man! Fokken money!' yelled Zuko, stabbing at the low-hanging light bulb, smashing it.

'Here, everything I have,' said the cripple, throwing his jacket towards Zuko.

'Don't fuck with me! Phone, fokken phone,' said Zuko.

'In the side pocket.'

'What's that chain on your wrist?'

'I'm diabetic. It's worth nothing.'

'Give.'

'I'm sick. Please. Just take what you want and let me go.'

The cripple was now on his knees and shivering like a pig that has just realised it has been lured into a slaughterhouse. Even in the semi-darkness Zuko was shocked to see how white the man's body was, almost luminous next to Candy, as if the only light in the place issued from his skin. Zuko had the man where he wanted him and relaxed his shoulders. He enjoyed the thrill of their nakedness, white and brown, and drew the flat side of his knife up to the white's face, making like he was giving him a shave.

'Is this how you do it in the salon, Candy?'

'Let him be, he is a handicap,' she said, pulling her knees up. 'You may be one in the next life.'

From outside, Jesus called, 'The people from the centre, they come. Let's go, man. Go!'

Zuko heard him run.

'What's it to you, my Candy?' said Zuko. 'You like the white? Maybe. You half-white gammie.'

'Fok you!'

Zuko pushed the man onto his back, knocking his walking stick into the corner. Zuko kneeled down and grabbed Candy by the throat with his left hand.

'You will offend me again? You minstrel,' he hissed.

He squeezed until no sound came from her throat and her eyes bulged unnaturally. Everything between them had the air of finality. The naked man got to his feet, gathered his clothes and car keys and limped heavily out the door.

'Your last trick, my Candy?'

She leaned back on her elbows to steady herself on the mattress and her hand landed on the man's walking stick. She grabbed it and, closing her eyes, swung it as hard as she could behind Zuko's head. The weighted brass pommel struck him above the ear.

'No, *your* last,' she said.

He released her and tried to grab the stick but she quickly got to her feet and swung again, this time catching the bridge of his nose. He stepped back, which allowed her to get a better swing. This time the stick swiped him heavily on the side of his head and he went down on both knees. Again she hit him. Candy stopped when she registered the violence of the blows, then dropped the stick and watched his flesh cleave as blood covered his head. It was her last independent thought. Zuko locked eyes with her and in one motion lifted his knife into the air, burying the full length of the blade in her belly.

IX

The morning after, Zuko kept his head down, allowing time for Candy's body to be found and taken away, and for the first response police to leave the scene. He spent the weekend thinking, not about money or the next hijack, just thinking. The events of that night got confused with the previous evening when he saw off the two thugs who attacked Candy on the street. Both touched something inside, something he couldn't describe, as if they were two halves of a whole.

He wondered if he should leave Mandela for another township: Gugulethu or Langa were bigger ponds, bigger fish. Start again. While washing off Candy's blood at the standpipe the previous evening, Zuko had fleetingly considered a substitute girl, a thought that angered him now, but he didn't know why. The images of that night returned to him. The dead weight of Candy's body falling on him, the ugly sound of her head hitting the floor and, later, the hot blood, dark, thick, heavy, turning cold on his arm and neck replayed in him again and again. It reminded him of the first time he had killed. It was suddenly hard to imagine a substitute for Candy. The troubled closeness that existed between them, now destroyed by his own hand, had kept alive a deeper relationship, the earliest he had known.

SAPS officers came and rested their hands on their hips and spat in the dirt. Nothing new here: before now they'd dragged stab victims out of the latrines by the main road; they'd picked out the burnt bodies from the remains of shack fires; they'd cradled babies with their heads smashed against walls by men who believed that defiling an infant would cure them of their diseases. The police soon left. When Zuko heard there had been another neighbourhood murder since Candy felt his blade, he came back into the light. On the third day Zuko kicked at Lucky Lulama's door and told her to see to his splitting skull, still bloody and weeping from the thrashing Candy gave him with the walking stick.

'They say you found her,' said Zuko.

'It is true,' said Lucky Lulama. 'And so terrible, neh. I called SAPS but those fuck brains couldn't find their own balls with a mirror.'

'Sho. You know it what happened?' asked Zuko.

She seemed hesitant, and turned to fill a basin and cut some bandages. Zuko was pleased when she broke the silence.

'They say a white man was behind with Candy and he brought a knife,' she said. 'There are such wicked men in the valley.'

'Is true. I ran, but he stayed and chopped her,' he said. 'It is too-too bad.'

'White's can fuck you up too,' she said. She put down the scissors. 'I found something else.'

From behind the bar she retrieved a walking stick with a heavy metal top.

'I took it before the police arrived. Was I right to do it?'

Zuko snatched the cane and inspected the brass end in the shape of a lion's head, speckled dark red.

'It is my blood,' said Zuko. 'It is the stick of the cripple, he hit me lucky. Wherever he is, he is limping. I will take it, but stay silent. Nothing good will come of speaking to the police.'

'Sharp.'

Lucky Lulama put her attention to Zuko's wounds, dabbing them with antiseptic.

'You must see a doctor for the cut, neh. It is too deep. They will put stitches.'

'I will not die. Do your best.'

'I can clean your wound, it is all I can do.'

He winced as she dabbed his bloody scalp.

'And if anyone did speak to SAPS,' he said, weighing the walking stick in his hands, 'their time would be over in the township.'

'I know it.'

Jesus's big mouth would have made it common knowledge by now that Zuko was at the scene on the night Candy died, but he was sure he was not observed leaving the shack. He also believed that Lucky Lulama would accept whatever he told her. She was not someone who had favourites. She had beer to sell and she didn't care which girls drew in the men.

Neither wanted to talk more. She wrapped his head in gauze, re-dressed the razor cut on his neck, then treated the scabby scar on his forearm with antiseptic.

He left the Lucky Strike and, on seeing Jesus at the standpipe, realised he had left his knife at home. He had felt light and insubstantial all morning. Now he knew why.

'That was some shit, my bruh,' said Jesus. 'You well fucked up. You look like you came from a war.'

Jesus was the last person he wanted to see.

'You know what happened?' asked Zuko.

'Yo! We all know. You never know what is around the corner. But how, my bruh?'

'Things was crazy down there.'

'I told you – never in your own neighbourhood,' said Jesus, 'and now this.'

'It was cool until Candy talked to me kak.'

'*Ja*, but the white guy brought a knife?' said Jesus. 'Why kill a chick after being robbed? It makes shit sense.'

Zuko had assumed too much. Jesus didn't know. For once, Jesus was wrong.

'He was a kaffir-hater, I could see it,' said Zuko, touching his head.

'Who is he? Was he off-duty SAPS?'

'Nah.'

'You too cool,' said Jesus, laying a rare hand on Zuko's shoulder. 'He could have cut you serious.'

'It was dark, the light was out. He hit me lucky.'

'Fok! The cripple always brings a stick,' said Jesus. 'But Candy, bruh? Sho!'

'It is done. I took the score and ran and thought she was behind me.'

Following the conversation with Jesus Zuko's urge to flee to another township receded. Later, the gossip among the women queueing for water at the standpipe told him that word had already spread that Candy had been murdered by a white man. The story grew to become a white policeman in a bakkie. Then people talked about how there were two of them in plain-clothes who pretended to attend the Christmas concert at the community centre but pursued Candy following a shakedown. It was what they wanted to believe. Zuko said nothing to fuel or dampen the speculation. He didn't need to, the story was confused enough. That afternoon two coloured detectives used the Lucky Strike to question the regulars and a few neighbours, but nobody admitted to seeing or hearing anything, and they went away with empty notebooks.

X

The two sisters were sitting outside Antonio's in the street-side patio under a length of tinsel strung between the ribs of a parasol that kept them in the shade. One drank Appletiser, the other sipped from a glass of sauvignon blanc. A plastic miniature Christmas tree balanced on the table between them.

The smaller of the two women – dyed black hair and matching eyebrows, linen suit, her neck, wrists, ears and ankle laced with gold – faced the beach and idly watched the Zimbabwean traders sell trinkets to tourists. Beyond, she traced the coloured township up the mountainside towards the Sentinel, the dark peak overlooking the bay. She lit a cigarette and exhaled, which ended in a sigh.

'Ag, what do you have to do to get food in this place?' Rhea said. 'They all on go slow? We the only ones here, for God's sake.'

'It's Monday,' said her sister, Cheri. 'Skeleton staff on Antonio's day off.'

'Quicker to train a baboon.'

Cheri pressed her lips together. Rhea was still shaking her head when a waitress placed two plates of food on the table.

Rhea struck a pose of mock outrage. 'What do you call that?'

'It's salad niçoise, madam.'

'Where's the niçoise?'

The waitress looked blank.

'You know what niçoise means? You don't, do you? Niçoise is a place –'

'*Nice*, you mean –' interjected her sister.

'Thank you, Cheri, *Nice* is a place where they grow tuna, which is why it's called salad niçoise. With me so far?'

'Yes, madam.'

'So where's my tuna?'

'On the top, madam.'

'That masticated mess from a can?'

'I'm sorry?'

'So am I. Take it away. I'll have a small pizza margherita.'

'It may take twenty minutes, madam.'

'This is what I'm talking about. I'm sick with hunger and you're refusing to bring me a simple plate of food.'

Rhea took out a handkerchief and dabbed the corners of both eyes as the waitress picked up the plate.

'Antonio will hear about this,' said Rhea. 'Don't expect a –'

'No, madam.'

'– tip.'

Her curt reply revealed too much of the waitress's thoughts. In that moment the two women knew everything they would ever know about each other and their lives lived at opposite ends of the world: one on the mountain, the other in the valley; one standing, the other sitting; one serving, the other drinking. And as far as Rhea was concerned, those worlds would never meet outside the provision of paid-for services.

A car parked up on the busy street and a middle-aged man got out. He was wearing tailored shorts belted on the last eyelet, a short-sleeved shirt that, despite his swollen waistline, was tucked in, and black sandals that revealed unclipped toenails. With his left hand he placed a sweat-ringed Panama hat on his head; with his right he leaned heavily on a walking stick.

'Hello Clive,' said Cheri. 'Howzit?'

'Cheri! My favourite sister-in-law.'

'Lucky you only have one, hey?'

He pressed the key fob and the white Mercedes-Benz burped quietly. He joined them at the table.

Rhea said, 'What are you having?'

'Not fussy,' said Clive.

'You can have my pizza when it comes. I'm not hungry.'

Cheri shot Rhea a glance but said nothing. Clive waved into the restaurant and called for a Windhoek lager.

'Is this the new cane?' asked Rhea.

'*Ja*, picked it up from the Af's market. It was time for a new one anyway.'

'Can you believe it, Cheri?' said Rhea. 'His cellphone and beautiful carved cane with the brass top were stolen from the car. A walking stick! What are they thinking, these people?

The cellphone can be replaced, but that was Daddy's old lion's head cane. Closest thing we had to an heirloom.'

'It was just a stick,' said Clive.

'Our last break-in they took a DVD player and all my teaspoons,' said Cheri. 'I ask you.'

'Drugs,' said Clive, happy to change the subject.

'Drugs on Villeroy and Boch teaspoons? What next.'

'It's how they cook it up,' said Clive.

Rhea did not want to talk about drugs. 'But why would anyone want to steal a walking stick? Probably used for firewood already.'

'Stolen, lost, what does it matter?' Clive said. 'My own fault. Forgot to lock the car. I'm happy enough with this one.'

The waitress placed a pizza and a bottle of Windhoek on the table.

'Howzit, Mpatuleni?' he said.

'O, you say my name too good!' said the waitress with a toothy smile. 'I am very well, and you, Mister Clive?'

'Gorgeous day,' he said.

'Most gorgeous!' she said. 'May I bring you something more?'

'No,' said Rhea flatly.

'Thank you, Mpatuleni,' said Clive. 'We'll manage from here.'

The waitress left.

'Why do you suck up to these Africans?' said Rhea.

'A smile can set the world right,' he said with a casual tilt of his head. 'And just to be completely accurate, she's Malawian.'

'Malawi was in Africa last time I looked,' said Rhea.

This good *rooinekke* bad *rooinekke* routine had long become tedious for him. The friendlier he was with black Africans the frostier Rhea became. She was too old now to change her attitudes, he knew that; he just wished she was more forgiving, more open to persuasion. Younger. In kinder moments he saw her brusqueness towards the gardener, the waitress, the bank teller, as grief for the lost world before Mandela and democracy, a time she always claimed to abhor. But now that it was gone, she acted as though every black person in South Africa had borrowed something without her permission, and had no intention of ever bringing it back. Regardless, most people saw her for what she was: rude, disrespectful, ignorant. Clive called her attitude 'blaming the blameless'. The people with whom she came into contact were not responsible for what she saw as the considerable ills of the country: they had jobs. They did not steal Rhea's car last winter, or break into Cheri's house and take all her teaspoons, or rip out the copper cable from the electricity sub station on Main Road.

Clive took a slice of pizza and bit into it as a newspaper seller approached. He bought a copy of the *Cape Argus* and was drawn immediately to the story on page one.

> 44 Murders – One Bloody Cape Town Weekend
> Cape Town lived up to its reputation of murder capital this past weekend, when between 4pm on Friday and 7.30am on Monday 44 people had died violently.

A total of 29 people were stabbed to death, 12 were shot and three were victims of assault and blunt trauma.

He became engrossed in the news story: the shootings in Mitchells Plain on Sunday night, the murderous gang fights in Valhalla Park early on Monday morning, the double rape and murder in Lavender Hill late Saturday night. The last two paragraphs were what he feared.

Police spokesman Lieutenant-Colonel Andre Fredericks highlighted the violent death in Hout Bay of a young woman who was stabbed to death sometime on Friday evening in a makeshift brothel next to the Lucky Strike tavern in Imizamo Yethu township.

He said: "We have reason to believe that the incident was preceded by an argument between the victim and her customer, who fled the scene, and who is yet to be arrested."

Clive folded over the headline and placed the newspaper on the table. He took a sip of beer while Rhea and Cheri talked as if he wasn't there. He watched customers step into the restaurant patio as he touched the cool glass and enjoyed the warmth of the sun on his back. He thanked God for them both. He pushed his hat back on his head and closed his eyes. Nobody saw him, of that he was fairly sure. Except the guy with the plaster on his neck who got cracked on the skull with his walking stick. At least it was put to good use. But the girl was dead. Fucking hell. The pimp must have finished her off after he ran. Now the police. But there's no reason why they should come looking for him. If her pimp did her in, he's the only one who knows Clive was there. That worked. He's no doubt ditched the sim and sold the cellphone by now. Can they trace these things? The medi-bracelet? Fuck it; probably in a ditch somewhere. Walking stick? Ditto.

Clive ran his fingers through the stubble on his face, a gesture which dug up an image from Friday night. That blade could as easily cut through his flesh, leaving his naked body on the putrid mattress. But this time it was – what was her name? It's never their real name. He'd had a Lola, a Lolita, a Lucy. Coco, was it? Chastity? A gurgle of laughter erupted from him.

'What's tickled your funny bone?' said Rhea.

'Nothing. Just... life.'

He pushed the newspaper across the table, as if distancing himself from the memory, and eyed a lithe Zimbabwean vendor across the road who was wearing Christmas tree earrings.

'People dying in our beautiful city for no reason,' he said. 'It could be any one of us. We don't know what lies ahead.'

Rhea picked up the newspaper and looked at the headline. 'They really are the nicest people, except when they're trying to kill you,' she said.

'Funny.'

'These murders happen in one place, Clive, you know that – in the townships. Let them live their lives and we'll live ours, thank you very much.'

Tempted by the smell of garlic and tomato sauce, Rhea put a slice of pizza on a side plate and picked up her knife and fork.

'You hungry now?' said Cheri.

'But hey,' said Rhea, ignoring her sister, 'lighten up. Especially after the few days you've had. You know, Cheri, he also lost his medical alert bracelet. What am I going to do with him, hey?'

'*Ja*,' said Clive. 'It was a hectic weekend.'

XI

The evening after getting his wounds dressed Zuko spent many silent hours at the Lucky Strike chewing over Candy's death. Lucky Lulama said she never trusted anyone who drove a white car – which accounted for a large percentage of the population of Hout Bay – and just because he was white didn't give him the right to ill-treat our sisters. She really had it in for anything white. She then poured Zuko a free shot of Johnnie Walker Red.

'Shame Jesus, Mary and Joseph are not here,' she said. 'I would have opened another bottle.'

She must be mad as a township bitch, thought Zuko.

None of the crew came in, and he said nothing when one-eyed Sara and the other girls failed to appear after dark. Passing them at the mini-bus taxi rank, Zuko was aware that they must have thought he was acting strangely but he allowed them to believe it was because Candy and all her income had been taken from him. One more thing to consider was that Jesus, Beauty and most of the immediate neighbourhood had witnessed the incident in the salon the previous week, and the black eye he gave Candy was the talk of the shebeen, so he would have to keep his head down for a few more days.

A man from the city morgue turned up asking about Candice Schippers' next of kin and her home address. He knocked on the shacks and houses on either side of the shebeen, but got nowhere. Zuko hoped that the regulars at the Lucky Strike kept quiet to shield him and his crew from closer investigation. More likely the truth was that they said nothing because nobody knew anything about her. Her face was so familiar on the street and in the Beauty Girl Salon that people assumed she had grown up in the township and had family close by. It soon became common knowledge that if her family could not be found she would be buried in the communal plot out near the airport.

The break in his routine gave Zuko time to consider the situation from a new perspective: what he had lost, what she had meant to him. He sensed a chasm opening up before him, a lifetime with no Candy. Despite their fights, their fractious history was something Zuko had come to cherish. Even their most violent fights were now remembered with something close to affection; he would begin a memory with a smile and end it wet-eyed. She made him who he was. The Madiba shirt – the only gift she had ever bought him – now seemed to signify the possibilities of a new Zuko. Sometimes a shirt was not just a piece of clothing. Now that she was gone, more than ever he wanted to ask her if perhaps she had a different view of their relationship, even as she headed for a shameful burial with the other township unknowns. He suddenly startled himself with the realisation that what he felt for her must have been love.

Two nights later Zuko provoked an argument with his current live-in girl, a heavy, satin-skinned Namibian with an unhealthy dependence on store-bought melktert. On the third night, he lost his patience and threw her out of the house.

'Look in the mirror! You blacker than me!' he said, emptying the shelves of packet food into a plastic bin. 'You no have class.'

'Ha! A no-school gangster tells me I no have class,' she called from the street. 'You would not know class if it bit your pygmy cock!'

He dragged her belongings to the open door then kicked them into the dirt. She screamed at the bolted door for twenty minutes before he opened it with a beer in one hand and a blade in the other. Silently she backed into the darkness. He did not expect to hear from her again.

Zuko opened a second beer, then a third and a fourth. He did not want to be alone, but didn't want the Namibian back.

With the feeling of an animal that had slipped its collar – free, yes, but also lost – he recalled arguments with Candy after which, as he remembered it, they soon made up by him cooking a special meal. The urge to look for her – and the shirt – was powerful, at least to look for the ghost of her and bury her in a named plot. It would not do for her to spend eternity lying next to no-name Ovambo gangsters.

But where to start? All trace of her seemed to vanish the moment her dead body hit the ground.

Her cousin with the cripple daughter might know.

The next morning Zuko went to the cousin's house, which looked more neglected than he remembered it on Candy's arrival three years earlier. Two light-skinned men were sitting on the step, smoking.

'Hello, my brothers,' said Zuko. 'I seek a family that lives here. Do you know them? They have two girls, one is a cripple.'

'We know nothing,' said the older man. 'The house is ours.'

'They live in a share with you?'

The man stood up. 'Only my family. We have rights.'

'It is not true,' said Zuko with caution. 'Another family owned this house. Where are they?'

Another man appeared in the doorway.

'Do you have a home, my brother?' he asked.

Zuko nodded.

'Then go to it. This house is ours now. I may bring my proof.'

The man's upper lip curled back showing his blackened teeth, then he slunk back inside. His image was replaced by two small children with lollipop-stained mouths who leaned out of the torn screen door. Soon, above their heads, the man re-appeared holding a .38 Special across his chest. The taped wooden handle showed that it was well-used, threatening. Zuko clocked the gang tattoo on the back of the man's hand and took a step back. He pulled his arms away from his sides and opened his palms.

'Blessings, my brothers,' Zuko said. 'I will not bring trouble. The house is yours, true.'

'True,' said the gunman, holding the children close with his free hand. 'No trouble comes to our door.'

The gunman and the other two men on the step all spat into the dirt. The children copied them.

Zuko backed away and the image of the glinting gun above the heads of the two children receded.

On the street corner Zuko bought a pack of cigarettes from a vendor.

'Where is the family from this place?' he asked.

'The mother, she got sick and died. The children, who knows. These gangsters took the house. We leave them alone.'

Without thinking he drifted uphill towards the Beauty Girl Salon. There was one other person who might know where Candy lived.

He was waiting at the container when Beauty arrived to open up for the day, sleeves rolled up ready for washing or work.

'Where is Candy's house?' asked Zuko.

She swung open the cargo door and wedged it with a broken paving stone. When the container stopped trembling she stepped up into the salon. She looked down on him, which, for the first time in Beauty's presence, made him feel small. He felt she could read him: No big-man ideas, just *tsotsi* kak from a country boy.

'I do not know,' said Beauty. 'Far, far on the mountain. I did not see her place. She sat with me in the early evening, but she worked elsewhere during the day. After her last date she always went home alone.'

She sucked her teeth and gave him a steady, quiet look, beneath which lay what he imagined to be a vast ocean of loathing, none of it needing to be said.

Eventually, 'What do you want, Zuko?'

Normally he would not allow her to speak to him so disrespectfully, but there was something in the air. There was guilt, a shared guilt that neither could seize. If he thought about it long enough he would realise that he was looking for someone to tell him how he felt. He tried to shake it off like a dog shakes off dirty water.

'The burial must take place,' he said. 'The family must claim her.'

'*Yebo!*'

'If not, the municipality will put her with the unknowns. It should not be.'

'Use your logic, Zuko. Candy must be in the ground or the crematorium by now.'

She picked up a bucket and jumped down from the container.

'I need water,' she said. 'I have to work, even if you don't.'

Zuko followed her to the standpipe. 'Do you know her family?'

'She did not tell.'

'From where did she come?'

'I know no more than you,' she said as the bucket filled. 'Somewhere in the Cederberg, as you know. Have you tried her cousin's place?'

'Squatters have taken the house,' he said.

'Then I have no more suggestions.'

Zuko headed back up the hill and thought again about the course of Candy's life in Mandela. He remembered she had worked at Antonio's restaurant while living with her cousin before moving in with Beauty. Then Candy came to him. After she left his shack she seemed to step off stage. Even her closest friend did not know where she had lived.

He felt compelled to search. He left his own neighbourhood, ignoring the bulges of cellphones and money clips in men's pockets, and disregarding unattended stalls of produce in quiet dead ends. He walked beyond the homes fitted with insubstantial locks that his boot could take care of; beyond the spazas with flimsy barred counters that were close to cut-throughs from where he could make his escape; and beyond the shacks that he knew were left open for children returning from school. He left behind those familiar faces who would make their excuses and leave whenever he appeared, and the down-at-heel shoes of the girls he could entice with a flash of his gold chain. And most of all he left behind the mamas and the pastors and the neighbourhood chiefs who gave up chasing him when their hearts began to burst and who could all go fuck themselves.

He continued on, behind the new houses painted from the palette of a child's colouring box, towards silver shacks in the informal settlement, which soon petered out into pitiful lean-tos. It was difficult to tell if the little cabins and make-do constructions were occupied at all. Around him now were the recent knock-up shanties covered with plastic sheeting built by new arrivals from African towns he had never heard of. This, thought Zuko grimly, is what Jesus calls 'paradise'.

He reached the eastern limit of the township and looked back across the valley towards the white estates going up on the southern side of Table Mountain and above Victoria Avenue. He could make out white bodies dotted on lawns and beside swimming pools accompanied by an echoey soundtrack of wailing alarms and barking dogs. He had taken in this view, from other locations, many times. It was like looking at a painting that slowly reshaped itself; occasionally a mansion would go up here, a security complex there, erasing another line of trees that led up to the sandy crag of the Karbonkelberg.

He turned to the sprawl of the township below, and the NGO-built homes that moved some of the longstanding population out of shacks. He could see the new houses with huts built up against the back wall and rented out to the ever-hopeful from Malawi and Zimbabwe and those, like him, from the Eastern Cape, squeezing four families into the space for one, making a buck any way they can.

Since the day he had arrived in Mandela Park Zuko accepted that change was the way of things. He noticed the constant flux because back in his village nothing had ever changed. The hills remained as they were when God laid them. They were there still, he was sure, like his mother's hut and the chicken pen, empty and forbidding. It seemed to him that every new wave of incomers to Mandela Park pushed everyone else into an ever smaller corner. People rubbed up against each other so tightly they were in danger of igniting, and the divisions were as starkly evident as those between him and the whites who drove Benzes down

Victoria Avenue. He saw all new visitors to the township as adversaries because they stood between him and his money. In fact the people in the township were more his enemy than the rich whites in the valley – their money was so well protected as to be deserving of respect.

He continued walking. Here, under his feet, nothing looked familiar. It was years since he had covered this stretch of the mountain. There were now rough roads where there had once been tracks, homes where there had been trees. He kept on, hoping to notice some landmark that Candy might have mentioned, but he only saw wary people emerging out of dark doorways and dogs snuffling for scraps. Women with worried faces carried babies with reddening hair, a sure sign of malnutrition.

Drawn by the stench of charred wood, he stopped outside a burnt-out cabin that had once been a spaza. Approaching from the opposite direction, the shopkeeper pushed his salvaged goods in a supermarket trolley down the uneven road, calling for business in an unfamiliar accent. The man's dirty feet flapped on the hard earth and his arms, too long for his jacket, gave him the appearance of a fast-growing schoolboy. He was tall, heavy lidded, with a prominent forehead. Somali. Some called them whites with black skin. There's always some foreigner finding a new bottom rung on the township ladder, and putting local spazas out of business. If they could make a penny on a sale, they would do it; for that, the rung above made them pay with machetes and firebombs.

Zuko bought a packet of biscuits, one of a few singed items in the trolley. 'I am looking for a girl,' he said, 'a beauteous girl-girl!'

'There are many girls in the neighbourhood,' said the Somali, dismissively. 'Pick your choose!'

Zuko took this as an insult and reached for his knife.

As he did so, the Somali said, 'I know you are *tsotsi*. They have burned my shop and looted me out. I am now not a man. There is nothing more you can do to me, my *tsotsi* friend.'

Zuko realised the absurdity of his own reaction and returned the knife to his boot.

'It is a particular girl I seek,' he said. 'One who is the colour of the sand on the beach.'

'I am Somali,' said the shopkeeper, moving on. 'I notice only Somalis.'

Zuko ate half the biscuits then dropped the remainder into the lap of a pipe-smoking old woman with a heavily scarred face who was squatting in the road. He turned into dead-ends, retraced his own steps and banged at every padlocked shack, hoping chance would intervene. When he saw two women emerge from a make-do cabin he reasoned that Candy may not have lived alone, so he began looking inside shacks occupied by old men or women with babies on their backs, an action that was usually greeted with abuse and the snapping of skinny dogs.

The long hours of the blazing afternoon turned to evening and he took another breather. He bought a Fanta and sat on a lacerated car tyre as a family of guinea fowls filed past. He was empty, and had spent the day dragging around the emptiness like a rock. He was looking for a murdered girl that he would never find and felt sorry for that. In the fresh light of this new place, guilt looked different. It was strange that after a lifetime of being blamed for things he did not do – and many that he did – people should think him innocent of Candy's death. Somehow he wanted to make it up to her, a futile thought that troubled him. He was not only sorry that he was looking for a dead girl and sorry that he couldn't find her, he was also sorry that he was responsible. He wished that he had not murdered the girl with the golden skin and a barbershop dream. There was a word for what he was feeling that he had never learned, but he did not need to know the word to feel it.

He shuddered and began to think that his day had been wasted. He thought about getting the crew back together. He could certainly use the money from a big score having already spent the few rands he took from the white with the limp. He hoped soon to return to the corner seat at the Lucky Strike or take his place on the bench in the shade of the Beauty Girl Salon where he would scrutinise once more the girls of Mandela Park, and then, and not for the last time, choose one and make her his own.

As he was about to admit his search for Candy's traces was beyond him, a momentary thought of Jesus brought back one of his insults like a regurgitated piece of goat fat: *For once, think. Use your brain.* Where would she live her life when she was not at the Lucky Strike? What mattered to her more than anything? The salon, the itch that had irritated him as much as her. Didn't she know that she wasn't the only one who had dreams. His own were buried too deep, not said – not when he left his mother under the pillow, not when he took her mirror from the bedside cabinet and walked the road going south until his shoes fell apart and his feet bled, not when he slept in a box that first week and carried his hunger like hate, and not when he made small-packet deliveries for the Nigerians. Every path had been an improvisation. With his bare feet and wild hair, people treated him as something feral. Even in the informal settlement the teenage Zuko was remarkable. His dream had been delivered like a still birth on his arrival in Cape Town when he saw Table Mountain for the first time and regretted leaving the ruined school books behind. He knew he could never return to his mother's home, so the thought of the books remained inside him. Perhaps he could acquire replacement copies. He would find the one with Table Mountain on the cover and once again write his name inside, then he would buy the one with the president's wrinkled eyes that replaced the old history. Reading them would be another matter.

The thought of these desires put new air in his lungs and galvanised his search once more. He tipped the last of the Fanta into the dust and called to a group of children playing with a rusty pushchair.

'Barbershop, hey? Beauty salon?'

They all pointed behind him to a hand-painted sign that read, "Man-hat-on Salon: We will be serious on your hair".

He pushed open the screen door and found a stylist teasing a customer's hair with two brushes. He described Candy in every way he knew how: her colouring, the Lucky Strike. The woman said nothing until he mentioned the black eye.

'You mean Candice?' she said.

'Candice, it is she.'

'She has not arrived for days. I have had to work her mornings. There is no answer at her place.'

'Where is?'

The sun was gone for another day and Zuko found it difficult to pick his way up the rough track to the shack the stylist had described. The irregular slope of the corrugated roof had a fresh layer of plastic sheeting and on the door was spray-painted the address: X246. A few metres away, full garbage bags were piled around an abandoned car that had somehow found itself wedged into the ground as if driving to the centre of the earth. The remains of a collapsed building in front made it difficult to reach the shack. The padlock was off but the door was fastened from inside.

He banged with his fist. 'Open!'

There was a movement within and he shouted again. 'Fokken open!'

He then heard a low voice. He stepped back and kicked at the door. Although the shack was leaning at a precarious angle, the door was fast. He dragged up an old beer crate and pulled himself up onto the roof and peered into the shack through a section of clear corrugated plastic. A girl looked up at him. For a second he believed he saw Candy. The feeling was so strong that, involuntarily, he called her name. He jumped down and yelled again.

'Who is within? Open up! This is not your home.'

There was the sound of three bolts sliding before the door opened a crack. He could see a pair of eyes retreating, like a duiker in a dark wood.

'I have come for Candy,' he said. 'Candice, so.'

'Candice has not been for days,' said a female voice.

'*Ja*, sister, I know. There was terrible shit down the mountain.'

The door opened a little wider. Inside was a girl in her early teens wearing a thin floral dress and flip flops.

'Who are you? You live here with Candice?' he asked.

'Who are *you*?' she answered. 'Did you get the letter?'

'Letter? I am a friend. I knew her down at the Lucky Strike.'

'But where is she now?' said the girl. 'We are hungry.'

Zuko swiftly took the blade from his boot. 'Who is "we"?'

'Do not hurt us. Please! She told us not to leave without her. We must wait for her.'

'There is someone else?'

Zuko shoved hard on the door and raised the blade to shoulder height. 'Show yourself, bruh.'

Tears brimmed in the girl's eyes and she fell to her knees. 'It is only my handicap sister,' she said.

He pushed past and stepped into the syrupy heat. The shack stank like a latrine. Two beds were arranged side-by-side; one was empty but on the other was what looked like a collection of human bones. Once his eyes were accustomed to the gloomy light he could see there was a body on the bed, all knees and elbows and ugly angles; the mouth was contorted, as if sneering at him. The girl, for behind his shock he knew it was a girl, was wearing nothing but a nappy and a man's vest. He saw that both girls had the same golden skin as Candy, and he lowered the knife.

The girl in the floral dress made her way to the bed and hugged her sister's contorted legs. Her tears were falling now.

She looked up at Zuko, and blubbed, 'Candice is our cousin. We are Mandisa and Mosa.'

XII

For the rest of the night Zuko's thoughts rested on shack X246, drawn to it like a terrier at a rat hole. He went to the Lucky Strike and listened to conversations about scores and football and girls, and Jesus giving out about the new South Africa. One of the bar girls asked him about the prominent bandages, and he had to admit 'A white caught me lucky,' ('Lucky Strike!' said Little Mabhuti) and that Jesus was responsible for the gash on his neck. Both explanations created some astonishment among the regulars, and angered Zuko.

He left the shebeen and walked to the Amazing Grace spaza for bread, then bought two portions of rice and chicken from a vendor at the kerb and, guided by the light from his cellphone, took the food up to the girls. He put it on the ground outside the shack and kicked at the door. Before it opened he was already heading back down the mountain.

He spent the next forty-eight hours at home without beer or dagga. It was a new sensation; it had been months since he had let two days slip through his fingers. Just being in his shack for such a stretch was a novel experience. During long nights, time lay before him like the ocean. He dozed and woke, dozed and woke. His eyeballs felt like they would crack, endlessly flitting over the evidence of Candy's time in the house: the purple sheets and curtains, the framed picture of Nelson Mandela nailed to the wall. These small things now crowded in on him.

He had spent his first months in Mandela Park robbing in order to gather possessions, as if that was its only purpose, until he realised that the permanence of things irked him. Then he dispensed with everything that was not essential, that he couldn't quickly salvage in a fire. Apart from his blade and the clothes he stood up in, that meant his treasured kitchen tools. They would never go. The surrender of material goods had only ended when he looked around the near empty shack one morning and thought: this is all I need to live the life I have chosen. His stripped-down existence seemed to acquire a new settled purpose. But Candy had changed all that. Possessions, including lost ones such as the Madiba shirt, meant something again.

Accompanied by a pounding headache, his mind returned to the events of the past week. Candy's absence had left a gap in his life that churned like a bug in his guts. Although he could not formulate the thought, physically he was aware that the pain of losing her was keener than the pleasure of possessing her. It was only a week since her death but she had left a coating that would not wear off anytime soon. He revisited significant conversations he may have misunderstood. He wanted to tell her that he would change;

no more the beating, the late nights at the Lucky Strike, the beery men in the shack behind. Although their relationship was now snuffed out by absence it was replaced by something deeper. He remembered her more fondly. Even the worst days together seemed enviable now.

Her ambition returned to him, an ambition, he decided, he must adopt as best he can. He would make it up somehow, but not to her, to another. Be careful what you wish for, his mother once told him, as if wishing was a foul habit like rubbing himself under the bed sheet. Now he wished to become part of what he wished for. He would change his life. Instantly his past seemed lost to him. Gone was the day he arrived in Mandela Park and slept behind the community centre before someone robbed the clothes off his back and left him bleeding in a ditch. Gone was the early lesson that violence was a potent currency in a neighbourhood where every man carried a knife in his boot. Later, the first score that seemed to be good fortune, the one that would define the adult Zuko, did not point towards a clear future, but rather stretched no further than the next robbery. He soon learned that the power came not from the weight of the weapon in his hand, but from the gasps it drew from his victims. Potential, where before he had none.

Zuko learned to fill his pockets. Like the newly-blind, he stumbled daily towards an uncertain fate, robbing the powerless and spreading fear wherever he showed his face. Tomorrow always seemed hazy, just beyond his vision. Now he looked back on his life and saw nothing following him down this road. He tried to look ahead and, for the first time since watching the village kids walk past his mother's hut to school, he wondered what would become of him. It brought on the sensation of floating.

On Christmas Eve, at the end of his second day of self-imposed exile, he walked up to shack X246 once again. He brought chicken and pap and a large bottle of Fanta and knocked gently on the door.

'It is I,' he called.

The door opened slowly and he entered. The shack smelled poisonous. Wet with sweat, Mandisa thanked him for the food and immediately took it to the bed where her sister lay. She pulled her up into a near-sitting position and spoon-fed her. Zuko picked up a box of bloody rags and soiled nappies and took it outside. He threw the box as far as he could. Taking a deep breath he scanned the surrounding shacks for a minute then took a laundry bucket full of scummy water that had been left under a washing line. He returned and placed the bucket by the bed for Mandisa to rinse her hands and face and do the same for her sister. With the door open for light, he could see clearly the meagre contents of the shack: a camping stove and enamel pot on the ground; two unmade cots, one occupied; dresses and blouses set on wire clothes hangers hooked into holes in the tin walls and roof; a table with a mirror and wash basin; and a drawerless chest on which were piled countless books.

The most compelling item in the shack was not furniture but human. He now noticed that the younger girl's two rows of teeth were mismatched, her jaw seeming to grind the food rather than chew. Mandisa held the spoon at Mosa's chin to catch the pap falling from where her upper lip should have been. Mosa's hands and feet, twisted at ugly angles, seemed to refuse to cooperate with her thoughts. Her fingers were frozen into claws. He felt an overwhelming desire to straighten the girl's limbs into something resembling her sister's, which were graceful and lithe. A spike of guilt reminded him that the girls probably hadn't eaten since he left the food at the door three days before.

'Good appetite,' he said, redundantly.

Zuko squatted in the doorway and allowed the girls time to eat uninterrupted. He watched Mandisa's glistening arm stretching with the spoon to reach Mosa's mouth. He followed the line of her fragile, bare shoulders, the stretch of her neck and the liveliness of her small breasts under the thin dress, her small nipples pushing against the fraying material. He knew she was aware of his gaze and he enjoyed the moment.

When the bowl was almost empty, Mandisa said, 'You have been three times, but still we do not know what has become of our cousin Candice.'

Zuko shifted on the dirt floor.

'I ventured to open the door yesterday, to ask for help from a neighbour,' she said, 'even though she told me never to leave my sister.'

Mosa continued to slurp food from the spoon.

'I will bring more,' said Zuko. 'What would you eat?'

'Food is very well, but we must know where is Candice.'

'She is dead.'

Mosa screamed and food slithered down her chin and onto her chest. Mandisa put her hand to her own mouth and with her other arm grasped her sister around the shoulder.

'How is it so?'

'A white from the valley,' he said, with more indifference than intended. 'She was friendly with him but he chopped her. Near the shebeen. Do you know it?'

'We know nothing that Candice does not tell us.' She held her sister closer, then corrected herself: 'Did not tell us.'

The two girls wailed, Mandisa's eyes tightly clenched, Mosa's boring into Zuko. He couldn't bear it and stepped out into the warm morning sun, closing the door behind him. He waited for the sound of crying to end before returning.

Mandisa was now scraping the bowl with dirty fingernails and feeding herself.

Through sobs, she asked, 'What is to become of us?'

'Where is your family?' he said. 'Why do you live like animals in a cave?'

'Candice *was* our family,' said Mandisa. 'She told us not to leave the shack without her, the neighbourhood is too dangerous. Our mother is no more; the TB took her. Our father is too much the drinking, and would treat me terrible. The house is lost and he lives in Gugulethu township with a new wife. He would have us back only if I sleep in his bed.'

Mandisa dropped the bowl. 'But where is Candice?' She swallowed a deep sob. 'Is she buried?'

'Some things I do not know. SAPS took her, the municipality may have buried her,' said Zuko without sympathy. 'What are you going to do now?'

The girls looked at each other and again wailed loudly.

Mandisa recovered herself and pleaded, 'You will help us?'

Zuko kept on. 'You say your pa is gone. Your ma is dead. But you have sisters and brothers?'

'No.'

'Only two? It cannot be.'

Mandisa touched Zuko's elbow and indicated for him to go outside. The sun, alone in the clear sky, was now oppressively hot. They moved into the shallow shade up against the wall of the shack. What Zuko thought was an empty, shy face in the dim light of their room, now revealed another quality, something that did not belong in his world. Her skin was the colour of milky coffee, the kind Candy would make him some mornings after sex. The girl's cheekbones were set wide and gave her face the look of a triangle, her chin tempting him to cup it. Her lips were pinched as if permanently hoping to kiss, and her tiny nose hardly looked like a nose, so seamlessly did it merge with her cheeks. Rather than look at him, her eyes seemed to rest on his, questioning, searching.

She sniffed wetly. 'Zuko, is it?'

'*Ja.*'

'Mosa understands as I do, so I do not talk bad things in front of her. Her body is broken, but her brain is worthy. There are only two of us, Daddy. We are not like other families. After Mosa, Ma did not want another handicap. She was afraid that a second cursed child would destroy her insides. Pa had a part-time woman, so he let Ma be.'

'That your ma should have two daughters, one so beauteous and one so foul is unspeakable,' said Zuko.

'What is "unspeakable"?' she asked.

'There are ways to dispose of such infants,' he answered.

Mandisa turned away and searched eagerly for the furthest point on the mountain.

'You discover us and bring us food, for which we are grateful,' she said, 'but I am thinking you are not a good man all through.'

'What?' he said. 'You should spend your life feeding and carrying and wiping shit from such a sister? Blood or no blood, such people have no place in the township. Life is hard enough.'

Mandisa turned back to face him. 'But I am thinking life is not hard for you.'

'Do not question me, girl. Have I not fed you where many would have let you rot in your own dirt?'

He meant for her to be both fearful of him and thankful; she looked as though she felt neither. Mandisa stood straighter and folded her arms.

'One thing to be clear, Zuko, *our saviour*,' she said, slowly, 'we are sisters together. Ma made me promise I would never leave her; Candice too. Live together, sleep together, eat together. Remain together. It is God's will.'

Then she turned and stepped towards the open door.

Zuko dismissed her with a flapping hand. 'Coloureds have always the attitude. Pah!'

Mandisa stopped in the doorway. 'We are not coloureds. We are proudly San.'

Zuko was left alone. Despite his turmoil, he had to admit he had found the trace of Candy that he was looking for. More than that, Mandisa looked like she could be her sister. The discovery of the reason why Candy worked the bar stool long after she should have moved on made him feel both sorrowful and whatever the opposite was.

He stepped onto a strip of ground that ran between the shacks from where he saw two figures approaching. The older man had a buzz-cut shave and carried a handkerchief in one hand and an expensive cellphone in the other. He was wearing a white suit jacket and shiny, pointy shoes. The other, a much larger, shaven-headed man wore a tight Yankees T-shirt and clean Adidas trainers. The jacketed stranger stepped up onto the collapsed shack lying awkwardly five metres away between Zuko and the track. Alerted by their arrival, Mandisa came to the doorway.

'So the mole emerges into the light,' said the jacketed man with a flash of gold-tipped teeth.

'Who arrives?' Zuko whispered to Mandisa.

'He comes for the rent. He has been banging.'

The man bowed slightly towards Mandisa.

'Banging, but getting no answer, my child,' he said in a West African accent. 'Who is this boy? Does he come to rob you or is he a sugar daddy who may cover the rent.'

He tilted his head as if sizing up Zuko.

'Where is the gammie stylist? I do not care who pays, but I will be paid.'

Zuko turned his full attention to the men. 'What is owing?'

Ignoring Zuko's question, the jacketed man said, 'May I ask your name, brother?'

'It is no concern. This is not my shack.'

'To be not gracious would be considered rude in my country. My name is Sunday Johnson, newly arrived from the glorious Republic of Liberia – there, you have it. I afford you such respect, and me and my good brother here would welcome the same in return.'

'Their mother and cousin have died and abandoned them,' said Zuko. 'They have no rands to give.'

'Dead? I am sorry for your circumstance, especially for their charming cousin. She had the beauty to turn kings into beggars and beggars into kings.' He smiled, seemingly at the thought of her. 'But forgive me, not only do you disrespect me, I also believe you do not understand my situation. I am a businessman and have not been paid what is owed to me. High-class accommodation comes at a price, even in a township.'

The other man grinned. He spread his feet on the dry earth and gripped his wrist in front of his crotch, an action that emphasised his shoulders.

'This is not your neighbourhood, is true,' continued the older man, seeming to appeal to Zuko's better nature. 'We can see what you are. We have names for your kind in my country; you endeavour to dress like an American rapper but you look like township trash. However, here, in this territory, you have no... jurisdiction. Have you heard such a word? You, *tsotsi*, are in my juris-*dic-tion*.'

The younger of the two strangers, who had not yet spoken, bent down into a ditch and picked up a discarded wooden chair leg. Zuko looked for escape routes as Mandisa stirred behind.

Zuko asked again, 'What is owing?'

'With late payment for overdue monies, two thousand rands. Plus two thousand on account.'

Zuko weighed up the two men. On a dark night, individually, he would cut them without a thought. But he had to be cautious. And if he spent more than a second to think about it it was because he was not only considering his own safety, but also the fate of the two girls.

Sunday Johnson took a step forward, tilting the remains of the shack underneath his well-shod feet.

'While you consider my simple request, I may say that I built that shack; I can tear it down. Like the one on which I stand. Unfortunately the family were in it at the time, but they soon evacuated. And they still paid me.'

Mandisa moved a step closer to Zuko, almost crouching into the well of his back.

'And I will do it again, with or without occupation,' Johnson added.

'The girls have not,' said Zuko. 'But I can cover small-small.'

'What is your offer, *tsotsi* without a name?'

Zuko dug into his jeans and pulled out a handful of notes and coins and offered them.

'It is all,' said Zuko.

The T-shirted man stepped forward and took the money. He counted it, then said something in pidgin English to Sunday Johnson.

'The money is not enough,' said Johnson. 'What is to be done?'

'I have no more for you,' said Zuko, bending down and quickly straightening up with his combat knife in his hand, 'only this.'

Johnson smiled, dabbed his forehead with his handkerchief, and said, 'I do not fight like a township dog. I am a businessman. I settle by business means. When you fuck off back to your Xhosa hole, the coloured girl is mine and the shack will not stand by this night. Is true.'

Mandisa whimpered faintly and Zuko put a hand on her arm.

Turning away, Johnson said, 'My barber thanks you for your pocket change. I hope we meet again; I have uses for an errand boy. Merry Christmas.'

The younger man called out, 'Jackal shit!' then raised the chair leg above his head like a machete and threw it through the open door of the shack. The back wall shuddered and something smashed. The man then turned and followed Johnson who was already carefully stepping towards the dirt road.

Mandisa ran into the shack. 'Mosa! Mosa!'

Before the two men were out of sight, Zuko said, 'This is some vexation I do not need.'

He followed her and saw that the thrown chair leg had smashed a wash basin, the soiled content of which was dripping over the lip of a table.

'What will you do?' he asked.

'You have asked us already,' said Mandisa. 'Will you help us?'

'I eat enough shit, I do not need crazy Liberians on my back.'

'But we are two; we are children. And Mosa!'

He looked away.

'Look at Mosa!' she said. 'I cannot manage. Where will we go? Or shall we be taken? We will be at God's mercy. Maybe your woman can help us. We will be no trouble.'

'There is no woman,' he said. 'I cannot care for such a cripple.'

Everything in him said run from the neighbourhood, but something stopped him. The previous week he had spent the best part of a day looking for the ghost of Candy; now that he had found it he wanted to hold on to it for a little longer. There was also something about the little scene in the dark shack that reached deep inside him: the wash basin and flannel, the smell of dirty washing, and on the bedside table, a mirror. Then his mind alighted for a moment on the possibility of Candy's resurrection, the return of something precious.

'Stay!' he said, and ran off between the shacks.

He returned after twenty minutes dragging a shopping trolley half-full of groceries and placed it on a flat piece of ground beyond the collapsed shack.

'What is to be done?' asked Mandisa. 'Ah! I think I know, Daddy.'

'I had money in my boot,' said Zuko, 'and bought the trolley from a torched Somali.' He smiled his first smile of the day. 'I bought everything in it also.'

Mandisa grabbed a Checkers shopping bag. 'It is true, you will take us?'

'Now-now! The Liberians will return. We must leave their juris-*dic-tion*,' he mimicked.

Mandisa exhaled an exhilarated laugh, then tried to show Zuko how to lift Mosa.

'I know how,' he said, and pushed her away.

He placed one hand under the crook of a knee and the other around her neck then gently carried Mosa out into the sunshine. Mandisa threw some bedding into the trolley and when Mosa was placed on top she covered her with a dressing gown. Mosa's head lolled back on the edge of the trolley, and she struggled for air.

'Her head needs support,' said Mandisa, 'or she will suffocate.'

She lifted Mosa's head and settled her on the bedding. She looked like a broken doll with her left leg precariously angled out of the trolley, her two twisted wrists approximating hand signals and her head shrouded in a jumble of clothes.

'Bring what you need. Hurry, child,' said Zuko. 'But no room for books.'

Mandisa ran back inside and collected two large handfuls of clothing and piled it on top. Amongst the jeans and blouses and underwear was a man's shirt with a familiar multicoloured swirl. It felt like the fulfilment of a promise.

'More!' she said, and ran back.

She returned with clothes on hangers and a wholesale Noxzema carton, frayed and tatty with use.

'Cousin's private papers!' she said.

'It's Christmas! We go,' said Zuko, and pushed the trolley away from the shack towards the roadway. 'Pull from the front. Pull!'

The commotion of the wheels on the uneven ground soon drew a crowd of children who joined in the game of pushing the trolley down the mountain.

'Fanta for everyone who pushes!' said Mandisa.

The trolley soon gathered momentum and skidded this way and that, almost out of Zuko's control.

'Do not push her over and out of the cart!' he admonished the children. 'She is broken enough!'

In response, the girl yelped and seemed to scowl.

'Mandisa, is your sister in chaos?'

'No, Daddy Zuko. She is laughing!'

'*Yebo*! Push!'

When the children saw him smile they all sang: 'Dad-dy Fan-ta! Dad-dy Fan-ta!'

Zuko joined the chanting. He had begun the morning annoyed, but now laughed. He laughed at the strange neighbourhood in which he found himself and the idea that he had brought food to the needy on Christmas Eve; and, as much as he was troubled by Mosa's stare, now awkwardly recumbent in the trolley, he also laughed at Mandisa's boldness. Mostly he laughed at her colouring and spirit, which reminded him of the one person he wanted to be reminded of. Three days ago she had wept with fear at the sight of his blade; today the teenager who called herself a proud San answered back like one of his favoured girls.

Making their way down the dirt road between the shacks, he noticed for the first time all the street barbers and salons, some dressed with half-hearted Christmas decorations glittering in the sun: Home Girl Salon, Tempeh's Braiding Temple, One Luv Hair, and all the yellowing photographs of women with outrageous hairstyles and hastily crayoned faces layered with gaudy makeup. Guiltily he wondered how Mandisa might look once her tight cornrows and girlish buns over her ears were teased out. She was a woman, no doubt, he saw the soiled rags, and Candy's clothes in the trolley could almost fit her.

They reached the tarred road where the trolley rolled freely. The children ran to the first spaza they saw and Zuko retrieved some more cash from his boot.

The following morning, his legs stiff from being contorted for so long, Zuko woke to be surprised he wasn't a child, and his first thought to help his mother. His dreams rarely brought him any comfort. Occasionally she returned as a difficult memory, something he never went into in too much detail in the light of day. When his mother was alive, he acted the man of the house; when she died, he was an orphaned child. That was the top and bottom of it.

He reached for his cellphone: 5.35 a.m. Dewy light streamed between the window bars and settled on the fraying rug in faint stripes. He heard the rattle of the fridge door and sat up.

Wearing a thin nightdress and headscarf, Mandisa came towards him holding two steaming cups.

'Merry Christmas,' she said.

'Christmas?' he said, taking one.

'Really.'

He took a sip of coffee. 'Then I have-have no gifts for you,' he said. 'Don't expect anything.'

'To be here is a kind of gift,' said Mandisa.

There was a stir in the bed behind her. For a second Zuko had forgotten that this appealing vision did not come alone, and he slumped back onto the burst cushion. He watched as Mandisa rinsed a towel in a plastic bucket and wiped Mosa's face. She swung Mosa's legs over the side of the bed and sat her up with two pillows behind her back. She held a cup to Mosa's mouth and encouraged her to drink some coffee.

'You have a toilet?' Mandisa asked.

'Fill the bucket with water and take it to the latrine. I use the veld if I need.'

From behind, Mandisa took hold of Mosa under her arms and lifted her feet on to her insteps, then prepared to take her outside.

'Is this your chore every morning?' he asked.

'If not me, who?'

'But to live your life for another is... not natural.'

'But it is natural,' said Mandisa. 'You cannot live life just thinking of yourself. Anyway, God gives everyone a different plan. Mosa is part of mine.'

Her sister exhaled loudly, which came out like a growl.

'I have told you, Zuko. Mosa is hearing everything. She is part of the conversation, even if she speaks little.'

Wordlessly he dressed, picked up his cellphone and reached the door before the girls.

'As you say, child, it is part of God's plan for you. Not for me,' he said, and left the shack.

Zuko mooched around the becalmed neighbourhood all morning like a hungry tomcat. He scuffed from the Beauty Girl to the Lucky Strike — both closed — and to the taxi rank at the entrance to the township. Everybody was dressed for the holiday and had somewhere to go, someone to be with. On the walk back up the hill he stopped at a spaza, one he had robbed more than once. The Somali shopkeeper and his family were in the doorway eating a meal of chicken and beans.

'Christmas, hey?' Zuko said.

A man wearing a dirty white kufi stood up and wiped his eating hand on his robe. The family watched.

'It is not our Christmas, it is true,' said the man, 'but it is a day of joy, and there are not enough of them.'

Zuko dug his hand in his pocket. 'Marlboro.'

'Thirty.'

Zuko handed over the money.

'Joy, brother,' the man said, following him out of the store.

'*Ja*. Joy-joy.'

Zuko stepped away from the doorway, unwrapped the pack of cigarettes and lit up. He looked back to the family who had by now resumed their meal. The man must have made a joke because, as one, the family stopped eating and smiled collusively.

Zuko headed to a corner that had lately been taken over by vendors who sold vegetables and fruit from bakkies parked on some waste ground. At least two were not celebrating Christmas at home and had chosen to sell the dregs of their produce. He haggled for onions, tomatoes and aubergines, enough to make a meal for three.

On his return home Mandisa was kneeling in the sand outside his front door with her arms up to her elbows in a tin bath of soapy water working his Madiba shirt against a washboard.

'Careful with that,' he said. 'It is precious.'

'Of course.'

A thin rope, swaying above her and stretched between telegraph pole and gate post, was weighed down with his dripping trousers, underwear and shirts. A few metres away Mosa was sitting upright in the open doorway. Her shoulder was wedged under a chair seat that had been pushed hard against the door frame, and her legs folded underneath for balance.

Mandisa sang a song in time with her washing. Zuko put down the shopping.

'What is it you sing?' he asked.

'You don't know it?' she said.

'Of course not. I have only heard your language when Candy wished to vex-vex me.'

'Candice, Zuko, as she was baptised. She can vex no more, God save her,' she said. 'I only know one song by San, taught by my ma. We girls have lost the language of our distant cousins. The clicks are difficult. The song tells of how the San people were the first in Southern Africa, before the whites came, even before the Bantu.'

'Who cares who was first?'

'For belonging,' she said quickly. 'My dear ma said that our kind came from the desert to settle at Kouberg. To them it was like going to a big town, but I believe it is just a tiny dorp. I have never been. In the Kalahari the San were hunters and keepers of the land, in Cederberg they were kept by the church, but here in the city it seems we are kept alive by chance.'

Zuko lit a cigarette.

'You people only talk of the past. What of today? Tomorrow?'

'Tomorrow will arrive whether I summon it or no, and I can hardly wait for God to bring the new day to me. But what is a life? Only the story of what you have already done, not what you say you will do. How many dreams come true? How much time have you spent waiting for the future for it only to work out different?'

She rinsed the shirt in fresh water then squeezed it almost dry.

'Where do you learn to speak so tangled when you say you stay at home for your sister?' he asked.

'Exactly, it is true. Candice read to us every day, and I read to Mosa. The books we left at the shack, we shall never forget them. The stories are now in our heads.'

As though in agreement, Mosa wriggled her shoulders and scraped a chair leg on the step. Mandisa hung the clean shirt on a wire hanger and hooked it on the line.

Zuko drew deep on his cigarette.

'Even if you do not wish it, we must think of the future. This is a new situation. I never had two girls in the house. It may be what Candice would have wished, but I cannot care for such a one.'

They both looked towards Mosa.

'This cripple is your family, not mine,' he said, 'so you must see to her needs.'

'Of course, nothing has changed. I ask for nothing, only shelter and food.'

'I can share what room I have until we make a plan.'

'You can see I wash your clothes, bring your breakfast. We are grateful, are we not, Mosa?'

Her sister made a sound of consent and scraped the chair leg again which dislodged a thin length of timber that had been wedged under the door to keep it open. The visible end of the wood glinted gold.

'Where did you get this?'

'It was behind the couch.'

Zuko retrieved the walking stick from under the door, which swung heavily against Mosa's shoulder.

'Mosa needs support —'

'Do not touch-touch my things. Leave the stick where it was.'

'There was nothing else. She needs —'

'Leave it!'

Zuko held the walking stick at eye level and, at the weighted end, inspected traces of his blood, traces of his last contact with Candy. His gaze shifted from the golden lion's head to Mandisa kneeling in the sand, now looking wretched. Without willing them his thoughts were taken over by superimposed images of Candy on the floor of the shack with the knife in her belly and Mosa rolling down the hill in the trolley. He tried to make sense of the two events and failed. Were they somehow connected?

Picking up the bag of food, he headed inside. He hid the stick behind the stove, which he lit, then put on a pan of water and laid out his kitchen tools.

Through force of habit he rifled through the girls' few personal items that were pushed to the end of the bed. On the floor he spotted the Noxzema box that yesterday Mandisa said was filled with Candy's private papers. Inside was a stack of white envelopes, sealed, with writing on one side. Just the words made him suspicious. He lifted them out and inhaled. Zuko then tore one open and retrieved three pages of black, scrawly writing. Even though the act revealed none of its contents, he believed it brought him a tiny step closer to her. He thought less about what the words themselves might mean and instead considered the hand that wrote them, the pressure of the pen, a greasy thumbprint, the crease on the edge of the page. To him, they belonged in a museum, or at least deserved to be stored in a place of safety. His eyes swam as he carefully replaced the envelopes and returned the box to its place under the bed.

Turning his attention to cooking for three, he was infused with the thought that he had just adopted a burden. So why did it make him feel so good.

XIII

Cape Town, Boxing Day. The central bus terminal was teeming. Anna Schippers had never seen so many people so determined to get somewhere else. It reminded her of termite hills on the donkey track into Kouberg. Anna approached a taxi driver sitting in an empty Toyota Corolla.

In Afrikaans, she asked, 'Can you take me to this place?'

The black driver scanned the piece of paper handed to him.

'Ah, Mandela Park. They call it Imizamo Yethu now. I can take,' he said, 'but you must direct me to the address.'

'I have never been to the parish,' she said.

'Then we will get lost together.'

'*Ja*, but take the short way,' said Anna, swapping to English, and getting into the back seat.

When the taxi was full with a woman and child and two silent men, the driver set off. Anna opened her bag and felt for Candice's letter, something she had done countless times on the bus from Clanwilliam, which prompted her to replay the key phrases: *I am a broken woman... I have told Mandisa must send this sealed and stamped letter if I do never return.* The creased and crumpled envelope showed clear signs of Anna's anxiety; it now looked more like a discarded piece of litter than a sister's call for help. She expected this to be the last stage of her journey, which she simultaneously wanted to end yet go on forever. She was facing the possibility of being without a younger sister; now that the truth was coming closer, she didn't want to know.

The driver took a left on Buitengracht that led up Kloof Nek Road towards Table Mountain and through Tamboerskloof, a neighbourhood of elegant Victorian homes. The clapperboard buildings lined with filigree peeped out from behind six-feet high perimeter walls topped with electric fences. Anna looked out of the rear window at the skyscrapers of Cape Town and thought of the outlook from Bushman's View over Kouberg. Feeling the same thrill of excitement that Candice must have experienced on her arrival, Anna instantly regretted thinking her village contained all that she needed in life.

The single line of traffic crested the pass between Lion's Head and the cable car station, then headed downhill towards the sea. Out of the residential neighbourhood the ozone light seemed to turn the car yellow. She caught a glimpse of surf on Camps Bay beach and looked out towards a queue of container ships waiting to unload at Cape Town docks, further along the coast.

'So this is Camps Bay,' said Anna.

'Yes, lady.'

'The waves, the waves.'

'*Ja!*'

'What is beyond the sea?' she asked.

'America, hopefully.'

'The whole world, I think.'

'If you say.'

She looked down onto colonnaded mansions and brilliant-white apartment complexes on avenues that snaked down the mountain. Pristine 4x4s with closed windows drove up the smooth tarmac and joined the opposite line of traffic heading for the city.

'I have read about Camps Bay in a magazine,' she said. 'The richest people in the world live here, it is said.'

'Richest and idlest.'

'Why you say?'

'No taxi driver that I know lives in such a place. Camps Bay is serious exclusive, yo! They say Mugabe has a house here,' said the driver. 'And Elton John.'

'Of course. It would take much hard work to attain such a status,' she said.

'Where you from, lady?'

'The Cederberg. Do you know it?'

'I know it must be a long way from Cape Town. And I know that it would take a hundred lifetimes to earn the money to live in one of these properties. Unless you have come to squat.'

Anna took his remark as his wish to end the conversation. The two men in the back seat glanced at her as if wishing the journey would end.

'The world is there for everyone,' she declared. 'No one is privileged.'

They drove on in silence along Victoria Road that hugged the rocky Atlantic coastline. Such wild water. In comparison, Clanwilliam Dam was no more than a plunge pool. When they reached the top of Suikerbossie Hill the driver slipped into neutral and freewheeled into Hout Bay. Anna leaned forward and took in the wide valley surrounded by mountains on three sides and, on the fourth, a blue bay lined by a strip of sandy beach. Properties dotted the mountainside, some embedded in lush gardens, others in little knots of six or eight houses surrounded by high walls topped by the same electrified fencing she saw in the city.

She wound down the window and gawped. 'Such big hotels and guest houses. They are wonderful.'

'No, lady. One-family homes. Hout Bay is five stars all the way. No one is privileged, heh-heh!'

Anna said nothing.

On the opposite side of the valley there was a delineated area where hundreds, perhaps thousands, of smaller houses were concentrated in a tight wedge as if being forced up the mountain rather than across it. The area was bounded on both sides by thick stretches of plane trees that separated the neighbourhood from bigger houses.

'Mandela Park?' she ventured.

'Of course,' said the driver. 'Your destination is in there somewhere.'

A pall of smoke hung over the closest section, where Anna could see red lights flashing.

'There is a fire?'

'All the time, lady. When you cook in a wooden shack sometimes it goes pffff. Other times the veld is so dry it catches and spreads quickly like a bad joke.'

Outside the township, the people walking along the dusty footpaths that edged the tarred roads were all darker skinned than she; others drove open-windowed Toyotas with three or four sweating people in the back seat and often two more in front. Drivers cruised slowly, calling for fares by slapping the outside of their car doors, honking horns or blowing a penetrating whistle. As they reached the township entrance Anna could see that many of the homes were not houses but shacks built with an assortment of corrugated tin sections, rough-edged wooden planks, some makeshift boarding and torn plastic sheeting.

At a traffic circle she saw a large sign, which read "Imizamo Yethu – Mandela Road". She felt as if she was about to cross a frontier.

Everyone got out of the taxi.

'You are better to walk from here,' said the driver waving an outstretched palm.

Annoyed that he made no attempt to locate the address, she handed him five rands less than the agreed fare, grabbed her bag and got out of the car.

It took her an hour to find someone who had heard of the Man-hat-on Salon, then a boy led her on a thirty-minute slog up the mountain with the bag on her head. She gave the boy two rands then took out Candice's letter from her jacket pocket to double-check she had the right place. The sight of her sister's handwriting served to inject a little purpose into her resolve. The tinselled door was open and she stepped over the threshold of the little salon.

Inside was a sweating woman some years older than Anna who was wearing a shimmery wig of black curls, too-tight jeans and a red T-shirt who was engrossed in crimping a customer's hair. When she turned, Anna could see that her chest read "HIV Positive. Get Tested. Get Treatment".

'Hello, my sister,' said Anna, in English. 'I am looking for shack X246.'

'The place beyond, but it is empty,' said the stylist curtly. 'Candice is gone.'

'It is Candice that I seek. I have just arrived from the Cederberg.'

'You must be family,' said the stylist. 'You have the look.'

'I am Anna, her senior sister. Do you know the girls?' Anna asked, excited. 'Young ones.'

'All I know is Candice worked here mornings but stopped coming last week. There was no answer at her shack,' said the stylist. 'A man was looking for her some days ago.'

'Where would she go? Did she suffer misfortune?'

'This I do not know. Whatever happened, it was too sudden.'

'This man, you say, who was looking for her... who is he?' asked Anna.

'I never saw him before.' The stylist pointed the comb at Anna. 'Don't bring trouble to my door, sister.'

'I would not do such a thing. We women have too much grief.'

The stylist returned to the head of hair before her then looked at herself in the mirror and seemed to have a change of heart.

'He dressed like a *tsotsi*.'

'What is?' asked Anna.

'*Skelm*. Gangster. He called her "Candy" and believed she worked evenings at a bar near the tarred road. If she knew him, then trouble came to her door, sho.'

'You have helped me plenty,' said Anna. 'I will look for her and my cousins in all the shebeens in the township if I have to.'

'The Lucky shebeen, I do believe he called it.'

'Hopefully it will be,' said Anna.

'No, sister, there is no luck for a pretty one in a tavern.'

Anna turned to go. The customer said something in an unfamiliar language, then the stylist turned and put both fists on her wide hips.

'Sister, wait, where do you sleep tonight?'

'I have not thought about my own comfort, just to discover what has happened to my sister and find the little ones.'

'There is a bed in the back and running water.'

'O, such kindness.'

'My husband is working in the mines on the west coast, so I have room. I do not mind the company, I have only my six little ones.'

'I have five,' said Anna, stepping closer.

'I am Precious,' said the stylist, and lightly stroked Anna's palm. 'It is almost dark and too dangerous to be out. I will heat some food; tomorrow I can show you Candice's shack.'

The following morning Anna called the landline at the Kouberg mission church hoping someone would get a message to Jakobus that she had arrived safely. She prayed that Minister Johannes would not answer. It rang and rang. Futilely she called Jakobus's cellphone, but unless he was over the mountain closer to Clanwilliam she knew the signal would not reach him. He was probably already turning over the earth on their patch of ground alongside the river before the sun got too hot. Not being able to speak to someone from home made her feel alone. Alone, but also determined to finish what she had started.

After breakfast of porridge and Madeira cake, Anna and Precious made their way to Candice's shack. Anna took in the neighbourhood, a collection of ramshackle homes built on waste ground with tracks between them worn smooth by footfall. The shacks seemed to be erected with no obvious plan, the opposite to Kouberg's careful design by the Rhenish missionaries. Here, shaky doors faced every direction except the one she expected, cardboard and corrugated tin sides were so rudimentary that she wouldn't have described them as walls, and roofs were sometimes no more than plastic awnings. This Cape Town looked very different from the city she saw yesterday from the back of the taxi.

They reached shack X246. It was unoccupied. The cousins, who, according to Candice's letter, should have been living here, had clearly moved on. Strangely, the doorway was littered with books, their pages waving in the wind. Inside, the place had the stale smell of having been recently vacated, but it was already picked clean of anything useful. Litter and soiled nappies were the only evidence of human habitation.

Before her arrival in Cape Town, Anna could not realistically picture her sister's new circumstances. But now that Anna had spent one night here, many of those gaps were already being coloured in. Even if she could not visualise her life, she would never have imagined this. The shack was not much to show for three years in the city.

A family arrived and began unloading belongings from a handcart. A woman carrying bedclothes approached the shack.

'Leave this place!' she called in an unfamiliar accent. 'I have paid the rent. It is mine!'

'With blessings,' said Anna. 'Do you know where is the lady who lived here? Candice Schippers? And two young ones?'

'It is ours,' she said, pushing past.

To encourage her to open up, Precious said, 'Zim? Welcome to the neighbourhood.'

'We are Mozambique,' she said plainly. 'And this is now our shack, you hear.'

The woman's four children, dressed in charity cast-offs, stared at Anna with cheerless expressions.

'Stay well,' said Precious, and stepped away.

'Maybe she and the girls moved to another place?' said Anna.

'I do not wish to think bad thoughts,' said Precious, 'but there has been a difficulty here, no doubt. Your sister has left in a hurry, not with a plan.'

The two women walked towards the tarred road.

'The shebeen must be our next stop,' said Precious. 'We will not give in until we find your sister. The Lucky shebeen is not in this neighbourhood, I am sure. But to locate a bar, we must ask a drinker. There are plenty in Mandela Park.'

As they got closer to the tarred road, the shacks turned to houses, some painted, and satellite dishes and furniture – both inside and outside the houses – became more evident.

'So, you have come from the Cederberg,' said Precious. 'Candice spoke of it. I believe it is not such a place like Mandela Park.'

'No,' said Anna. 'There is space to breathe. Mountains, but not full of shacks. People, but not living on top of each other. Children who play in the streams and amongst the rooibos, not with the dirt and the filth.'

'It is a heaven on earth?' asked Precious.

'Paradise.'

'Candice would often be in tears to talk about it,' said Precious. 'She wanted to return, but not before she would have her own salon. She carried that dream like a pack on her back. Are they all your colour in the Cederberg?'

'Most, but not all. San we were in history. You would call coloured. We are different, are we not?'

'No, Anna,' said Precious. 'We are the same.'

The two women hugged.

The morning seemed to drip with heat. With no tree shade, the search through the township was arduous, especially for Precious who was twice Anna's size and carried most of her weight on her hips. Naturally curious about barbering in other neighbourhoods, Precious moved from salon to salon asking people queuing for haircuts and styles and shaves if they had heard of the Lucky shebeen. Near the main entrance to the township they came across a shipping container barbershop called Beauty Girl Salon. Within, two women were having knotty hair extensions applied.

'Good day, sister. Do you know the Lucky shebeen?' asked Precious.

'The Lucky Strike, you mean,' said the stylist. 'It is close.'

Anna stepped forward. 'You know it?'

Beauty, for it was she, took her hands out of her customer's hair, and stepped back. 'Ayi! You have the very look of Candice!'

'You know my sister?'

Anna and Precious stepped inside. The container rocked a welcome.

'Knew her, girl. Knew her. The city authorities were looking for her family and now you are here. You do know the sorrowful news?'

'No, no, no!' Anna held on to the edge of the container and eased herself into a chair. 'I am not ready for bad news.'

'It is terrible,' said Beauty, shaking her head. 'She is dead, for sure, a week past. We know it to be true.'

Precious sat down next to Anna and pressed her to her bosom. Anna howled.

When she recovered enough to speak, Anna said, 'Inside I feared it. But I hoped, always hoped.'

Beauty introduced herself. 'We were close, it is a terrible tragedy. I have lost a friend, but you have lost a sister. I am sorry for you, and I am sad for all of us.'

Beauty told the women what she knew about Candice's death at the hands of a white man. She described her container salon dream but said nothing about her life at the Lucky Strike. Rather than finding the answers Anna was hoping for, Beauty stirred more questions.

Another stylist took over Beauty's customer and the three women went to see Lucky Lulama who was in the back of the shebeen taking in a delivery of Castle beer.

'This is Candice's sister from the Cederberg,' said Beauty. 'She has come for knowledge of her passing.'

Lucky Lulama embraced Anna. 'My sympathy, sister.'

Anna said, 'Tell me what you know about Candice.'

'Candy, she was called.' Lucky Lulama stopped. 'It is best you see the spot.'

She handed them each a warm Coke from a crate, then the four women went to the shack behind. She lifted the latch, pushed open the door and took Anna's hand. 'Come.'

The two women stepped into the darkness, here and there pierced with occasional points of light from minute holes in the corrugated iron roof. The dirty air was laced with sweat and rotting wood.

'This is the place where my sister's life ended?' said Anna, unable to hide her distress. 'Pitiful. As far from God's gaze as can be imagined.'

She stood next to a hollow in the wall where a window should have been; instead, someone had nailed an offcut of corrugated iron.

'What is this dark shack with only a mattress on the floor?' she asked. 'What would draw our Candice to such a place?'

Beauty and Precious remained silent.

Lucky Lulama said, 'A young girl must make her life any way she can, neh. We all loved her, you must remember that. We would want no harm to come to her.'

Precious said, 'This is news to me. She was a good stylist. I did not know she was a bar girl.'

Anna dropped her pretence that she was too naive to know the shack's purpose. Her disgust was replaced by simple curiosity about her sister's last night in this Godless place. The three women described what they knew in turn: Lucky Lulama said she was at the community hall concert on the evening Candice died; Beauty was at home; Precious recalled her absence at work the following morning. Anna was troubled that nobody had any direct knowledge of her sister's last moments. And what of the young cousins?

Precious said, 'Where there are girls working, men benefit, no doubt. Lucky Lulama, Beauty, you knew her better. Who was her boy?'

The two women looked at the ground.

'Do not open that wound,' said Lucky Lulama. 'Allow her unhappy history to rest. Look for the white man who chopped her if you have to, neh. That is where you will find your answers.'

'But for now,' Anna said, 'all I have is you, sister. Please help me how you will.'

Lucky Lulama seemed to disentangle her thoughts. 'I closed the shebeen early that night, but there are some things I do know.'

The other two women stopped.

'Tell, sister,' said Anna.

'Candy... Candice's boy is called Zuko,' said Lucky Lulama. 'The man who attacked her had a fine walking stick. He hit Zuko with it. He was cracked here and here.' She indicated her ear and head.

'How do you know such a thing?' asked Anna.

'I found the stick the following morning when I came upon her cold body. The carved stick was as heavy as a knobkerrie and had a golden top.'

'Why would a white come to such a place with a valuable stick?' asked Anna.

'It is not unheard of, neh,' said Lucky Lulama. 'They come for the girls when they can't keep it in their pants. Slumming, they call it. Zuko called him a cripple. Lame.'

'Is he in the jail?' asked Anna.

'No, he escaped into the night. Zuko said he drove a white car.' Lucky hesitated. 'But do not tell him that I am telling you this. It is difficult to run a shebeen. I need the bar girls, and Zuko's crew look after them. Usually. Please understand, my sisters.'

'This man Zuko is a, what you say?' asked Anna.

'*Tsotsi* we should say in the township,' said Precious. 'The man who came to my salon to search for her, it must be him.'

'And Candice was one of his girls?'

Nobody answered. The more she considered the inferences and assertions of her new friends, the more Anna was convinced that there was a mystery to be uncovered.

'Sisters, is this the life Candice made for herself willingly? It is unbelievable.'

She felt a hand on one shoulder, then the other, gestures that created a shared sense of solidarity.

'So this was the news that she was ashamed to tell us in her home village,' said Anna. 'This is what stopped her from calling all those years. Now I understand. But bar girl or barber, she was my sister. What would she do if *she* came looking for *me* in this place?'

'She was good people,' said Lucky Lulama. 'She did not deserve a knife in her belly.'

Anna took a moment to assess everything and everyone concerned with this new situation, both the living and the dead.

'I have come not only to discover Candice. Her letter said she was caring for our cousins, two young girls.'

The three women's faces showed their surprise.

'We did not know,' said Beauty.

A hundred thoughts flooded through Anna, first of which was the reason Candice had left for Cape Town, the reason Candice said she 'Could not live with such a wicked sister.' Had she told these people why she had parted from Anna and her family?

Anna forced an outward change of purpose. 'If our places were swapped she would search for this killer. Surely SAPS can find him. Where is the walking stick?'

'Zuko took it,' said Lucky Lulama. 'But do not go to him. His kind will not speak to the police, for any reason. He believes he will be set up.'

Anna was grateful for what now felt like an investigation, which she hoped would mask the hollow despair she felt in her stomach. Until the white was caught, all questions seemed to point to Zuko. The women left the shack and held each other in a circle.

'Your Zuko may not speak to SAPS,' said Anna, 'but he may speak to me.'

XIV

Beauty said that the surest way to find Zuko was to wait for him to show at the Lucky Strike. He would appear sooner or later. That evening Anna stood with mamas and children at the public standpipe across from the shebeen. A few steps away vendors tended smoking braziers, turning mielie cobs and pieces of offal with their fingers. Beauty remained out of sight and agreed to point him out, although she hardly needed to. Soon after nine o'clock a shared taxi drew up and a man got out. He wore a sports-branded T-shirt under a leather jacket, brilliant white trainers and baggy blue jeans. The man's most striking features were the tatty bandages on his neck and head. Anna reached him before he opened the shebeen door. He turned.

'*Molo sisi*,' he said.

'I believe you are Zuko,' she said.

'True.'

'Forgive me, I do not speak your isiXhosa. I am told you knew my sister.'

He seemed to examine her as he might a new enemy. His face considered a dozen thoughts.

'Leave me,' he said, walking on, 'I have business to attend to.'

'Candice, it is,' she said. 'I was called from the Cederberg to discover her, but I have learned that she is recent passed.'

He turned back and relaxed his expression.

'*Ja*, terrible. A white from the valley chopped her. I have nothing for you.'

'Do you know where is two children, girls? They are family.'

'Why should I?'

'They are aged around fourteen and ten, one is very disabled. If they are alone, only harm will come to them in such a place.'

'Lady, don't bring your troubles to my door. You will have to look elsewhere.'

Anna was hoping for more, so she tried another tack.

'They say you knew Candice well.'

'Who said?'

'People in the neighbourhood.'

'They should keep their business to themselves,' he said. 'I have no news.'

'You saw her on the night she was killed, they say.'

Anna went to lay a hand on his elbow but he instinctively moved away before she touched him.

'I saw nothing,' he said. 'The white hit me with a walking stick and I ran. Don't you see my bandages, woman?'

'Yes, you have bandages, and you also have the walking stick.'

Zuko stopped.

'Do not get tangled in this matter. Return to your farm, or wherever you live, and leave it alone.'

'If the limping man killed Candice, we can find him,' said Anna. 'The tavern owner said the stick –'

'The shebeen queen knows nothing.'

'She said the stick has a golden top. Such an item may be one only. If we find the owner, we find her killer.'

'You cannot hope to find the man. I have more chance of playing for Kaizer Chiefs. Leave it.'

He reached for the door, then turned back.

'You have the colour,' he said. He seemed to think again. 'Sister, you said you were called from the Cederberg to search for Candice. Who called you?'

'Our cousins, Mandisa and Mosa. The letter said they had been abandoned but they are not at Candice's place.'

'You have been there?'

'*Ja.*'

He punched his fists down into his pockets and hunched his shoulders.

'What is your name, sister?'

'Anna Schippers.'

'Lady, the stick is already sold and I used the money to pay for flowers I sent to the morgue. So please, I can do no more for you.'

'Did you speak to SAPS?'

'Do you think the police help us in the township? One more murder in Mandela Park is one less for them to worry about.'

'But if you are the only one who can identify the white man, why would you not help me?' she asked.

'The night was dark, I could not see his face.'

'But still, the walking stick –'

He turned away and entered the shebeen.

The situation that Zuko believed was under his control was being taken in a new direction. No doubt she was family, the resemblance was too strong – was this the sister Candy had spoken of, the one whose actions made her flee the Cederberg? Somehow the girls had managed to contact this woman. Now that he thought of it, he remembered Mandisa mentioning a letter and believing that was the reason Zuko had come to the shack. It was getting complicated, but for now, instinctively, he thought it best not to mention the girls. He had a vague plan for one of them, and he didn't want this woman to interfere.

XV

The following day, rather than the early start she had promised herself, Anna overslept, exhausted from the journey to the city and her discovery of Candice's fate. It was after eight o'clock when she stirred, despite the sound of music videos playing in the salon on the other side of the thin bedroom wall. She woke to an image of her sister with a white man who, after abusing her in a stinking shack, attacked Zuko with a weighted stick then stuck a knife into Candice's belly. The white was now walking free, free to end someone else's life, to traumatise their family, destroy another township dream. The thought offended her embedded sense of natural justice. Too many unsolved crimes were being committed in the new South Africa; perhaps now was the time to take a stand. Anna also had to admit to a disturbing wave of revenge, a new emotion that worried her. Nevertheless she allowed it to flow through her.

Precious already had a customer in the salon, so the solitude in the bedroom helped Anna plan the day. She had fallen asleep with the idea that she should find a way around the obstacle that Zuko posed and take another path to the truth about her sister. But she had the persistent thought that Zuko held, if not the answers to all her questions, then at least, perhaps unwittingly, the key to solving the mystery.

But first she needed to share all the new things she had seen and heard since arriving in Mandela Park. She called Jakobus. The line did not connect to his cellphone but she tried the mission church landline again and the answerphone soon beeped. It did not seem right to repeat into a machine the bare facts of her sister's death, such as she knew them. She would wait until she could speak to Jakobus, by which time she would probably know more. She left a message that confirmed there was bad news, the worst, and that she would stay on for a few more days to tie up some loose ends and arrange transport back to Kouberg for 'a respectable Schippers burial'.

She then went to the police station at the entrance to the township and found a waiting room filled with the desperate and the hopeless. In front of her was a distraught woman explaining the circumstances of her son's death in a gang fight the previous night. Behind her, a man brought in a young child in his arms who had what looked like a gunshot wound to the stomach.

'This is not a hospital!' yelled a policewoman before coming to his aid.

Another officer came to the desk.

'I have information that can help find my sister's killer,' she told the duty officer. 'Candice Schippers.'

He rifled through some paperwork. '*Ja*, a case docket is open on this but the officer dealing with it is already assigned to another murder.'

'I can describe the man who killed her,' she insisted.

'Save it lady, speak to the officer on the case. Look what I have to deal with,' he said, indicating the office full of people. 'Get a paramedic to that child, man!' He turned back to Anna. 'Have you been to Salt River morgue? Near the docks?'

She shook her head.

'One thing at a time, lady. You need to identify the body. Got it? Then you arrange the despatch of the deceased, but not till we tell you. Good luck.'

He looked over her shoulder. 'Next!'

She noted the cellphone number of the officer assigned to the case then walked to the main road hoping to find a mini-bus that could take her to the morgue. As she waited, she took in the busy scene before her: white women whooshed by in 4x4s, often with a young one in a baby seat, like nursery chauffeurs; white men in rolled-up shirt sleeves and deeply tanned arms drove bakkies loaded with black men in blue overalls sitting precariously in the open backs; black women in flip-flops scuffed out of the township along the dirt path. The divisions appeared starker than those in Kouberg, where everyone seemed poor and had the same colour skin.

To a blaring Bob Marley soundtrack, the boisterous mini-bus ride to the city was in direct contrast to her inner thoughts, which were troubled by guilt and sorrow, now lying on a bed of dread at having to identify her sister's body. Her guilt came from the reason Candice left Kouberg for the city; her sorrow from never reconciling her sin with the one person to whom she told her secret.

A combination of the heat and noise in the mini-bus and her apprehension at visiting the morgue made her retch up her breakfast into an abandoned plastic bag. The man beside her moved to another seat and called for the driver to pull over, but she insisted that she continue to Salt River, afraid that were she to abandon her mission she might never return.

Ten days after her death, her sister's body looked sunken and doll-like. In lurid contrast to the clinical smell of the room in which she lay, there were traces of make-up and glitter still visible on her face, which also showed signs of a bruise around one eye. The assistant at the morgue confirmed that the cause of death had been established – 'penetrating abdominal trauma', he called it – and the police enquiry was still open.

Anna remembered what Zuko told her about the money he made from the sale of the walking stick.

'Did flowers arrive for her?' she asked.

'Flowers in a morgue, lady? You crazy,' said the white-coated man. 'Sign here to take responsibility for the burial. The body will be released when we receive clearance from SAPS. She's no pauper now, she's yours.'

From the window seat in the minibus taxi on the return to Mandela Park, Anna couldn't shake the image of her sister's body laid out on the sliding table. She thought of another flake of her flesh lying now not in a municipal facility but returned to the earth in one of her ancestors' hunting grounds. There was mystery only over the most recent death. She saw no irony in her determination to discover Candice's killer, while the first, the anguished fruit of her own body, was still lying where she placed it ten years before. Unmarked, save for her red scarf she placed there on Christmas Day.

The mind can provide many excuses for wicked behaviour as long as it feeds on a closed circle of justification. Despite unwisely sharing the details of her actions three years earlier with her sister, while the secret stayed with her and Jakobus it remained part of their history. What she did not want, now that she found time to reconsider it, was for it to become part of her current life.

As she entered the township, Anna felt as if she had achieved something by assuming responsibility for her sister's body. The fleeting spirit of accomplishment encouraged her to examine a bigger question. Where is the man who killed her? In a city the size of Cape Town she could spend a lifetime looking for one man; and who was to say he lived in Cape Town at all. She must convince the *tsotsi* with the bandages to reveal more information about that night.

She returned to the standpipe near the Lucky Strike until the sun dipped over the mountain. When Zuko arrived and noticed her approach, his watchful expression turned to one of amused annoyance.

'I have no more for you,' he said with exaggerated emphasis.

'Zuko, I was unkind the other day. I questioned you, when I should have been consoling you.'

'Leave me be, woman.' Then he stopped and seemed to study her. 'What is "consoling"?'

Anna stepped up to the entrance of the shebeen. 'Giving comfort for a hardship.'

'I have suffered hardship all my life,' said Zuko, holding open the door. 'Now return back to your Cederberg.'

'We have all suffered,' said Anna, spreading her palms. 'But how do you fight back? How do you show God that you can recover and carry on?'

Zuko gripped the door handle a little tighter and looked her up and down.

'We both loved Candice,' she said, 'and we both miss her. We have that much in common.'

Zuko allowed a man to pass between them into the shebeen then let the door swing close and sat on the step, leaning back on his elbows.

'You are strange women from the Cederberg,' he said. 'Different to our kind.'

'How so?'

'Others would have taken the hint and fled. People don't mess with me in this neighbourhood. You don't give up.'

'Did you give up on Candice?' she asked.

'Do not disrespect me. I was there the night she died, is true, but I cannot go back and change the past. You cannot change your past, which also may hold secrets.' He left a pause, seeming to gauge her reaction. '*Ja, sisi*, Candy spoke of you and the reason why she left the mountains.'

She held a straight face. Surely Candice would not have told this man her secret, broken the pact she believed they had made.

'We all have done things to regret, Zuko.'

'Some regrets you must carry with you like a stone in a shoe... until one man chooses to share it with others.'

He wasn't fishing; he was threatening. If Candice had told him the reason why she left Kouberg three Christmases past, Anna had to keep calm and not show how worried she was. If she ended the conversation now, he would take it as an admission of guilt.

'Perhaps you will carry her with you, as I do,' she said. 'When you lose somebody who means a lot to you you still echo with them after they are gone. Do you feel that sometimes, Zuko?'

'Yo. After a night at the shebeen my head still buzzes with the sound of the music.'

Anna was happier with the joke than Zuko, which signalled that the conversation had moved on.

'I am thinking of something painful, Zuko, more like a bee sting.'

'But even the sting goes away.'

'Some stings never go away,' she said. 'Regret can go deeper than any mistake.'

She hardly recognised her own boldness. After two days in the city Anna was acting like a different person, someone who might intimidate the version she left behind.

Zuko spat in the dirt.

'I regret nothing.'

Anna grabbed the moment to regain control of the conversation.

'Do you believe sometimes that you are the one good person amongst those who do wrong?' she asked.

'Hallelujah to that.'

'Are you from Cape Town, Zuko?'

'Eastern Cape.'

'You came to find your future, as Candice did?'

'*Ja*, find my fortune,' he said, raising his eyebrows. 'And the rest.'

'What did you find?'

'A squatter camp on the side of a mountain.'

'Would you not have been happier where you came from?'

'In the mud hut? Chickens in the pen? No, I take my chances in the city.' He fingered the gold chain at his neck. 'I have prospered where others have failed. My story is not all misfortune.'

'Yet you live in Mandela Park.'

'One day I will live like the whites in the valley,' Zuko said. 'Why not? The future is here, we have to grab it with both hands, they say.'

Anna moved into the shade and settled on the step next to him.

'Would you like that life down there? Living behind electric wires, behind bars, the more you own the more you fear losing? Perhaps you should value your family more, and the people you love.'

Zuko shifted on the step. 'Fok. You speak English but I do not understand all your words. You talk more than your junior sister.'

'You left family in the Eastern Cape?' she asked.

'Not any I wish to see.'

He grabbed the bottom edge of his T-shirt and used it to wipe the sweat from his face, then left it pulled up, exposing his belly.

'Lady, stop digging with your questions.'

She said nothing. He left a pause.

Finally, 'Did you find her?'

'Yes,' said Anna. 'Salt River morgue. The docket is still open; the police are dealing with it.'

'Do not depend on it. Nobody saw anything.'

'Except you.'

'You know everything I know.'

Anna shuffled an inch closer to Zuko.

'Tell me more about that night.'

'How can I tell you more about the darkness? It was dark-dark, that is all.'

'How old was the man with the limp?'

'Just another white daddy. Grey.'

'That helps. And the car?'

'A white Benz, how many more times?'

It was the first time Anna had heard the type of car mentioned. Getting information from Zuko was like picking a lock. She wondered why he was so reluctant to share what he knew. Maybe he would let something else slip. She picked again.

'So we know the man was a white who lived in Hout Bay.'

He nodded his assent. She had guessed correctly. Searching for a man in the city was one thing, but looking for a grey-haired white with a limp who lives in Hout Bay and drives a white Mercedes narrowed the field considerably.

Zuko stood up and straightened his T-shirt.

'You will not find such a man. And if you do, perhaps other secrets will be discovered that you hoped would remain hidden.'

The following morning Anna needed to lose herself in unfamiliar surroundings. She took a shared taxi to Mariner's Wharf at the far end of the beach and, sandals in hand, walked barefoot along the edge of the rushing water on the pale, hot sand, hundreds of miles from scenery she understood. There was a merry atmosphere on the strand: tourists paddled in the shallow waves, white couples walked dogs and coloured families played football or lay on the sand, some under parasols. She passed two black boys burying their father up to his neck, which turned her thoughts to the plot reserved for the Schippers at the edge of the little cemetery on the road out of Kouberg. She stopped and looked across the wide bay to four orange-vested kayakers battling the surf. She idly dug a shallow hole with her foot and wondered if Jakobus had got the seed potatoes in the ground.

With sand crusted between her toes Anna reached Chapman's Peak Hotel and took a table on the open deck facing the wide arc of the sandy bay. She noticed how she was ignored by the street vendors selling beaded Christmas trees, who followed white tourists until they were told to clear off. She asked for a glass of tap water from the waitress and, while she waited, read through a menu listed with items she could not afford. A table promotion read "Chapman's Peak Hotel: The Social Crossroads of Hout Bay". The reverse side listed expensive cocktails that, even at "a festive 33% off", seemed barely credible. What must these people earn to afford such prices.

The road was busy. Without thinking she scrutinised every white car that headed up Chapman's Peak Drive.

The waitress returned. 'Ready to order?'

'Nothing, thank you, sister,' said Anna.

'If you don't eat, you don't sit,' said the waitress, snatching up the menu.

'May I ask a question. How many people live in Cape Town?'

The waitress sucked her teeth. 'I am a waitress not a tour guide.'

'Tour guide? Yes, a tour guide would know.'

'The tourist office is not far.'

There was something in her now that wanted to quantify the size of the task before her. She drank the tap water then followed the waitress's directions to a Cape Dutch-style building on a leafy road a short walk away. It was quiet and empty of visitors.

The woman behind the desk said the current population of the city was four million.

'Four million!' Anna could not hide the pain in her face.

'No one really knows. The townships are growing like wildfire. Almost half are coloureds, like us,' added the woman.

'And whites?' asked Anna.

'Much less, maybe fifteen per cent. In the summer, more, with all the tourists.'

Anna had not reckoned on the killer being a tourist. But even so.

'What number is fifteen per cent of four million?'

The woman slid a calculator across her desk and prodded it.

'Six hundred thousand.'

'Yo!'

'A big number.'

It looked like a hopeless task. She needed to narrow it down.

Anna thought again. 'How many live in Hout Bay?'

'That's a different story. I can tell you more precisely.'

The woman tapped the keys on a computer keyboard.

'In our last census there were eighteen thousand people living in the valley, mostly whites; plus minus thirty-four thousand in Imizamo Yethu, mostly blacks from every African nation; and a few thousand in Hangberg, the coloured area near the harbour.'

Put like that, isolating the neighbourhoods, the task seemed a lot more manageable.

Anna walked back up to the township and headed for the Beauty Girl Salon. A music video was pumping out of the TV on the wall as Beauty crimped a teenager's hair.

'How is, Anna?' asked Beauty.

'I saw Candice at the morgue.'

'O, my sister,' said Beauty, and gave her a brief hug.

'I disgraced myself in the mini-bus taxi; everything came up, not just my breakfast but also my distress and grief and confusion,' she said, holding her mouth. 'My mind is in chaos. It did not feel real to see her body. She did not *look* real. She wore much make-up but it could not hide a bruise and cut over her eye, which must have happened before the night of her death.'

'It did. She and Zuko had a wild relationship at times.'

Another incident that pointed back to Zuko.

'I must arrange for her to be removed to the Cederberg. The police still have a docket open, but Zuko thinks –'

'You saw Zuko again?'

'Yes, outside the shebeen. He says the police will do nothing.'

'Perhaps Zuko *hopes* the police will do nothing,' Beauty said to herself in the mirror. She then focussed on her customer's reflection, pointed the rat-tail comb at her, and said, 'You heard nothing!'

'No, mama.'

'Now, leave us; here is rands, go for soda. Come back in ten.'

The girl jumped out of the container, leaving it trembling in her wake.

'Do you know more than you tell, sister?' asked Anna.

Beauty said, 'She was not my family, is true, but I am also in trauma since Candice came to grief. Township life is not the platteland, as Candice called it.'

'What do you mean?'

'I mean nobody knows what happened that night, only Zuko. But he is not one you should question if you want a quiet life. I am lucky, Jesus is my boy. But to be true, sho... you are unsafe around that *tsotsi*.'

Anna digested the threat. She had already worked out that Zuko knew more about her sister's last night than he was telling, but she had believed it was due to his distrust of SAPS. Perhaps he was hiding something else. Beauty was one of only three potential friends she had in Mandela Park, so she tread carefully.

'It is a fine salon, Beauty.'

'Thank you. Jesus, he arranged it, even though it shakes like an earthquake.'

'It is what Candice always dreamed of.'

'True. And Zuko promised her many times. But many times he disappointed.'

'It seems Zuko stirs in many pots,' said Anna. 'Does he rule over you?'

'Not while I have Jesus.'

It was now or never.

'Then help me find the man who killed my sister.'

Beauty opened her mouth to speak, then exhaled noisily like air leaving a balloon.

'Please, sister,' said Anna. 'Forget Zuko. He will remain Zuko whatever you do. He does not have to know that we are searching for the white. He gave little information, but enough to start a search. Think about it. The man who murdered my sister is walking the streets of Cape Town, do you not see the need for justice? The need to protect the next girl who has a container salon dream? And even if you do not, somehow I must explain my sister's sorrowful death to our clan when I return with her to the Cederberg.'

Anna heard footfalls on the steps outside. The container rocked.

'Here is my Jesus,' said Beauty.

Anna turned. Standing over her was a powerfully built dark-skinned man with a flat-top hairstyle who wore a lined suit jacket over a white singlet.

'We shall help you find the truth, wherever it may lead us,' he said. 'It is time to put this trouble behind us.'

'This is my man,' said Beauty.

'You will help?' asked Anna.

'Fo' sho,' he said. 'I heard everything you said. Fuck Zuko. I am beyond caring what he thinks. If he doesn't get one impression he will get another.'

'I am so glad for you to be here,' said Anna, tearing up. 'I have thought about the task ahead and I am overwhelmed.'

'Wait, I will bring some tea,' said Beauty, 'the kettle has boiled.'

She poured hot water into three cups and threw in three tea bags. Anna sat forward in the spare chair and spread a piece of paper on the counter next to a pen she was given at the tourist office.

'It is maybe an impossible task to find this man,' said Beauty. 'You are not in your home village where you know all by name.'

'True, true. But hear me,' said Anna. 'The tourist lady said there are four million people in Cape Town.' She wrote the number on the sheet of paper. 'Is a big number, for sure. But we must discount those who may not be in suspicion. So, only eighteen thousand whites here in Hout Bay.' She wrote another number.

'Still a big number,' said Beauty, sipping her tea.

'But smaller.'

'It is a true total if you believe this man does live in Hout Bay.'

'The way Zuko said it, I believe the man is local,' said Anna. 'Now, how many are children?'

'Whites have small families. Some poor souls have none.'

'Say every third white is a child.' Anna scribbled a calculation. Then she crossed it out and started again. 'That means twelve thousand adults. Half of those twelve thousand must be women, yes?'

'Smaller!' said Beauty.

'Smaller!' said Anna. 'That leaves six thousand white men in Hout Bay.'

Beauty reacted to Anna's excitement. 'How many drive a Benz?' she said.

'Ayi! One in ten? And a white Benz? Say one in twelve for the easy calculation.'

'Even smaller!' said Beauty slapping her hands together.

'Five hundred. That is less than live in my village, and I know everyone there! How many of those five hundred white men who drive a Benz and live in Hout Bay also walk with a stick?'

'Small-small!'

'Correct. A handful, maybe.'

'We are searching for him without leaving the salon. You are a marvel, Anna.'

'Now it is not such a big number for me.'

'For us,' said Beauty. 'We are with you.'

'Thank you, sister.'

The two women embraced. Jesus looked on.

'But we cannot stand on the roadside and wait for him to drive past,' he said.

'No,' said Anna. 'We must go where he would go. He must fill his car with petrol, so one day he will show at the Shell station.'

The mention of the station seemed to cool Jesus's interest in the whole project.

'True, but he can fill anywhere in Cape Town, not just Hout Bay,' he said. 'And even if a white Benz may show at the Shell station he will not get out and show a limp if the attendant pumps the fuel.'

'Where else must he go?' asked Anna.

'The Mainstream shopping centre. He will shop for food.'

'The beach? He may have a dog and take it for a walk.'

'A restaurant.'

'But which one? There are many in Hout Bay.'

'To the doctor to repair his limp?' said Beauty.

They all laughed.

'Zuko said the man left behind his walking stick, and he sold it,' said Anna. 'Perhaps now he needs a new stick. Where would he buy such a thing?'

'The Sunday market on the green.'

'You have something,' said Jesus.

'This is not such a large task,' said Anna. 'We are not looking for one person in four million, as I say, but one in a handful. And we are not one but three looking for this man. We can do it. We each take a path and look for him. Jesus, the filling station.'

'No,' said Jesus quickly. 'Beauty, you take the station. I take the beach.'

'Okay,' said Anna. 'I will ask at restaurants near the bay.'

At that moment the teenage customer jumped back into the container with her hair in a tangled Afro.

'Please, mama,' she said, pointing to her head. 'Do something with this.'

XVI

It was New Year's Eve. Zuko returned home with two bags of shopping and placed them on the stove then opened the fridge and took out a large bottle of Coca-Cola. As he swigged heavily he leaned back on the low cupboard and caught a foul whiff. He looked in the direction of his occupied bed where Mandisa was changing Mosa's nappy. Disgusted, he left the shack and spat out the mouthful of Coke.

Soon Mandisa joined him on the step. She was wearing one of Candy's dresses.

'My sister must be cared for,' she said, imploring.

'I know all about it,' he said, lighting a cigarette.

'But I have to do it.'

'You are not the only one. I have done it for another when I was younger than you.'

'You had a cripple brother?' she asked.

Zuko hesitated before he said the word. '*uMama*.'

'Ah. Then you are not angry, as we believed.'

'Mosa believes I am angry at her cursed condition? Not angry, happy. Happy that I do not have her twisted body.'

She waited for a neighbour to finish hanging washing on a line, then said, 'We thank God each day that you have taken us in.'

'Where would you be now?'

'The landlord –?'

'That bomboy Liberian meant business.'

'*Ja*,' she said with mock dread. Her face soon creased into a smile that mobilised her features.

He turned towards her, smiling broadly. 'Did you see his shoes? Hah! Like he was going dancing.'

Mandisa snorted with laughter.

He felt on good form. 'And the jacket! Like a five-star waiter!'

'Remember the trolley!' she said.

'We got out of that shit. Pick n Pay: I picked you up but we didn't pay.'

Mandisa now had her face in her hands, breathless with laughter. All of her pleasure flowed through him; it felt like sharing a long satisfying drink.

'Let him tear down your shack,' he said, 'maybe the gorilla will spoil his new shoes.'

'Too, too much,' she said, and wiped her face with her palms and dried them on her skirt.

Zuko followed her action and left his eyes on her legs. Not since the moment outside Candy's shack had Zuko noticed how much she looked like a full-grown woman. Or at least could pass for one. She had fine legs and a pronounced buttocks that would cause a stir sitting on a bar stool. Her plummy, wet lips fascinated him, and the point of her chin accentuated her long neck. He raised his eyes to her tight, stringy necklace, at the loose shirt, and the translucent skin beneath. Her small teeth were not white but perfectly even, and appeared to nestle in her mouth, doll-like. Her smile flickered something within, a light that he had not yet fully appreciated, and he could imagine what she would look like ripened. She was all potential, like a letter addressed but not yet posted.

What had seemed impossible a few days ago was becoming almost inevitable. It was time to see what was hidden beneath the loose top and over-sized skirt.

'Do you like to visit the barbershop?' he asked.

'The salon? Any girl would,' she said.

'Then I will arrange it.'

'But where?'

'No, a stylist will come here.'

'And Mosa?'

'Mosa too, if you wish. Then some new clothes.'

'O! You are a good man, Zuko.'

'I am not all bad, as some say.'

'Then can you put us in school?' said Mandisa. 'I have not been since Mama died. When Candice took us in I would stay at home to care for Mosa while my cousin worked, by day and by night. The neighbourhood was very dangerous so she told me never to go outside while she was away.'

'She was a good woman.'

'I am glad you say it. It makes me happy to remember her through the sadness.'

'You remind me of her, fo' sho –'

He couldn't finish the sentence. He turned away and looked over the tin roofs while he regulated his breathing. With the rare insight of a child, Mandisa averted her eyes until he regained his composure.

'I know you miss her too,' she said.

'Too-too bad.'

'And school?' she said.

'We will talk about it in good time.'

Mandisa rinsed her hands at the tap.

'Do you want food?' she asked. 'I will make as well as I can.'

'*Ja*, but no pap. We can cook together. I have brought pork chops and broccoli with brown rice. We will all eat well tonight.'

'A feast for Old Year's!' said Mandisa, skipping up the step into the shack. 'What will the new year bring?'

While Zuko and Mandisa cooked, Anna was making her way down Victoria Road towards the Hout Bay shopping district. She had spent every available minute of the last three days out of the township to immerse herself in this otherworldly life of luxury, home of the man – and the car – she was seeking. She walked from the leafy neighbourhoods of Scott Estate to the large mansions of Hanging Meadows, from the new security complexes towards the Karbonkelberg to Rhodes Drive. She had even taken the snaking mountain road to the top of Constantia Nek and peered through every fence and gate. If she was greeted at all it was with suspicious looks by whites who came to the gate with their dogs and told her to move on. Even black gardeners made their distrust clear by swearing something in a language she didn't understand. She asked waitresses in restaurants, attendants in petrol stations, and sales assistants in stores if they had seen a white man with a limp. Nothing. When she found a white Benz in a car park she would wait until someone got in and drove off before she could be sure it was not the one she was looking for. She had never noticed Mercedes-Benz's before; now she saw them pass by every few minutes. And every second car on the road was white, which made it difficult to concentrate on anything other than scanning cars with the three-pronged badge and scrutinising the interior for a grey-haired white man, ideally one who was holding up his walking stick. She felt ridiculous.

As the evening wore on and dusk covered Hout Bay she became aware of an irresistible drift of people towards the bay. As she got closer, she noticed lampposts displaying posters advertising "South Africa's biggest New Year's Eve Celebration". It seemed like the whole of Hout Bay was heading for the beach. She called Beauty and followed the crowd. As she reached the strand she could hear the first thundering chord of a rock band. There was a surge towards the stage, which left space for her to easily follow the line of cars parked along the sea front. She counted two white Benzes in the first row of cars and five more in the beach car park. She couldn't watch them all. A parking guard wearing an orange bib leaned against a battered Toyota and counted a handful of change.

'I'm looking for a man, hey?' Anna said.

'Yes, Ma.'

'A white man with a walking stick. You have seen him?'

The man put out his palm. 'Yes, Ma.'

'Seen him tonight?'

'Yes, Ma.' He shook his palm. 'He was here.'

The guard had a thick accent, not South African. She enunciated her words more clearly.

'A man with a walking stick was here tonight? Was he in a Benz?'

'Yes, Benz.'

'Which one?'

'I cannot say.'

'Cannot? Are you truthful?'

'Whatever.'

Anna sighed and scanned the beach. The man spat. She tried again.

'Was he limping or not?'

'Yes.'

'Which one?'

'The man with the stick.'

'No, I mean – What did he look like?'

'A grey daddy and a woman.'

Anna handed him two rands.

'Which way did they go?'

'To the beach,' he said, waving his hand in no particular direction, 'with all the others.'

She looked down to the crowded strand. Should she wait for the man's return to the car park or begin an immediate search of the beach? She couldn't wait.

'Do you have a cell?' she asked.

The guard picked an old Nokia with a smashed screen out of his pocket.

'There will be more rands for you if you call me when the man returns.'

'Two rands cannot buy bread, Ma.'

'Ten rands, then. What is your number?'

He told her and she thumbed it into her phone, then called him.

'Now you have my number. Call me when you see him. I will come quick with money. You will eat tonight.'

'Yo!' said the guard as he ran for a tip from a driver leaving the car park.

Anna received a call from Beauty and told her her location. She then walked to the edge of the beach wall and noticed that most of the younger, barefooted crowd were dancing, pressed around the stage. Many older people wearing fleeces and long trousers sat on fold-up chairs near the low wall that divided the sand from the beachside houses. Most people had a drink in their hand.

Anna walked slowly along the wall, her gaze flitting from man to man. If they were on their feet she looked for an unsteady gait; if they were seated she searched for a walking stick close by. But the beach was so crowded with people and picnic paraphernalia that it was difficult to get a close look at anybody.

Beauty arrived with Jesus, who had clearly been drinking.

'The cripple is here,' said Anna. 'Somewhere. A car guard saw him arrive.'

'What does he look like?' said Beauty.

'Grey hair. That's all I have, but we will notice him walking.'

'Jesus –'

'Happy Old Year's,' he said swinging a limp arm across Anna's shoulders.

'– wait at the car park. Beauty and I will split up and look in the crowd.'

After two hours the two women found each other again. No luck. They walked on in opposite directions and continued the search. After another two hours Anna found Beauty sharing a bench with a coloured family swaying to the music.

'It is nearly midnight, Anna. There are always fireworks. Afterwards, the man will find his Benz and drive away. We should wait near the cars.'

At that moment an explosion shook the air and a thousand yellow, blue and red stars fell from the sky, then another shower of white, blue and green. The South African flag had never looked so beautiful. The crowd roared as everyone looked up to the cascade of light and the band struck up the national anthem. The sound was deafening with booms and hissing rockets that crackled and echoed off the water. The singing of the crowd brought on a profound loneliness.

'We go,' said Anna.

She instinctively reached for her cellphone. Missed call. She pressed redial.

'Bring my ten rands,' said a voice.

'He is there?' she yelled down the phone.

'Here. Yes. Bring money.'

Anna shouted to Beauty, 'He is at the car park.'

Beauty took out her cellphone and pressed the contact for Jesus.

'Where are you?' said Beauty into the phone. 'You must wait by the cars.'

She ran behind Anna as she listened into the phone.

'So, you're not with the cars!'

They found Jesus on their way back to the car park. His zippered jacket was bulging.

'Many opportunities on such a night,' he said with a stupid grin. 'Boys must have their toys.'

When they reached the car guard he pointed to a large white car in a queue of traffic waiting to leave with a white man at the wheel and a woman in the passenger seat.

'Benz E Class,' said the guard. 'Sweet.'

'That is the car,' said Jesus.

'How do you know the car, Jesus?' asked Anna.

He didn't answer. Anna stored this fresh piece of information as she attended to more immediate concerns, namely confirming that the driver was her man. She found a ten rand note in her pocket and gave it to the guard.

'What do we do?' asked Beauty.

'I must be certain it is the man before I approach him,' said Anna. 'I must see his walking stick or this man will cause me big trouble.'

'Follow him,' said Jesus. 'Take a car and go where he goes.'

Anna hailed a shared taxi with the front bumper hanging off and a single headlight shining on full beam.

'No room for three,' said the driver.

Jesus told the four passengers to get out and find another taxi. They didn't argue. All three got in and told the driver to follow the Benz.

'Like in the movies,' Jesus told the driver. 'Without observation.'

The driver glanced at his new passengers in the rearview mirror. 'I want no trouble. I have a family.'

Jesus threatened something in isiZulu and the driver reluctantly selected first gear.

They followed the Benz as it drove through Hout Bay at a funeral pace, probably slower than the taxi had ever moved. It reached the lights at the bottom of Suikerbosse Hill and took a left.

'Helgarda Estate,' said Beauty. 'I worked for a family up here.'

'I worked this neighbourhood too,' said Jesus, and sniggered.

The district, lit with ornate street lamps, was quiet, the roadway litter-free and clear of parked cars. The tarred road turned to red cobbled brickwork overhung by jacaranda trees and palms. Large houses loomed left and right behind high fences, some with boats in the driveway and large TV screens flickering in rooms beyond burglar bars. The taxi slowed almost to a stop as the Benz took another left. Anna looked out of the side window and peered through a gate to a house with a dog sitting bathed in a security light above the front door. She was transfixed as in a dream. She wanted to own that house, pet that dog, watch that TV, and have that life for herself, anything but confirm the identity of her sister's killer.

Jesus, who had been opening up the cellphones he had acquired on the beach, leant over Anna and threw three sim cards and an emptied purse out of the open window. Beauty glared at him. Anna pretended not to notice.

The Mercedes-Benz stopped at a wide metal gate on wheels that slowly slid open from right to left. The taxi driver killed the headlight and parked a little further down the road. When the gate was fully open the white car drove into a large compound.

'Security complex,' whispered Jesus.

The small housing estate was surrounded by a high fence, electrified on top, behind which were communal gardens and a swimming pool eerily lit blue. The gate closed. Anna got out of the taxi and pushed her face against the bars. She could just see the car pull up in front of a garage door on which a sign read: "ADT Armed Response". Beauty and Jesus joined Anna at the gate. The driver's door of the Benz swung open. One leg emerged from the car, then the other, shortly followed by a walking stick.

XVII

The taxi took Anna, Jesus and Beauty back to the township. There was no conversation. Anna's silence sprung from her belief that she had reached the bottom of her investigation. Now what? Beauty seemed to be withholding her thoughts about the whole affair. Anna would get her to share them soon. Jesus dozed.

The township streets were teeming. Most people had bottles or cans in their hands, there were braais aflame with boerewors and chicken pieces, and all the spaza shops were open. There were more people on the roadway than Anna had ever seen during the day.

'Should we not go to SAPS?' said Anna. 'We know where the cripple lives.'

'The police, is it?' said Beauty. 'They put one thing straight and leave a dozen others crooked. Anyway, they will do nothing at this time. We can do no more for Candice tonight. She is sleeping, at peace. Why not come out with us.'

'I can't, I am so tired, I will call Precious and go up to the salon,' said Anna.

Beauty would not hear of it.

'It is Old Year's, Anna. Everyone is out tonight, including Precious.'

Anna looked up and down the road, which now resembled a carnival. 'Goodness! It is unbelievable. After midnight! Kouberg is silent at this time.'

'*Yebo*!' said Beauty, raising her arms and shaking her midriff. 'That is why we live in the township.'

Jesus took out the cellphones from his jacket.

'I will sell these and see you later at the Lucky Strike.'

He slapped Beauty's rear end and joined the drift of humanity down the street.

Anna could not hide her thoughts on how Jesus had acted tonight. Her expression must have invited explanation.

Beauty said, 'He is a good man, but he gives in to the devil inside. It is something he will have to change if he wants to stay with me.'

Anna felt better for the acknowledgement of her feelings.

'We all have good and bad inside, that is why God has given us the option to choose good. I am sure he – and you – will make the right choice.'

The two women embraced.

'Come,' said Beauty, 'my place is not far.'

She put an arm on Anna's shoulder and they strolled up Mandela Road.

'I must share something with you, Anna. Jesus and I have spoken of it. We feel unease since Candice died.'

'What is it, sister?'

'Is it not curious that a white cripple would kill, even one that comes for a bar girl?'

'Of course,' said Anna, 'but you say crime is common here in the township.'

'It is. We live with it every day. But usually our black brothers are killing our own. A white man in a township after dark is bold, but to bring a knife and kill a girl? And then to attack and chase away such a one as Zuko?'

'What do you say?' Anna asked.

'I say that someone who cut Zuko on his head would not now be living in the valley. He would be in the Salt River morgue instead of your sister.'

'And?' Anna continued the conversation in her head. 'You think Zuko killed Candice?'

'I cannot say for sure,' said Beauty.

'Why do you only tell me now that you suspect Zuko when I have been in the township for five days?' she cried.

'I have seen you search Mandela Park like a lion looks for its cub, and my heart hurts for you. I have thought, What would I do if it was me?'

Anna tried to line up her thoughts. On the brink of confronting the man who she believed took her sister, another door was opening.

'But now that we have found the white,' said Beauty, 'I would ask him to tell us what happened.'

'But maybe he is a wicked man. The police is best for him. Even if he did not bring the blade and kill Candice, he has much to lose.'

'True. But is he more likely to talk to us than to SAPS, to tell enough for us to prove it was Zuko.'

Anna was not convinced.

'What will his family say if they knew he went to the Lucky Strike for a bar girl?'

'Fo' sho,' said Beauty. 'He may talk to us to protect his secret. If he tells us lies, and it seems he did it, we will then go to the police and he will be taken for murder. But if he can prove Zuko was the one, we go after him. To hell with the white, I do not care about his situation. After all, Candice would now be alive if he had not come to Mandela Park.'

Anna walked on in silence, picking her way past revellers on the street.

'What does Jesus say?' she asked.

'First to say, he has problems with Zuko. Zuko hates anyone who would diss him. Jesus is my boy, he is schooled and has read books, real books not just messages on his cell. Zuko hates him for that. Jesus believes he is capable of anything. Chopping one of his girls is only one of the possibilities.'

Anna winced.

'Do not go to SAPS in the morning. First we should hear the white's story,' said Beauty. 'We three girls will go together for safety. We leave Jesus here or he will scare the man into silence.'

They reached Beauty's house, which she now shared with her parents and sister, and played host to a constant stream of visitors throughout the night. Anna felt in the way and reluctant to enter into the Old Year's spirit, and looked for an opportunity to return to her warm bed next to the Man-hat-on Salon. No chance. No matter what torment she was going through, celebration was in the air, in every boom of music from the street, every burst of laughter, and every firecracker.

Beauty pulled her into a sweaty bedroom and opened a wardrobe like she was performing a magic trick.

'Tonight we entertain ourselves.'

She held up blouses and skirts, shoes and dresses then threw each in turn onto the bed. Anna was far too small to fit comfortably into any of her new friend's clothes so Beauty asked a neighbour's daughter if she could borrow some jeans and a sparkly top. Anna's old sandals would have to do. Then Beauty mixed and matched in front of a full-length mirror until she was pleased with what she saw. When she found an outfit she liked she loudly sucked her teeth and air-kissed her own image, then asked Anna, '*Mhle*?'

Anna didn't need a translation to know that Beauty was dressing for male attention. She eventually chose high heels with plastic flowers on the insteps, a swishy low-cut dress – orange with a yellow tasselled hem – and a white feather boa. The outfit was topped with an outsized wig of gold and chestnut curls that fell past her shoulders. An hour later the two women headed towards the Lucky Strike down Mandela Road arm in arm, one striding out, the other more reluctant, like two mismatched characters entering stage right.

They passed a group of men on a step swigging from cans who loudly jeered them with rude comments.

'Eat it up,' said Beauty, swinging her hips with emphasis.

Lucky Lulama had placed one of the sound system's waist-high speakers at the shebeen door – 'to attract passing airplanes,' joked Beauty – around which were gathered a broad cross-section of the neighbourhood, some seated on chairs they had dragged from home. Old Year's had brought out the pimps and the prayerful, the garish girls and the grimly formal, the drunks and the dry. Inside the shebeen it was mostly the former, who were covered in a shared, glistening sheen of sweat, like a herd of wildebeest in rut. Young men wore new suits like fancy dress pimps and draped themselves over giggling women.

As soon as Beauty entered, Jesus spotted her and called, 'Chaka Khan in the house!'

She found two seats close to Jesus who was at a table with a small group of musicians: a guitarist, a penny whistle player and someone who slapped a box between his knees to keep time. Gyrating women took turns singing into a microphone connected to the sound system. The ceiling was dripping.

Even above the raging volume of the music and the din of the crowd it was impossible to ignore the room-filling presence of Lucky Lulama, dressed from neck to toe in yellow topped with an outsized blonde wig; she seemed to be everywhere. Anna noted that she was in drink and was loudly directing waitresses to bring beers to hard-to-reach tables or run out for food from the street braai for customers. Occasionally she would take the microphone from a singer and finish a chorus – and get the loudest cheers. In her quieter moments, Anna caught Lucky Lulama eyeing her, more than accidentally, like the shebeen owner had something to say.

It was inevitable Zuko would show. He looked high, and wore a basketball jersey and baggy trousers rolled up to his calves. The tongues were out of his trainers and the laces dragged on the floor. He picked up a full, unattended bottle of Heineken from the nearest table and joined two other men in a corner.

Beauty squeezed Anna's hand. 'Say nothing.'

It was unnecessary; Zuko ignored their table.

Anna felt like the only sober person in the township; the longer she stayed at the crowded shebeen the lonelier she felt. Other people's joy was like being slapped gently about the face. She thought of her five children and Jakobus, she thought of her sister laid out in the morgue, she even thought of the shivering rooibos. But the thought of the dark roadway back up to the Man-Hat-On Salon kept Anna in the bar longer than she would have credited before arriving in Cape Town. Few things now were as unpredictable as the dark streets of Mandela Park. Then again, most events that had occurred in the past week were new to her. It was going to be difficult to describe her time here when she finally returned home.

Lucky Lulama passed through the crowd and sat in a space that didn't exist between Anna and Beauty.

'You are finding what you seek?' asked the shebeen owner.

Despite the festive atmosphere, Anna had no time for small talk.

'Tonight maybe I saw the man who killed my sister. We did not speak but I know where he lives, in a large house across the valley.'

'Sometimes the eye misses the obvious, neh,' said Lucky Lulama.

Beauty leaned in to the conversation. 'What do you mean, gogo?'

'Some mysteries are solved before they should even be considered. Pah! It is clear to some what occurred that night.'

Lucky Lulama, wet-lipped, was spitting on Anna with every plosive consonant.

Anna said, 'Forgive me, but may we talk in the morning?'

Lucky Lulama furrowed her brow, as though cut with a knife. 'I will be sober then, my tongue may not work so well.'

Anna took a gamble. 'Did Zuko kill my sister?'

'May I put it another way,' said Lucky Lulama, swaying a little. 'When was the last time a white, who was not a police, killed one of ours in Mandela? It is rare, rare as snow on Christmas Day. We believe Zuko's story because it is what we want to believe. It makes no waves: SAPS file the report; he finds another girl to sit on my bar stool; the men come and buy my beer. We continue as before, neh.'

Anna looked over Lucky Lulama's shoulder and caught Zuko's eye.

'He is looking, is he not?' said Lucky Lulama.

'Yes, gogo,' said Anna, before looking away.

'We put up with Zuko like bad weather, as if it is something we cannot change. But I.Y does not need him; the Lucky

Strike does not need him; and poor Candice did not need him.'

'Why do you reveal all now, gogo?'

'There comes a day for all of us when we must decide whose side we are on.' Lucky Lulama shifted her considerable backside a little closer. 'Maybe the new year has put some steel in my soul.'

'Please tell me what you know.'

'I know that *tsotsi* like I know my own tits. I told you I found the golden stick, hey? Zuko took it because he did not want the white to be found.'

'He is part of this mystery,' said Anna.

'As certain as mud follows rain in the township. Secrets fascinate, but the truth can be wicked.'

Anna was not certain what she meant. Beauty squeezed Anna's trembling hands that had pushed themselves together in prayer.

'What to do now, gogo?' asked Anna.

'The white has all the answers. You must talk to him and beg him to come forward, but Zuko must not know. He is quick with the blade, so stay out of his way. Anyone who talks about your sister is in great danger.'

'Do not be concerned,' said Beauty, 'we have a plan.'

XVIII

On the first day of the new year Zuko ducked through the thin strip of trees that marked the northern boundary of the township, passing a fresh huddle of shacks in no-man's land which lately seemed to spring up overnight like strange shipwrecks. He skirted the first line of large properties surrounded by high walls and fences. Excitable dogs within heard him push through the thick bushes and barked until he moved on to the next property, seeming to pass him on from guard dog to guard dog. One property had thick metal railings topped by an electric fence. Through the bars he could see a swimming pool and a boma strewn with the debris of last night's braai: ribs chewed to the bone, toppled beer bottles, half-filled glasses. There was no dog. All was quiet. From where he stood, the house did not appear to be overlooked and the ground floor sliding doors were not gated. He scanned the roofline of the house for CCTV cameras and infra-red sensors. Clean.

He took out his combat knife and attacked the loose, sandy soil under the fence. When he had dug a hole the size of his head, he stopped and listened. Nothing. He put his hands through the metal bars and dug on the other side of the fence, scraping the soil out through his side and throwing it behind him like a fox on a snake hunt. Soon the hole was big enough to crawl through. He lay on his back and pulled himself under the fence into the garden. He paused and listened again. All still.

Of course, this was not the first time Zuko had entered a property uninvited, but it was the first time that he was interested in how these nameless scores lived their lives. The coloured gammie had told him that he would not like to live like these people. He wanted to see who was right.

The number of whites who had swimming pools always amused him. If he owned a house like this he would not waste the electricity it took to run the pump that kept the water clean, and even if he did, he could not envisage himself sitting next to it for so long that he would need to jump in to cool off like so many did. It made no sense, and the extravagance seemed excessive. The braai, caked with the remains of chicken and red meat, was something more useful. And even then, it always seemed to him a caveman's way of preparing food: a blunt instrument of torture for ingredients that deserved respect.

He sat on a sun lounger set on a raised section of decking next to the pool and scanned the garden. Protea bushes and dense ornamental grass on both sides hid him from neighbours. The closest sound was the drone of the pool cleaner working its way blindly around the bottom of the pool. In the middle distance an alarm wailed and drew his attention to life beyond the fence. Peeping out from a defensive line of trees, he saw the roofs of shacks and he wondered if this was one of the pools he had seen from the township.

It was too hot to sit for long in the sun so he made his way towards a sliding glass door covered by an awning. He stepped into the shade, cupped his eyes and peered into the house. Immediately inside was a dining table and chairs and, beyond, a large kitchen. There was a stillness that he recognised as an empty house. He tried the handle – even in today's South Africa some people believed misfortune would pass them by – but it was locked. He took hold of the sliding door by the outside plate of the door handle and lifted it slightly. There was enough give to feel the door was secured by a thumb lock bolted into the top runner. The bottom section was tired and warped. Taking a firmer hold of the plate and with his left hand grabbing the other end of the door frame, he lifted it no more than two centimetres, enough to slip the double-glazed unit out of its runner. He then pushed it to one side and leant it against the fixed panel. He entered the house and waited for the alarm. All quiet.

His curiosity took him not on a search for cellphones and cameras or the safe – which, from experience, was usually fitted to the wall in the master bedroom – but rather to the kitchen. The sunny room was flooded with light from two huge windows that faced south down the valley towards the bay and surrounding mountains. All the surfaces were either polished wood or glass, which made it feel more like a car showroom. Everything gleamed with menace. He could see no food save for four green apples in a glass bowl on the counter.

He opened both doors of a silver, double-sided Miele refrigerator. The contents, a multicoloured swirl of packets and jars and short rows of matching bottles, brought a smile to his face. He appreciated the sight as he might take pleasure in a beautiful white woman or a red sports car. Unattainable. He closed the fridge then opened a cupboard. The door was gently weighted, which made the action of opening and closing an unexpected pleasure. Drawers needed only a light touch to glide open, then a delicate push returned them to their perfect, cushioned home.

He took an apple from the bowl and bit into it. He felt at home, and had a fantasy that he should cook a meal. His delighted response to the house made him think of all the other properties he and his crew had entered. The scores were carried out without a single thought for the lives of the people who lived there. He never knew their names or faces, or if they had jobs or children, or what they cooked for dinner – neither the first-timers nor the houses to which he returned three months after the first visit, to take the newly bought replacement products. They never learned.

Zuko quickly reached the second floor and checked all four bedrooms, each laid out as if for a magazine shoot. The largest looked out over the township, and he took a moment to locate his shack. He couldn't. It was just one in a sea of silver roofs now glinting in the morning sun. On most surfaces in the bedroom were framed photographs of smiling people – cycling, sunbathing, drinking, scenes as likely to be from another country; he studied them as he might a store catalogue. For one dislocating moment he imagined himself in the pictures, having had those experiences. Too much happiness; too much to lose. Back in the moment, out of habit, he checked bedside drawers for cash, and then opened wardrobes as if he was adopting these people's lives. He inhaled the clean waft of freshly pressed shirts and unscuffed shoes and ran his fingers along a row of stiffly regimented trousers. He checked the waist size. Too big.

Downstairs, adjacent to the kitchen, was an immense sitting room with a double height ceiling and galleried landing. He opened more doors. Inside one room was a shiny, black piano and an empty fireplace into which he threw the half-eaten apple. More than the odour of the long-extinguished fire, there was another distinctive smell that tapped a memory. Books. Every wall was lined with bookshelves that stretched from the floor almost to the ceiling. A stepladder, essential to reach the top shelves, leant against a door frame. Like an animal in another's territory he followed the shelves around the perimeter of the room, touching the books with his fingertips, some spine-end showing, others face-on. An image returned of the books left behind in Candy's shack. Perhaps he should have made room for them in the shopping trolley.

He soon found a hardback with a picture of Nelson Mandela on the cover. He held it in both hands. It was not the same book as that given to him by cousin Maphule, but still, he opened it and inhaled. Everyone, even whites, agreed that Madiba was a good man, so it was not surprising that books were written about him and that he would not be forgotten. But all these other books? All these other people? Did their lives just happen to them, or did they go out and create their own stories? Whatever the answer, they were honoured and remembered, not lost and forgotten. What could these books teach him? He wondered how many he might have read if he had been schooled. Perhaps none; perhaps all. Maybe he could start now.

He was drawn to a set of hardcover books with blue covers and embossed writing on their spines. He caressed them snugly in his hand, one by one. The covers were a little scuffed but the gold lettering stood out boldly against the blue. He flicked the feathery pages, which were covered in tiny print and interspersed with occasional line drawings. So strong was the aroma that he didn't need to put the books to his face to recognise their age and significance. The pictures in one particular book featured a small boy in various scenes, mostly in distress. They were vivid enough to tell a story in themselves without reading the words. He slipped it under his jacket with all the satisfaction of pocketing a smartphone. He had seen enough. He returned to the dining room and listened for a few seconds... just the hum of the pool cleaner. He smiled at his own restraint in not ransacking the house.

'I have a book,' he said out loud.

Then he noticed a silver laptop peeping out from under a sofa cushion and took that too. 'And Apple Mac.'

He stepped out onto the patio, lifted the door unit back into its runner and pushed it to. Then he ran.

In a similar neighbourhood across the valley Clive unrolled the garden hose, connected it to the tap on the far wall of the open garage, then rinsed the Benz on the driveway, one of eleven identical drives in the complex, most of which were home to German saloons or 4x4s. He took care to hose the car's roof, around the wing mirrors and under the wheel arches. He killed the water then picked a sponge out of a soapy bucket and covered the car with suds.

Cradling a mug of coffee, Rhea came to the front door wearing long shorts and orange Crocs.

'Leave it for the garden boy, man,' she said. 'No point having a dog and barking yourself.'

'I enjoy it,' said Clive. 'Anyway, I don't expect anyone in the township to be in a fit state this morning after last night's festivities.'

'*Ja*, those ridiculous speakers outside the shebeens echoed down the valley till five. That boom, boom, boom sounded like we were being invaded. Which we are, of course, with squatter central spreading. They were setting bonfires again.'

'No, Rhea, that was a shack fire. The radio news said ten were destroyed.'

Rhea took a sip of coffee. 'And wear your hat, or you'll look like one of them.'

Clive opened the rear door of the car and slipped on his straw Panama.

'I'm surprised you're up,' he said. 'You sounded rough first thing.'

'Give me a break, Clive, it was Old Year's. If I can't enjoy myself at this time of year, well –'

She stepped into the garden and carefully pulled the scabby heads off a couple of her favourite hibiscus.

'When you're done, turn up the irrigation in the front garden,' she said, 'these are not getting enough water. It's so damn hot.'

As she turned to go, she glanced towards the estate's outer gate.

'Not again! I'm not having it this year, Clive.'

'What?'

'Begging, job search, rummaging in the bins, whatever they get up to.'

He followed her gaze. A coloured woman was standing outside the gate peering through the bars.

'She'll move on soon enough,' he said.

'Ag, man, just deal with it, will you?'

He stopped wiping the windscreen.

'Here,' she said, 'your stick.'

He threw the sponge at the bucket and missed, then reluctantly limped towards the gate.

'Don't give any money,' called Rhea. 'Don't encourage them.'

Clive wiped his palms on his shorts, lifted his hat then ran a damp hand through his thinning hair. As he got closer to the barred gate he could see the woman was well dressed and had the small, fine features of a Bushman. Not the usual scavenger.

With indifference, he said, 'What you want, hey? Who you looking for?'

'I do believe, *meneer*, that I look for you.'

'And?'

'We have much to talk about.'

Clive tried to recall whether he knew the woman. 'And?'

'It is not correct that we talk through these bars.'

'You can see I'm busy. What's going on?'

The woman's face dropped.

'It is a matter to be discussed with sensitivity,' she said. 'It is about my sister who has recently passed.'

'I'm sorry for your trouble,' said Clive, turning to leave, 'but I have nothing to give. Move on before I call ADT security.'

'*Meneer*, two weeks ago my sister – a young San girl, like me – was killed by a knife in a shack behind the Lucky Strike tavern.'

He turned back. She continued.

'A white man was there, with a walking stick, who drove a white Benz such as the one you are washing.'

She pointed at the car behind him. He couldn't help but look over his shoulder towards the wet vehicle, as much to hide his reaction as to give him a few seconds to recall the incident with the light-skinned girl and the *skelm* with the bandaged neck. The quote from the newspaper returned to him: *We have reason to believe the incident was preceded by an argument between the victim and her customer...* He felt dirty and trapped... *Who is yet to be arrested.* He was immediately presented with another predicament: Rhea was still standing at the front door observing them both. He took two paces towards the gate.

It was time for the new Anna to speak. 'Talk to me now,' she said slowly, 'or *I* will call ADT.'

'Not here,' he said with urgency. 'I'll meet you somewhere.' His thoughts spooled through a list of safe spaces. 'Go to Chapman's Peak Hotel near the beach, I will meet you there in an hour.'

'You will be there for sure?'

'You can bank on it. Now go. Don't come back here.'

An hour later Clive's Mercedes-Benz turned right out of the complex and headed down Victoria Road towards the bay. The woman, looking insignificant and out of place, was standing outside the hotel when he arrived. He pulled up and lowered the passenger window.

'Get in.'

She pulled the heavy car door and Clive flipped the central locking as he pushed hard on the accelerator. Her face showed bewilderment and a little panic, as if he had lured an animal into an unfamiliar trap. Or was he the prey? *Now what do I do with her.* The woman stared out at the sights of Hout Bay rushing past. The only sound was the whoosh of the car engine and the creak of leather as she settled into her seat. Like the threat of far-off thunder, their lives were about to change, but to what? It was for him to break the silence.

'So, do you work at the shebeen or what?'

'No, *meneer.* I come from a long distance. Cederberg.'

'I can tell your accent isn't local, hey.'

Small talk over, Clive parked up at a viewpoint overlooking the bay, the one known for a recent series of vicious muggings. The car park was quiet apart from two tourist buses arranged side-on to the bay so that the Chinese passengers could get a clear photograph of the panorama without getting out. Clive leaned into the back seat for his walking stick and Panama hat and eased himself out of the car. He waited while the woman clumsily found the door handle, exited the car and swung the door closed before he pressed the key fob. He then limped a few steps and sat on a concrete picnic table. Anna stood a few paces away.

The Sentinel across the bay was ablaze in the morning sun. There was a breeze coming off the water which created shallow cresting waves that were chased by diving gulls and cormorants, and sent pied crows soaring up the cliff face like kites straining on invisible strings. Below, the curve of the white sandy beach was dotted with people and colourful parasols and taut windbreaks. A fishing boat sailed into harbour. Happy new year, thought Clive.

'I have come to discover the truth about my sister,' Anna said, stepping forward. 'Candice Schippers.'

'Candice? Doesn't ring a bell.'

'Some know her as Candy.'

Candy. So it was.

'And you are?'

'Anna Schippers.'

'Who knows about this, hey?'

'Only good people who seek the truth.'

Clive lifted his feet onto the bench seat, placed the walking stick across his knees and looked out towards Seal Island. His speech was coming out in short bursts. He didn't want this woman to think she had anything over him, even though they both knew she did.

'Have you spoken to the police, hey?' he said.

'They are too busy to send anyone. My sister was not the only poor girl to lose her life at Christmas.'

'What do you want from me?'

'I need to know what happened to my –'

The occasion seemed to catch up with her as she pursed her lips tightly and tears, refusing to fall, filled her eyes. As she searched for a tissue in her pockets she looked small and insignificant, out of her depth. He felt like he wanted to slap her hard across the face, slap her back to the Cederberg. She wiped her cheeks with a loose sleeve and continued.

'You were there that night, is it true?'

Clive scanned the coastline once more as if searching for a way out of this. Then she tightened an already tight screw.

'We have your walking stick,' she lied, 'the one with the golden top.'

Emptiness overwhelmed him.

'It must be valuable,' she added.

He couldn't help releasing an expression of recognition.

'There's every likelihood it was the same night,' he said.

'Is that a yes? They tell me it was December eighteenth. Friday before Christmas, the day of the community concert. Were you there?'

Yes, he was there. He was never likely to forget it. It was the moment he would have given anything, the car, the contents of his safe, everything he possessed, to get out of that stinking shack unhurt. He was lucky to have only lost his cellphone and some cash. He had already replaced the medi-alert bracelet; Rhea missed the walking stick, but he had covered his tracks on that. Now he wanted to scream out how close he was to death, how much he loved life and didn't want it to end.

Something about the view across the bay and this woman's routine courtesy made him want to clean up the city, right here and now, grab his friends and the Neighbourhood Watch and ask, Do you know what's happening in the township? People killing each other, ruining what could be a paradise for all of us. We're living in the most beautiful city on earth, and this is how we treat each other. That's what he wanted to say and do, but this woman's presence reminded him that he fell far short of what he believed were his own charitable ideals. His utopian fantasy for South Africa was nothing more than that.

The tourist buses moved off, the sound of their ticking engines replaced by the rush and swirl of the wind. They were alone. He walked to the perimeter of the parking area then kicked a stone over the cliff edge and listened to it skitter down towards the water. Unconsciously he tried to calculate how high they must be. He turned to face the San woman with the Dutch name, now standing plainly before him. What would be the likely consequences if he went to the police and told them what he knew? He wrote a newspaper headline in his mind: "Valley Man Implicated in Murder of Township Prostitute". He wouldn't get out of it unscathed. Maybe he could do a deal with this woman: information for anonymity. Perhaps he could pull in a couple of favours from buddies at the yacht club. Charity funds were always disappearing, and he knew who had light fingers. They would have as much to lose as him, so wouldn't they help him clear up this mess? The woman broke the dizzying churn in his mind.

'I never saw the sea before I came to Cape Town,' she said.

Clive got his racing thoughts under control and looked across the water once more. This is what beauty looks like, and what fear feels like. He wondered if she too was forcing down her emotions.

'The world is full of new things, even at my age, hey.'

Anna pointed out to sea. 'What is out there?'

The space between them had instantly been filled by the vast expanse of the ocean. He felt better for it.

'Next landfall, Antarctica. Snow, ice.'

He wished he hadn't added the last two words. It sounded patronising, and something told him that the woman was shrewder than she appeared.

'Were you there that night?' she asked, quietly now.

'I had nothing to do with your sister's death. Do I look like someone who would kill a young girl?'

'I do not know what a killer looks like,' she said evenly.

'Not like me, that's for sure,' he said, with belligerence, lifting his stick as if offering proof.

'Were you there?' she asked again.

Silence, only broken by the shuddering wind coming up the mountainside.

'*Meneer*, if you did not kill Candice, you must help me prove who did. We know you were there.'

'Who's "we"?'

'Others who would look for my sister's killer. One found your walking stick with the golden top.'

He said nothing.

'We have no proof, but we believe the killer to be a Xhosa in the township – my sister's boyfriend one time, a *tsotsi* called Zuko.'

'Then leave me out of it. Why accuse me of killing her?'

'I did not accuse you. I asked if you were there, only.'

Clive jabbed his new walking sick at the dried earth.

'I was just passing through, I meant her no harm. The guy burst in with a knife and robbed me but she grabbed my stick and belted him with it, across the head. Fuck, I thought *she* was going to murder *him*. Even in the dark I could see blood everywhere, she was really going for it, man. I ran for my life.'

He felt as if he had taken the first breath after coming up for air. Since that night he had been desperate to share the details of the most terrifying moment of his life. Without knowing it he wished for a confidante, a confessor. If he could have been sure they would keep a secret, he'd have paid someone to listen before now. Now he had blurted it out to this courteous, unassuming woman wearing a headscarf and plastic shoes.

'Was he called Zuko?' asked Anna.

'How do I know?'

'How did he appear?'

'Just a black guy with a big fucking knife.'

'Such a description is common in the township.'

He let out a short belch of laughter at the unintentional humour.

'Point taken. What else... he wore the usual sports gear, had a bloody bandage on his neck.'

'It is him,' she said with finality. 'But you must identify him in person.'

The mention of the bandage brought the *tsotsi's* features back to Clive: the lip spittle, the geometrically shaven hairstyle, the leather jacket. A pulsating wave of nausea swept through his body. He licked his lips and breathed deeply.

'Look, maybe there's something I can do to help,' he said, with a more forgiving tone. 'But that means not involving me with SAPS. You'll get nowhere with that bunch of arsewipes.'

Clive made Anna promise that if he pointed out Zuko in the street, she would keep him out of it. It was the best he could hope for.

The man didn't offer his name, but on the drive back to Chapman's Peak Hotel he was checking for cars at a traffic circle over his right shoulder when Anna pulled down the visor to block the sun's glare. There, slipped behind a thick elastic band, was an identity card: "Clive Greenberg, Registered South African Tour Guide". She quickly flipped back the visor. Double-parked outside the hotel, she gave him her cell number, then insisted he call her on his new phone. She saved his number in her contacts as "Clive Greenberg", then showed him the screen.

'So you know this is not over until I discover the truth about my sister's death.'

She got out and the car's wheels spun as it merged back into traffic.

Anna was feeling a little light-headed after the extraordinary morning. The air up in the rich neighbourhood had seemed lighter, unsoiled, the sun more forgiving along the leafy avenues. Even the cool air that brushed over her face in the car had seemed cleansed of impurities. The streets of Hout Bay had looked a lot less threatening from behind a windscreen of a Mercedes-Benz.

As she reached the township and walked past the waste dump she was hit with the enormity of the task before her. She was already regretting not taking Beauty's advice that they both approach the white man together. He seemed to order the conversation, but she should have pushed him to answer more detailed questions about that night. She thought she could achieve more without Beauty, certainly without Jesus. She was wrong. She had felt like a child. The moment got to her, and she was overwhelmed; overwhelmed not only by her sister's death and having to deal with this man in a car probably worth ten years' income, but the very fact of being in Cape Town. She had never stayed in a township before, or dealt with the police or visited a morgue, or even seen the sea or sat in a Benz. It had been a week filled with new experiences, each one seeming to push her further away from the reason she was here. But why was she here, was it really for her sister? And what of her two cousins who sent the letter that fuelled her visit? Through it all, one thing was becoming clearer by the day: Zuko surely killed Candice, and probably has knowledge of the two girls. The two events must be linked; she just had to find a way of proving it.

She walked to Beauty's house and told her where she had spent the morning. Beauty's face crumbled.

'Are we not together, Anna?' she asked.

'I woke very early and could not wait. I had to meet the last man to see my sister alive.'

'Maybe not the last.'

Jesus came out of the back room. He lay on the sofa in his boxer shorts and flicked on the TV.

'Not now, Jesus,' said Beauty.

He switched off the TV and lay back with his legs over the armrest.

'Was the white there, Anna?' she asked.

'Yes. And I spoke to him.'

'Ah! What news?' asked Jesus.

'He said he did not kill Candice, as we suspect.'

Jesus sat up. 'What is this? You said the white killed your sister. That is why we followed him last night.'

'Things have changed,' said Anna. 'Lucky Lulama seems sure that Zuko was responsible, Beauty too. The white does not deny being there that night but he left as she was fighting with Zuko. It was she who cracked his skull with the walking stick.'

'Will the white tell everything that happened?' asked Beauty.

'I do hope. He said he will identify him.'

'Do you now go to SAPS?' asked Beauty.

Jesus stood up. 'You go to the police and you go alone,' he said. He pointed at Beauty but kept his eyes on Anna. 'She is not with you on this.'

'Jesus, I will do as I must,' said Beauty. 'I am your woman not your bitch.'

Jesus wiped his face with an open palm. 'Do not bring police to my door. I will end up in the jail with Zuko.'

'He must pay for Candice's murder,' Beauty said.

'The danger is too great,' he said, raising his voice. 'Candy was a casualty, not the only one, and there will be others. It is life in Mandela. Bring SAPS here and we are all under suspicion. They will find another reason to put me in jail if they do not find her killer.'

'But Jesus,' said Beauty. 'We know who is her killer.'

'I do not want to hear it,' he said.

'You know what I am saying.'

'Not for my ears,' he said, walking towards the door. 'I will deal with Zuko in my own way. It is time someone put us all out of our misery and eliminated that piece of shit. If I don't do it, who will?'

Beauty winced. 'You say you do not want SAPS involved and yet you threaten more violence. Where does it end? Jesus, the police is the only way to deal with him. Once he is in the jail Anna can return home with a settled heart and you can decide what to do with the crew.'

'The crew can screw, that is not my concern,' he shouted. 'I will survive, I am sharp. But I do not need more kak in my life.'

Beauty would not back down. 'If he kills Candice one day, he may choose another tomorrow. Will it be me? Or you?'

Jesus stopped pacing and turned to Anna. 'You have brought nothing but trouble to our door. Return to your Cederberg. Take Candy with you and bury her in the mountains with the other coloureds. Leave us alone. If you do not tread carefully out of here, I cannot protect you from others who may wish you harm. You must decide.'

Beauty put her arm on Anna's shoulder. 'No, Jesus, *you* must decide.'

Jesus put his hands over his ears, and shouted, 'FOK! FOK! FOK!'

Anna's mind was whirling. She had to separate the facts from guesswork – and then decide what she was going to do about it. She had come to Cape Town to find her sister: fact. She had found her lying on a slab in the mortuary: fact. Now what? Lucky Lulama and Beauty were risking their own safety by telling her what they knew, so she had to accept their suspicions were well founded. It was surely more than a guess that Zuko killed Candice. She also knew that the tour guide was the most important witness. And, judging by Jesus's response, it was even possible that he also had a hand in her death in spite of his offer to help search for the man on Old Year's. Meanwhile the letter that brought her here now felt like it had been sent by ghosts. Although she had never met the cousins, she somehow felt close to them. There seemed only three possibilities: they were safely taken in by a new family; they had already suffered a terrible fate;

or they were being hidden. Jesus refused to tell her where Zuko lived so she would have to confront him on neutral ground. In any case, it seemed unlikely that a man like him would take in two helpless girls.

When Jesus told her to bury Candice in the mountains with the other coloureds he unwittingly pressed an old wound that would not easily heal. It brought to mind her children. She called home.

'Jakobus, is that you?'

It was a relief to speak in Afrikaans.

'*Ja*, it's me.'

'I can hardly hear you.'

'I tried many times to call. I even called the church but no one answered.'

'I'm here now.'

'Where are you that you pick up?'

'I am in Clanwilliam to buy seed.'

'Jakobus, I have terrible news.'

'The minister told me the message you left on his phone.'

'Candice is passed. There is much to tell, but for now I will say that my sister died by the hand of another. She was killed with a knife.'

'Ah, it is too terrible. Sweetness, I wish I was there with you.'

'*Ja*, me too. SAPS will not release the body until they investigate her death.'

'Is someone charged with her murder, is that what you're saying?'

'Not exactly. But people in the township know who it is. It will take some time.'

'When are you coming back?'

'I can't say, Jakobus. Township life is not as it is in the Cederberg. The city! O! Also, Mandisa and Mosa are nowhere to be found. No one has seen them.'

'That is too bad. Anna, there is a situation here that needs you.'

'Are the children well?'

'All fine. Another situation, I mean. One that is ten years old.'

Anna recognised his change of tone. 'Jakobus, I will not speak of it on the cell. Leave me be to deal with my sister, then I shall do what you want.'

'It is urgent, I must tell you.'

'No, not now. I have too much to do. You do not understand what I am going through.'

'I feel the same,' he said.

'What?'

'Nothing. I will deal with it as best I can until you return.'

'Very good. Better for you to call me next time you are in the town and can get a signal.'

'But soon, sweetness, soon.'

XIX

The Mozambican hairdresser arrived from outside the neighbourhood to fix the girls' hair. The styling took most of the morning and Zuko remained within earshot to move the conversation on between her and Mandisa whenever she pried. Mandisa chose wide braids woven tight to her scalp that ended in a short bob; Mosa had her Bantu knots retied.

When the stylist took a drink of water from the tap, Zuko said, 'Show the beautiful one how to use make-up.'

'I will pretty her.' She turned to Mandisa. 'What is your age, girl?'

'Do not mind such things, just show her,' Zuko said.

The stylist handed Mandisa a mirror then took out mascara and lipstick from her make-up bag and turned her back to him.

She lowered her voice as she applied the mascara to Mandisa's flickering eyes. 'Where are your parents, my angel?'

'I have none,' Mandisa said.

'Who is this man? An uncle?'

'No. He has taken us in. He feeds and cares for us.'

'I think you care for yourself, and your sister.'

A man came to the door and negotiated with Zuko for the stolen laptop, which allowed the stylist to speak more freely.

'Does he mistreat you?'

'No, mama.'

'That does not mean he won't. Does he take you to his bed?'

'No.'

'Not yet.'

'He spends many nights away and comes home very late,' said Mandisa. 'Do you know something that we should know?'

'I know his type. Has he taken you to meet men at the shebeen?'

'No. I never drank beer.'

Zuko came to the door. 'How goes?'

The stylist stepped away. Mandisa was transformed. Blue and yellow eyeshadow, rouged cheeks, thick red lipstick, pencilled eyebrows and curved lashes like animal traps achieved the effect he was looking for. Candy recreated.

Mandisa lifted up the mirror to her face. She didn't recognise herself.

Zuko whistled. 'Yo! *Abafana* will be in a line at the door.'

Mosa looked at the stylist, who shot her an unmistakeable glare of warning.

'Leave the make-up,' said Zuko, pulling out his newly acquired wad of rands.

The following evening Jesus went to the Lucky Strike intent on confronting Zuko. One way or another Zuko's actions would bring SAPS back to the neighbourhood, something Jesus couldn't afford to happen. If Zuko was threatened with jail, he would drag Jesus down with him. Overnight he grew to understand Anna's predicament and it had become clear that, not she, but Zuko was the source of all his problems. He wished for him not to be in the neighbourhood at all, and was ready to take the necessary action. Who would miss him?

Lucky Lulama told Jesus that Zuko had not been in all day, so he continued up to the Beauty Girl and looked in from the roadway. Beauty was sweeping the floor in preparation for lock-up.

'I will be home late, Jesus. I am going up to see Anna who's staying with a stylist called Precious. She needs a friend, and I want to be there for her.'

'No problem. I must tackle Zuko. Enough is enough.'

'He is here,' she said, pointing over his shoulder with her broom.

Jesus looked back to see Zuko slink out from between two shacks, the swirling pattern of his Madiba shirt vivid in the evening sun.

'Long time no see, bruh,' said Jesus.

'You have miss-missed me?'

'No. But we must talk.'

'That is all you do, Jesus, fokken talk.'

Beauty stepped down from the swaying container, handed Jesus the key, and said, 'I cannot witness another argument. Lock up before you go.'

Zuko stepped past Jesus up into the salon and looked down on him on the bottom step.

'Have you been fighting with your one?' he asked.

'We have talked about you, Zuko.'

'Have you made a plan?' Zuko laughed. 'Fixing the world with a pen and paper?'

Jesus remained on the step.

'Someone enquires after Candy – her sister.'

'The gammie is there every time I turn around,' said Zuko. 'She will soon go back to the mountains.'

'I do not see it. She sticks to the task like a fly in chakalaka.'

'She is of no concern.'

'She will soon be your concern, Zuko. We found the white who was with Candy that night.'

'We?'

It hardly mattered now what Zuko knew.

'The sister found him,' said Jesus.

'The cripple?'

'It is so. I recognised the car and saw him with my own eyes. He knows the truth.'

'*Yebo*. He killed her.'

'He says not.'

'Of course he does. Either way, he will not speak to SAPS. A white with a black chick in Mandela has much to hide.'

'Not if he is accused of her murder. He will then have nothing to lose by speaking out. He can identify you, bruh.'

Zuko paced the salon, rocking it to and fro, noisily grinding the concrete step.

'What happened that night, Zuko?'

'I told you. I ran and thought Candy was behind. The guy must have brought a knife.'

'There are many who do not believe that.'

'Then they can go fuck themselves.'

'But I have to look out for my own situation,' said Jesus. 'If SAPS come for you, you must leave me out of it.'

'So now we are not a crew-crew?'

'It is time we went different ways, Zuko. Ask Jonno and Little Mabhuti what they want to do.'

'You trying to screw me, now. You were there that night just as I was.'

'No, not just as you were. It was another one of your no-brain scores that ended in chaos. You chopped her, do not deny it.'

Jesus traced out the likely fight about to happen. He was aware of the knife in his waistband and thought it best to get Zuko away from the salon and deal with the situation cleanly in a quiet cut-through between shacks.

'I will lock up then we will go to my place,' said Jesus. 'We must sort this tonight. Make a plan.'

'Another fucking plan.'

Zuko kicked over a chair then slammed his hand into the side wall, which sent a crack splintering across the new mirror.

'It's all fucked up.'

He turned to look at his fragmented image. His jacket swung open and Jesus could see a book in Zuko's pocket. He moved to the top step and snatched it.

'Now who is looking for answers in the pages of a book?' said Jesus.

'Return it.'

'Ah, ah!'

'Give me the fokken thing.'

Jesus jumped to the lower step and held the book away from Zuko, reading aloud the title from the inside page: '"Oliver Twist, or the Parish Boy's Progress". So you have found yourself a book. The parish boy can read! It is a miracle!'

Zuko swung a kick at Jesus, just missing his head. Jesus threw the book at him and jumped into the salon, which shook violently. Both men reached for their knife as the street outside became strangely deserted.

Zuko cut the air between them with his blade, hissing, 'Your time has come, *Msunu Wako.*'

'You are more trouble than you are worth, Xhosa shit.'

Zuko slashed the air wildly. Jesus flung his arms wide and skipped around the container, then he dragged the overturned chair between them. He lunged for Zuko, stabbing his upper arm. Zuko winced at the pain but managed to deflect the next attack by raking his blade along the back of Jesus's hand, which sent the Zulu's knife skidding out of the salon. The container rolled left and right as Jesus leapt out after his knife, which had clipped the crumbling concrete step and landed underneath. He reached for his blade as the cement block steps cracked and crumbled next to his head. The open end of the container lurched violently, dropped three feet, and came to rest on his hands. Jesus lay screaming as every loose item in the salon spilled out on top of him.

With the strong sense that people were watching him, Zuko returned home but did not immediately go inside. His arm pulsated as the blood from his injury seeped through his jacket and down his forearm onto the back of his hand. He sat on the step and gathered his thoughts with the detached feeling that his life was taking place in front of his eyes. It seemed like Jesus was ready for the fight yet he came off worst. He must still be there, hands trapped. For the first time he imagined the weight of the container. Whatever his injuries, they will no doubt be more lasting than Zuko's knife wound.

Someone would have seen them fighting. So what? Accidents happen. It was as though Zuko had rid himself of a problem without really trying. The cause of the fight? A book. He took the hardback out of his pocket and thumbed through it, leaving some of his blood on the pages. The smell of the paper hit him and he quickly returned the book to his jacket. Maybe Jesus will recognise the twist of fate if he ever gets out from underneath the salon.

One problem was solved. He opened his front door to another. Mosa was in her usual position on the couch watching TV, her head lolling on a pillow. Mandisa was at the stove, barefoot and bare legged, and wearing one of Candice's dresses belted around the waist, emphasising her hips.

'I wanted to thank you for our new styles,' she said, stirring something in a pot, 'so I will cook for you tonight.'

'How old are you, girl?' he asked abruptly.

'Fourteen,' she said, turning to reveal a hint of cleavage under a deep V neckline.

'Looking sweet.'

She rolled her eyes, but seemed to appreciate the compliment. She licked her sticky, reddened lips.

'We love our hair, don't we Mosa?'

Her sister gurgled approvingly.

Zuko lowered his voice. 'Listen, girl, we must make a plan for the future. We cannot go on like this, living in a home for cripples.'

Mandisa lay down the spoon. 'If you put us out, we must find our family. Mama would say the only family we have are in the Cederberg. But where is that?'

'Fo' sho. Your difficulties are double with your sister on your back.'

'That will not change. I cannot give up on her.'

'We all move on, girl. Even I. I walked from the Eastern Cape at your age. Shit happens, but you survive.'

He was still full of adrenalin from the fight with Jesus and decided not to release the energy on her. Mandisa was not the problem in his life. She turned back to the stove. He stepped up and put a hand on her shoulder.

'What cooks?' he said.

'Chicken and fried rice. Pap for Mosa.'

'Spices? Make a sauce,' he said.

'With what?'

'Anything. You must learn that I eat only quality.'

'I used what was in the fridge.'

'Here, some rands,' he said, handing her everything in his pocket. 'Buy what you would eat in a restaurant.'

'I have never been inside a restaurant. And I have not been in a shop for months, I would not know what to buy.'

'Well, ask someone in the store. Say you want sauce ingredients.'

'But what?'

'Surprise me! Just go! Keep walking downhill until you reach the main road. Your sister will be fine-fine for a short time.'

Mandisa checked herself in the mirror then opened the door.

'You may keep the change,' he called after her.

'*Yebo!*' she said, then disappeared.

Zuko opened a bottle of beer, turned down the two pots to simmer and leaned against the stove, appraising the contorted figure reclining on the couch. He reached behind the stove, the new hiding place for the brass-topped walking stick, and took it in hand.

'It is too bad you cannot eat real food,' he said. 'It makes life worth living. I cooked enough pap in my time. I was a good son.'

He moved closer to Mosa. Her eyes settled on his.

'What do you think of?' he asked. 'What occurs inside you? Do you feel as others feel?'

She shuffled on the couch and emitted a whimper like a small animal.

'Speaking in sounds only is not all bad,' he said, tracing a halo around her head with the stick. 'Sometimes I wish my girls said less.'

He pushed the walking stick under her chin then traced the metal ferrule down her body, ending at her twisted feet. The girl's fragility was simultaneously energising and paralysing; she rallied something in him, yet brought him to the edge of disgust.

'You are a sight,' he said, standing up. 'You disturb me.'

He went out to the step swinging the stick, and put his bottle down next to a basin of Mosa's dirty nappies. It reminded him of his mother's bucket next to the chicken pen, and brought back the mornings and nights he cleaned her, moved her to the pot then back to bed. The feeling that it would never end. Until he ended it. Now, years later, another cripple. It had only been nine days since he pushed her home in the supermarket trolley, but she and Mandisa had already made themselves part of his life. If he was honest, before he found Candy's old shack, he would have admitted that he was looking for comfort in a new routine. Mosa's care was now part of the package.

His thoughts were being pulled in opposite directions. Despite the burden, he could not deny the thrum of satisfaction he felt each night that he had succeeded in providing food and shelter for one so deformed. It had not only become his duty, it was his alibi, proof that he was not all bad, as some say. He was now haunted by this disabled girl who stirred buried thoughts, ones he thought had been left on the long road from the Eastern Cape.

Another part of his mind was taken up with the fine presence of Mandisa. Recently he found himself looking forward to seeing her. If the other reminded him of his mother, Mandisa was Candy without the ambition. She it was who he desired. The quickest way to return to the early days of Candy's time with him would be to separate the two girls. Permanently, if necessary. It would be best for everybody.

He re-entered the shack and lay the walking stick by the girl's side. Mosa had slipped a little off the pillow and was swallowing anxiously with her tongue darting in and out of her mouth. He stood above her and took a slow swig of beer. They remained locked in a strained silence for minutes.

'What troubles you, eh? Cannot breathe? I can fix that.'

He snatched the pillow from behind her head and taunted her with it as she threw her arms this way and that, clawing wildly in the air.

'It is of no concern to me if you are here or not,' he said. 'We must take what we want, and your sister is what I want.'

He put down his beer and took the pillow in two hands, holding it to his chest, then he sat on the edge of the couch and brought his face to hers, closer than they had ever been. He was taken over by another voice.

'Have no fear, I know how to do it,' he whispered.

Mosa regained the use of her tongue for a moment and launched a fat oyster of phlegm into his face. It shocked them both. A new coldness ran through him and he brought his face back to hers. His lips glistened with a mixture of his and her saliva. Her eyes bulged and he felt like pushing his thumbs into them, squeezing them like berries through a sieve.

'With a face like yours you spit in mine? Have you seen yourself?'

He dropped the pillow, reached for his mother's hand mirror and squeezed next to her on the couch. 'Look at the face your mother gave you.'

She growled at her reflection and a little regurgitated food dribbled down the side of her cheek.

'Are you hungry? You prefer baby food? But I will not make you pap for the rest of your days. It will be a life of misery, for us both.'

He felt the stolen book digging into his ribs. He took it out and pushed it into her face.

'Have you not learned to read? The children are walking to school without you... past the chicken pen with books in their bags.'

Mosa squirmed and wriggled up the couch, which supported her thrashing head and helped her catch a desperate breath. Her eyes rolled up towards the ceiling. He allowed the book to drop on the floor.

'Do you have the vertigo?' he said. 'I know what that's like – we all want to make patterns in the star-stars.'

He turned the mirror and caught his own reflection before tilting it slightly to angle it towards the open door. He imagined his cousin Maphule standing there: *The future comes disguised... if we want something we must grab it... it is our time and nothing must hold us back.*

He took the mirror in his left hand, as his mother used to, then quickly smashed it against the arm of the couch. He stood up and, stepping over the splintered glass, kicked his beer bottle into the shack wall. A violent, jittery energy seemed to leak through his pores, like unspent life. He didn't know whether he wanted to hit something or caress it, make something or destroy it.

'Now, girl, you smash my mirror and spill my last Heineken. You home wrecker.' He moved towards the door, intoxicated, but not from the alcohol. 'I will get some more beer, and vodka – it is time your sister learned the ways of the township. Better me than another man.'

His thoughts turned to Candy and the first time he spiked her drink, which made him kneel down and take the Noxzema box from under the bed. He looked back from the open door. 'Look after the homestead while I am gone. Don't talk to those bomboys, you know what can happen when you mix it with the neighbourhood *tsotsis*.'

XX

The terrified screams, distinct above the township hubbub, seemed to come from the direction of the Beauty Girl. They lasted for a few seconds, then ended abruptly. For some inexplicable reason the cries made Anna feel homesick. She called Jakobus.

'It is good you called,' he said with urgency. 'The situation needs you to return.'

'I cannot, Jakobus. I have much to do here for Candice. I do not want to explain on my cell.'

'Anna, this is serious. We expect the police will come to Kouberg soon.'

'What has happened? The children?'

'Your living children are all well,' he said with precision. 'But the other... when you went to Bushman's View on Christmas Day, someone followed you.'

'There is nothing to see. It is difficult to reach.'

'Not that difficult, Anna. It is known why you went there. Someone has found the grave of our absent child.'

She gave out a whine. Then silence.

'Are you there?' Jakobus asked.

'Who found it?'

'Not it. Him. For now, it does not matter who found him.'

'It matters to me. Who?'

'Minister Johannes.'

The name hit her like a misery from a past life.

'He came to me after you left on Boxing Day,' said Jakobus. 'He was out walking early on Christmas morning before service. He took another route to the mountain and saw you leave Bushman's View with tears in your eyes, which made him curious. It didn't take him long to search the cave and find your scarf on the grave. He waited until Christmas was over before coming to the house in a rage. It seemed he was angry not just as our minister but as someone with spite in his heart.'

'The minister is not all he seems.'

'Why do you say that?'

'I will explain when I return.'

'Anyway, when he heard that you had left he said he could not wait for your return. Anna, I swear I did not know what he was going to do —'

'What?'

'He returned to Bushman's View with a spade. The grave is dug.'

Her special place, her first born, resurrected with a common spade. She wondered if refusing him on Christmas Eve had something to do with the minister's actions. Would she turn back the clock if she could? Agree to his desires? Commit a new sin to cover an old one?

'Tell him to keep it to himself until I return,' she said. 'Better still, tell him to call me, we can work it out.'

'Anna, it is beyond that. He said that, of all people, you should know the difference between what is right and what is wrong. What does he mean by that?'

'How do I know?' she blurted.

The difference between right and wrong was becoming blurred, especially viewed through the lens of Mandela Park.

Jakobus continued. 'The minister tells everyone who will listen about his discovery. He says the child was not buried in the eyes of God and that you must suffer the consequences. The whole village knows the remains of an infant have been found on the mountain.'

'It has come to this, Jakobus,' she said, sobbing.

'The people are saying terrible things about us, Anna. The gossip is too cruel.' His voice cracked. 'We knew this day would come. You must return and explain all.'

'Say nothing more, Jakobus, to anyone. What's done is done. I will face my accusers when I return. I can do no more for our ill-formed child, but I can find the man who took away the life of my sister. For that I must stay.'

'But Anna, you must return so we can make amends for our sinful deeds.'

'I can make amends here in another way. I will bring justice for my sister.'

'This makes no sense. Leave the man who killed your sister. There is no more you can do for her. Return, I say!'

'I will stay, Jakobus – for Candice, for the little one, and maybe for me too.'

Her husband's distant voice mewed on as Anna held the phone at arm's length. She pressed the red button, then hurriedly made her way towards the Beauty Girl Salon and the source of the screams.

By the time Anna reached the salon, a large group of men were frantically leveraging scaffolding poles under the container, just enough to drag Jesus's limp body out from underneath. He turned onto his side and looked up at Anna in anguish, raising his head momentarily. The remains of one of his hands remained squashed into the bloody concrete step, the other dangled from the end of his arm before it detached at the wrist and flopped onto the earth with an awful permanence. People gawked then shrank away in horror. A crowd formed around Beauty whose face was hardly recognisable with grief as she wailed and threw her hands in the air then alternately slapped her thighs and her head.

'Jesus! Jesus! Jesus!' she screamed, wailing and slapping, wailing and slapping. 'God will punish you, Zuko! You are a devil! A devil!'

Jesus opened his eyes momentarily as she collapsed to the ground at his side. Lucky Lulama ran to comfort her.

A Toyota taxi, honking incessantly, eased its way through the crowd and stopped alongside the container. Four men lifted Jesus into the back seat, then Jonno jumped in next to the driver and yelled, 'Clinic, yo!'

'*Ja*, I know it!' said the driver, and lurched the car into gear.

'Wait!' yelled Lucky Lulama. 'His hands!'

An onlooker handed her a plastic bag and she knelt in front of the gaping container. She picked up the hand that fell in the dirt by a flattened finger and plopped it into the bag. The other hand was completely crushed; no more could be done.

'Take this,' she said, handing the bag through the passenger window, 'the other is no more.'

When Beauty could stand up unaided, Anna took her by the arm and they both followed the car down to the main road. The clinic receptionist told them there was no doctor on duty, and as there was no ambulance at the weekend, she had sent Jonno and Jesus in the taxi to look for a hospital in the city. The two women had no way of knowing where they had gone so Anna took Beauty home, where she dropped on all fours and vomited on her doorstep before taking to her bed.

Anna returned to the container. People seemed reluctant to leave the scene, including a huddle of small children sharing half a loaf of dry bread who had their eyes glued to the place where Jesus had been trapped. The container looked like a half-submerged ship with its cargo doors agape. At its mouth, Lucky Lulama was picking up the remains of the salon contents.

'The scavengers have already cleaned her out,' she said. 'The chairs have been taken. TV, video and all the styling tools and wigs have gone.'

Anna looked inside the container. 'Ah, it gets worse.'

The mirror was in shards on the floor, the sinks were ripped from their stands and torn modelling posters were fluttering on the walls.

'We cannot blame people who have nothing. They see a chance and they take it, neh.'

Anna whimpered, then realised for the first time in a week that she was thinking of something other than her sister's death.

'Did Zuko do this?' asked Anna.

'Who knows,' said Lucky Lulama, 'perhaps it was no accident: wherever he is, there is always trouble, as you know, *sisi*.'

'Others have troubles also,' said Anna, bending to collect a few stray hair rollers that had found their way into a muddy rain channel. As she straightened she noticed the step was still streaked red and buzzing with flies. She turned away.

'Bring a bucket of water from the pipe,' said Lucky Lulama

Anna forced herself to look at what was left of Jesus's hands. 'Should we not call SAPS?'

'He is in the hospital,' said Lucky Lulama, 'so there is nothing more to be done, neh. For now, this is not something for children to witness, we must get it cleaned up.'

In the gathering gloom of the early evening they rinsed the steps then swept the bloody remains into the open sewer, Anna quietly humming a mournful tune.

Lights were coming on throughout the neighbourhood as a man in a too-big black suit stepped into the road from a nearby shack and approached the women. Lucky Lulama said she knew him as a man of the church and community leader.

'Good afternoon, ladies, my name is Pastor Joshua. May I say what a terrible occurrence to happen in our neighbourhood this evening. Did the man survive this terrible tragedy?'

'We hope. He is called Jesus and is in the hospital.'

The pastor straightened his tie. 'It is not the first troubling incident at the container salon in recent weeks,' he said.

'You are right.'

'The salon seems to attract the wrong kind, like hyenas on a kill.'

'Beauty is a good girl, neh,' said Lucky Lulama, 'she has suffered much and is at the mercy of *tsotsi*s who threaten her and her business. Now her boy is mutilated and the salon is no more.'

'It is not only the salon that brings the wrong sort into our lives... other businesses also attract the dregs.'

Lucky Lulama rested her considerable weight on her back foot and folded her arms. Before she could respond, the pastor held out his hands.

'Shall we pray together?'

Anna took the pastor's hand and waited for Lucky Lulama to join the prayer. With eyes fixed on Pastor Joshua the shebeen owner raised her hands and made the tight circle. They all closed their eyes.

'God, for the love of Jesus, your son, and for our brother, his namesake, please save his life and bring comfort to our sister Beauty.'

The two women opened their eyes and waited for the pastor to let go their hands.

He continued, 'And in your mercy, help us rid this neighbourhood of the scourge that blights our community, wherever you may find it: demon drink, immoral women, poverty and ignorance.'

Lucky Lulama clucked. When Anna raised her head she noticed the darkening neighbourhood was now becalmed as silent men, women and children stirred in doorways up and down the roadway and in cut-throughs between shacks. These were the people Anna had largely ignored during her time in Mandela Park while she tried to settle her own piece of bad luck, the ordinary people, the mamas who spent evenings washing their children's only uniform for school the following morning, the gardeners and handymen who waited at the Victoria Road traffic lights for any kind of work that would make them feel they were part of something, the gogos who cared for the little ones left by their parents who were affected by the disease that left no family untouched. She knew instantly, in their stumbling, hesitant ways, they were also dealing with their own misfortunes, but silently, with dignity. She took a deep breath, one she had been meaning to take for the past seven days.

'Amen,' said the pastor, releasing the women's hands.

'Amen,' said Lucky Lulama, unwilling to hide a perfunctory note in her voice.

The pastor acknowledged the gathering crowd before addressing the two women.

'I now must speak frankly and express the voice of our neighbourhood on such an abominable incident. These residents desire that their voice be heard. Many people, watching from the shadows, saw the incident in the container between these two men. One, Zuko by name, is known to us already, and he knows our homes and spazas too well, not to mention robbing me of our collection box outside the God is Good Evangelical Church. We believe the injured man also runs with the wrong people, so perhaps it was a matter of time before an incident of this kind caught up with him – what some people would call collateral damage in a community somewhat less than God-fearing.'

Lucky Lulama nodded with a forced air of innocence. 'You can't touch me,' she said, 'I run a fine tavern. Cold beer and good food.'

'You, madam, are not the subject of our community's concern,' he said, 'but there are rumours, more than rumours, facts that are now common property about the bar girl who was killed two weeks ago behind your shebeen.'

Anna put her hand to her mouth and the tears that she had been willing herself not to shed since her arrival came in a flood.

Wetly she blurted, 'Candice it was, my sister!'

Lucky Lulama wrapped an arm around Anna's shoulder.

'Cry,' she said. 'Let it come. Feel better.'

The pastor continued. 'Madam, I did not know she was your sister, I am sorry for your loss. Then you have more reason than most to hear me out. The neighbourhood is alive with gossip; when it is too unbelievable that a white man, and one who walks with a cane, would come to Mandela and kill one of our own then we must deduce a more obvious conclusion. This Zuko was with the poor girl that evening and ended the night with a cracked head. I do believe she already had facial injuries from an earlier beating.'

The two women tightened their embrace and listened carefully as the silent crowd closed in behind the pastor.

'Now, either we rise up as a community or we fall as a community,' he continued, a little louder now, meant for everyone. 'My duty, my vocation, is to lead all the shack dwellers and householders to a peaceful and safe life in the eyes of God. If that means running someone out of the township to achieve it, then so be it. But we need everybody's help, including those who may be sheltering him, or providing safe haven, however unwitting.'

The pastor and the women were now completely surrounded by the growing crowd.

'The community is with me, as you can see,' said Pastor Joshua. 'Do you understand?'

'I understand,' said Anna. 'We have our suspicions also about this bad man. But before you approach Zuko I need to know that the white will identify him as the man he saw that night.'

'Madam, you may continue as you please; indeed, it may help our case.'

Anna immediately sent a text message: "Come now to the community centre to identify the man who robbed you".

The crowd continued to grow steadily. Anna hoped the threatening weight of opinion would push Lucky Lulama into action, or at least agreement.

Lucky Lulama clucked again, then finally spoke.

'Pastor, I hear you, neh. Do you not think that we also want him locked up? But if I make my wishes known he will come for me with a vengeance, and *I* would have to leave the township. If I survived. This savage *tsotsi* is as unpredictable as a squatter camp fire.'

'Then we work together for the greater good. Agreed?'

Anna's cellphone beeped. She read the message, then wiped her eyes and licked her upper lip. 'Agreed.'

'Amen,' said Lucky Lulama.

The pastor turned to the now restless crowd and addressed them stirringly in isiXhosa, which drew sounds of defiance and a few cheers. It was quickly decided that Zuko had to be tackled by enough people that for his own well-being he would choose to move on. First, they had to corner him somewhere for a confrontation. Lucky Lulama suggested the shebeen was the obvious location as he would likely show up there soon enough.

XXI

Once the scene outside the Beauty Girl subsided, Anna took Lucky Lulama aside.

'The white man is coming now,' she said. 'He texted. I told him to stay hidden and pick out Zuko when he comes to the shebeen, then let me know by message if he recognises him. Until then, give me half an hour with Zuko. I must hear it from him that he killed my sister, and why.'

'Anything you ask you can have.'

Soon enough Zuko slinked out from the space between the Amazing Grace spaza and an abandoned car and, from a distance, followed Lucky Lulama back towards the shebeen. More mamas and old men than usual were on the street seeming to make conversation to cover the fact they were watching and waiting. Before entering the tavern Zuko tucked the cardboard box under his jacket and rinsed his face and bloody arm at the standpipe, then took a long drink. When he opened his eyes, Anna was standing before him.

'Have you heard the news on Jesus?' she asked.

'*Ja*, I know it. It was his own shit container balanced on concrete blocks. Who is to blame?'

Zuko pulled up the end of his T-shirt and dried his face.

'We must talk, Zuko, about the other matter.'

'Accept that Candy is passed, we have nothing more-more to say to each other.'

He spoke as if to end the conversation and walked on.

Anna's cellphone beeped and she read the message: "That's him."

She felt weak as she followed him to the shebeen door.

'I believe we have a common ground, Zuko. To find her killer.'

'Why do you look in the township for a white in a Benz? He will not return before Kingdom Come.'

'Perhaps we can work together to find him. Two should find him quicker than one. May we talk?'

'I am going in,' he said, gripping the door. 'It is lucky you are here. I have something for you.' He tapped his jacket.

She followed. The bar, dark and dirty, looked more threatening empty of customers than full. Lucky Lulama stepped behind the bar, put her fists on her hips with a forced air of innocence and looked from one to the other and back again.

'What a day!'

Zuko approached. 'Heineken.'

Two steps behind, Anna said, 'Water, please, gogo.'

'I will make you tea,' said Lucky Lulama, leaving for the back room.

Anna followed Zuko to the corner where she had spent New Year's Eve with Beauty and the musicians. They sat on two benches side by side separated by a shallow wooden barrier. If they leaned forward they could see each other; sitting back they faced the bar and could pretend they were alone. Alone or not, Anna was frightened in this hostile place, his refuge. Frightened of the conversation ahead of her, and frightened that he wouldn't talk. How to ask the first question? Simultaneously they both leaned forward. He took out the cardboard box from his jacket and placed it beside him on the bench.

He surprised Anna by asking, 'What is your story, sister?'

'You mean —'

'I mean when your story is written in a book, what will be remembered?'

Zuko, though apparently mocking, was allowing her to talk. That had to be a good thing.

'I was the first born, then Candice, we are two sisters only. I reached standard nine in school. I married a good man and gave him five children. I am satisfied in the Cederberg, but Candice wanted more. Like you, she was drawn to the city like buck to a waterhole, but I fear she did not find the happiness she wished for.'

'Who is happy?' he said.

'Despite my troubles, you are looking at a happy person.'

Lucky Lulama placed a mug of tea and a bottle of Heineken on the shared table then returned to the bar.

'You country people believe life is so easy,' he said. 'Pick a life and live it. Many of us without schooling have to take to get by.'

Anna responded with a look of disapproval.

'Why should we not take what we need?' he said. 'It is our time. Look down the valley to the houses in the rich neighbourhoods. That is my future.'

'A future stealing from others?' said Anna. 'No matter how much you fill your pockets you will still live in a shanty town.'

Anna knew she was pushing her luck; she may lose him altogether.

'Like me, you have no schooling,' she said, 'but the difference between us is you believe it holds you back. I don't. It is for you to write your story every day, as you say, like the book of your life.'

Zuko shuffled and crinkled his eyes. 'Let Jesus do the writing.' His face transformed into a smirk. 'Maybe not anymore.'

Anna closed her eyes and leaned back. The pulsing conversation made the tavern seem hotter. She looked directly ahead to the bar.

'I mean you can change your future if you choose, Zuko.'

'That's what I'm telling you, lady. Don't you listen? You have no idea what we go through in Mandela. Go back to the mountains and be happy with your donkey carts and rooibos and leave me to make my own way.'

'The reason I am still here is to find my two young cousins and learn what happened to my sister and bring her back to the Cederberg. A man is living with guilt in Cape Town. I wish to shed him of that guilt.'

'You think the man who killed her will thank you for that?'

'Together,' she said, leaning forward, 'together we can unearth this mystery.'

Zuko took a deep swig, held the beer in his mouth for a few seconds then swallowed loudly.

'Maybe we can discover another mystery. A mystery that is known by no one alive, except me. A mystery that lies buried in the Cederberg.'

The tavern was now airless as a vault. *He knows. He knows.*

'You say you were mother to five children, but we both know it was six,' he said. 'Candice told me about the dead infant when we first met, and begged me never to tell. I have not repeated it until now. It was the reason she left you and her life on the veld. It pained her to say it, but she said you were wicked.'

Exhaustion flooded through her.

'We are closer than you think, *sisi*. You sent an infant to its grave – and dug it – for your convenience, your disappointment. Did you not feel God was punishing you with a snow boy child?'

'It is not for you to judge me,' said Anna.

'I am not judging. I am reminding you that we all carry guilt. Something we would change if we could.'

For ten years Anna had kept her secret in a sealed compartment. Even Jakobus never mentioned it. It felt sordid to be talking of her first born in a tavern with such a man. And yet now seemed the moment to unburden herself.

'I have suffered with my shame,' she said. 'Yes, shame. I was ashamed of my child. And I have been ashamed of myself ever since.'

'My people call them *isishawa*, cursed; cripple by another name.' He sneered. 'Did you sell the body parts for muti?'

She felt pain in every muscle and sinew. Her coiled stomach felt raw. It was her turn to think. She had rehearsed the words of her confession for years yet she wasn't ready for this.

'I was still a teenager and dreamed of a wonderful life, and that included perfect children. I could not bear it that God sent me an albino infant. Was he testing or punishing me? Did he want me to suffer for misdeeds in a past life? The child, a boy, was born at home with only his father and my mother in attendance.'

Anna replayed in her mind the difficult birth, the crying, the shock realisation of what she had created. She now sobbed for the infant.

'Nobody else knew the truth. I was frightened he would be abducted and sold to sangomas. He was born very sickly and may have died as a babe anyway... I know that is no excuse for destroying one of God's children, but if people knew where he was buried they may have dug up his body to make muti. Some say such a child is proof of a profane union, so others may have accused us of marrying within the family.'

There was another pause. The only sounds were Lucky Lulama stacking beer bottles and the thump of distant music from a crackly speaker. A loose window screen somewhere banged. Anna expected to feel lighter, unburdened after sharing her secret, but she didn't. She was overwhelmed with guilt and wanted someone to hold her.

'How are *you* guilty?' she asked. 'Earlier, you said we all carry guilt.'

Another pause.

'Tell me,' she said, leaning back. 'We can share our secrets and ask for forgiveness together.'

She felt like she was tuning an instrument, tightening strings, afraid they might break.

Zuko let out a sigh that turned into an elaborate throat-clearing. He spat a dirty gob on the floor.

'Can a child commit a sin?' he asked. 'Can a child commit a terrible deed and be responsible, even though it saved two people from lives of misery?'

Anna did not expect the conversation to go in such a direction. An air of revelation hung thick in the space between them like a prayer.

'An innocent must be forgiven, Zuko. Sometimes children make dreadful mistakes.' She allowed him a moment to think. 'Did you commit a terrible sin when you were a child?'

'What if I did? I have not paid for it. I have not suffered.'

'O, but you have, Zuko. I know how you have suffered.'

'You are a bad woman, and –' he squinted, as if weighing up the wisdom of finishing the sentence, '– I was a bad child.'

'I feel your pain,' she said.

'I feel your guilt,' he replied.

Another silence as Anna blinked rapidly at the ceiling. The shebeen remained empty, Anna willing the door to stay closed until she got what she came for.

From behind the barrier, he said, 'A child kills a mother; a mother kills a child. We are two very different, and maybe the difference is the reason for our sin. When I left Ma under the pillow, I promised myself a future. My sin had a purpose: my freedom. I am not guilty; I am free. You are trapped forever.'

'Did you push the pillow into your ma's face?' she asked.

His silence told her that he did.

'In the eyes of God, Zuko, murder is murder. Thou shalt not kill.'

'It is only murder if you are found out,' he said.

'You will be found by God.'

'He left me a long time ago.'

'But surely you must struggle to live with your actions,' she said.

'As you do? I cope with it by not thinking about it.'

'Have courage,' she said.

He snorted.

'Ask anyone in this neighbourhood who they fear most. I have the courage of a lion.'

'I don't mean fearlessness, I mean the courage to admit you sin before God, the courage to say what you desire in life and failing before all. Courage is knowing the size of the mountain ahead of you and carrying on anyway.'

Anna stretched forward and took a sip of tea before leaning back into her seat. It had become a curious conversation, or not just a conversation but rather a deep form of communication played out in a place accessible only to them, from where it was possible to withdraw in a blink whenever they wished to return to the here and now. They had already reached unexpected territory. But at least Zuko was talking, conversing as opposed to snarling veiled threats. She pushed still further.

'Do you dream of her?' she asked.

She thought of Candice and heaved a dry sob. He remained silent.

'You watched your mother die under your own hands. You cannot forget that.'

'I think of her,' he said. 'Sometimes. But I cannot remember her face, it has become distant in my —'

She waited a beat then leaned forward, but when she saw his wet eyes she darted back. Lucky Lulama was noisily busy in the back, which gave them both a minute to compose themselves.

Zuko wiped a sleeve across his face and nose. 'I look back and it feels like remembering the life of a different person, like watching it on TV or, ha!, like reading a book. If I could bring her back I would.'

'You wish to make amends?' she asked.

'What is that?'

'Even though you commit a sin, a person can make amends by doing good for someone else. The minister in my village has a word for it, that I cannot now recall. It is meant to prove that you are not all bad, a sign that good still lives inside no matter how black the heart may seem.'

A fierce gust of wind shook the Lucky Strike and a window slammed open, which brought in the low, pressing thrum of the gathering crowd on the street: the shuffle of feet on the sandy earth, urgent murmurs, the creak of makeshift doors. Still no one entered the tavern. Anna feared what might happen before she reached the question she was here to ask. She could sense the gathering storm, but Zuko seemed unaware of everything except their conversation.

'I entered a house in the valley yesterday,' he said. 'You said I would not want to live like the rich whites, so I went to see what I was missing.'

'I didn't mean you to —'

'No harm was done. It was quiet. The house had a room full of books. I have never seen so many.'

'Like a library?'

'I have never been to a library.'

'So.'

Zuko recalled this morning flicking through the pages of the blue book, the edges purple with his blood.

'They say you can learn a lot from books. What would I know if I had read them?'

'The knowledge of the world,' she said.

He conjured up one of the full-page pictures, a line drawing of two boys pickpocketing an old man.

'Could those books return to me what I have lost?' he said, stroking the page in his mind. 'You are not the only one to miss your sister. Could they teach me how to bring back the touch of her fingers in the morning? Or the painful wait for her to arrive home from the tavern? Or the joy of lying on the dry earth and imagining a new life in the stars?'

'Books are books,' she said softly, 'life is life.'

Zuko's reflective mood left a hanging pause that needed filling. Now was the time to ask directly about Candice. Anna had to know from his own lips. She leaned forward, about to speak, but unexpectedly Zuko was holding out the battered Noxzema box.

'I have no use for these,' he said, handing over the envelopes, 'I cannot read the words. They were your sister's, and you should have them.'

Anna sifted through the stack of unopened letters, every one addressed to her. She gasped. On the back of each envelope was a date, the earliest of which was the week Candice left the Cederberg. The most recent was December 17th, a week before Anna arrived in Cape Town.

'What do they say?' he asked.

'It will take time to read them all. It seems Candice wrote to me but did not post the letters.'

'Does she write about me?'

'Probably,' she said.

'Then you will know the whole story.'

'Letters from beyond the grave.'

'I wish I had the same,' he said.

'From your ma?'

'From both. Without them I am like a lost dog, never to return home.'

The confessional atmosphere was disturbed by the raw sound of a siren. Anna sensed that life on the street outside was speeding up. There was running, distant shouts. The thump of bass-heavy music stopped.

'Shack fire,' said Zuko, idly.

'Can you smell it?' she asked.

'Not yet, but I know the signs. It is a good time for my kind. People run to help put out the fire but leave their own homes unlocked.'

'Someone has kicked over a braai,' she suggested, hoping to return to the question that was searing through her.

'Or a cooker,' said Zuko.

The words triggered something in him. He stepped up to the door and looked out into the dark. From her seat Anna could see the low cloud reflecting a muted orange.

'What is it, Zuko?'

'It is my quarter.'

He ran.

By the time Zuko reached the fire, his neighbourhood was in uproar. Shacks were ablaze, smoke billowed from every window and door, flimsy walls were collapsing to the screech of warping tin roofs. People – whether shack dwellers or passing opportunists – were stripping homes of everything they could carry. Unattended infants were everywhere screaming into the yellowed night. The smoke obliterated everything beyond the first line of homes along the road, including his shack which was in the centre of the flames. A fire truck stopped fifty metres away, from where hoses were quickly rolled out.

'Mosa! Mandisa!' yelled Zuko.

'There are girls in there?' shouted a firefighter.

'My girls!'

'Stay back.'

Zuko approached the flames but was repelled by the heat and smoke. A screaming figure came to his side. It was Mandisa.

'Mosa is there!' she screamed. 'God save my sister!'

Anna arrived, breathless. 'Is it you, cousin Mandisa?' she asked in Afrikaans.

'How do you know, mama?'

'I am your cousin, sister to Candice from the Cederberg.'

Mandisa broke down and buried her face in Anna's shoulder. 'O, Candice, Candice!'

'Is Mosa in the fire?'

'Yes, cousin. I went to town for food. I should not have left her. She is helpless.'

Zuko looked at the two cousins in turn and weighed up his options.

A firefighter turned the nozzle on the hose and a great rush of water soaked them all.

'We'll do our best to get her out,' he said.

'No, I go,' said Zuko.

He zipped his leather jacket up over his nose and ran between two blazing shacks. He hardly recognised his own neighbourhood with all the familiar markers now either burning or caved in. He jumped over fallen tin roofs, which buckled and swayed under his trainers, then he slipped and fell onto a blackened, smouldering couch that had already been doused by the fire hose. He got up, filthy now, and picked his way towards his shack, which had imploded like a half-slumped house of cards. The purple curtains were burning on their tracks like flaming flags. It was the saddest thing he had ever seen. He pushed at the burning door and lifted away red-hot sections of corrugated roof, burning his hands. Flames singed his hair and he could soon smell his jacket melting. The back wall of his shack had caved in, collapsing the roof at a precarious angle against the opposite wall. It was possible Mosa could still be alive underneath. He calculated that if he kicked in his front door the whole structure might fall, so he pushed in the wooden shutter covering a window, hoping to force his way through the metal bars. But each kick of the bars made the structure ever more hazardous. He ran to the other side of the shack and ripped off a section of burning plywood, just enough to crawl through. One of the iron roofing sheets had collapsed into the room and the flames were being drawn skywards through the hole. The shelves holding his pots and pans had fallen on top of the two-ring stove, which, together with the sagging back wall, created a fierce bonfire around the propane gas bottle. His eyes were drawn to a curious burning strip on the floor alongside the couch: the walking stick was aflame and the golden lion's head shimmered. Next to it, the book was already incinerated, the flaking pages borne into the air one by one like black angels.

Mosa, eyes open, looked both serene and terrified. Prepared for her fate.

'I am sorry,' said Zuko. 'I will not abandon you.'

He thrust himself into the inferno that engulfed the couch and picked up the girl's contorted, searing body. The propane bottle beside them hissed for two seconds, then exploded.

XXII

The fire, the worst anyone could remember in the Cape, was finally brought under control the following evening. Whenever the fire service believed it was doused, an overlooked pocket of embers would reignite and burn fiercely until the firehoses could reach. Zuko and Mosa were two of four casualties to die in the fire, which city officials declared 'a miracle' considering the devastation. Electricity was cut, roads were impassable, water was scarce. For a month, in both the black and white neighbourhoods, aimless figures carrying ragged bags and blankets wandered the streets of Hout Bay like so many dazed refugees. Some squeezed into shacks that survived the fire and waited for the authorities to deliver shack packs. At night, many who could find no shelter took to the mountain with their salvaged goods, afraid to leave them unattended. Many people who did not lose their homes in the fire lost possessions to looters who emerged like cockroaches every evening after dark. Nobody was challenged. Little Mabhuti and Jonno took advantage of every opportunity.

Despite an incident that produced so many losers, there were some winners. One such, Sunday Johnson, cash to hand, made his presence felt among the ruins. As the newly destitute waited for the municipality to come to their aid, he parked his Audi 4x4 at the limit of the tarred road before the embers had cooled and, with calculated largesse, provided materials for the homeless to build their own shacks on plots he now adopted as his own. Within three days he was receiving rent on a dozen shacks. He then sat back and assumed the largely unappreciated role of slum landlord.

A week later the container salon was still agape. Because of the crazy angle at which it had come to rest, it was impossible to shut the doors so not even a makeshift business could take up residence. Nevertheless, settled as it was, the salon was now more stable than it had been for years. No more swaying when people stepped in. Pastor Joshua made the most of the shrine-like space, now an ugly symbol of the township's sins, by using the empty shell as a satellite location for his God is Good Evangelical Church. The pastor knew that a corner had been turned when Jesus, the ends of his arms still wrapped in thick bandages, came to pray. When the bandages came off, he could be found reading library books to children at Sunday school, turning the pages with his stumps.

What of the lame man who drove a Benz and risked his life to be with a coloured girl, who, the gods might suggest, was predominantly responsible for the chain of events that affected so many lives? His life continued as before, except he never again set foot in the township. The police quietly dropped the investigation into the young prostitute's death, such as it was. They did not interview the white with the limp; there was no need for him to officially identify the body of the *tsotsi* with the wounds on his neck and head and scars on both arms. The experience made Clive wonder if his wife had a point after all – let them live their lives and we'll live ours.

The Lucky Strike was now home to stunned, quietened customers. Following the fire there was less neighbourhood money for beer and girls as regulars spent all their spare cash putting their lives back together. Lucky Lulama cleaned out the shack behind the shebeen and set up a rudimentary salon. She bought two chairs, an unplumbed sink, some basic tools and a large mirror. Beauty rented the space and paid off the equipment week by week until she owned everything. She couldn't forget the girl that came from the Cederberg with the barbershop dream, so she paid someone to erect a sign: "The Candy Shack Salon".

With cousin Mandisa in tow, Anna returned to Kouberg with the bodies of Candice and Mosa. She also carried her sister's letters, which contained every detail of her life with Zuko, at the Lucky Strike, and her dream of opening a container salon. But that was not the most pressing story she would take home. Anna claimed to know the difference between what was right and what was wrong, and she now admitted to herself that once in her life she had been wrong, abominably wrong, and despite shutting the episode into a closed cell, she acknowledged that she had carried her guilt for ten years like a depraved trophy. As a way of returning her first born to her thoughts, in the moments before sleep each night she summoned an image of what the child might look like now, the eldest of her six children. It helped her sleep more soundly.

Confessing to Zuko was like having a tooth pulled: the pain was sharp but the healing could now begin. Somehow the pursuit of her sister's killer and all the other experiences in Mandela Park prepared her to face the consequences of her sin that had festered since she buried the pale infant with the blue eyes at Bushman's View. She had explained it to Zuko in the shebeen, so why could she not now testify to the police, her extended family, Pastor Johannes? Kouberg would punish or ostracise Anna as the village elders saw fit, but she looked forward to the time when she didn't shoulder the secret alone. Until then she would do everything she could to remind people that she was not all bad, as some say.

END

If you have enjoyed this Inkstand Press book
please tell your friends and mention *Mandela Park* on
social media.

Follow
Facebook: Alan Whelan Author
Twitter: @ACWhelan
Web: www.alanwhelan.co.uk

....

Other titles from Inkstand Press

THE BLACK STARS OF GHANA by Alan Whelan

EMPIRE ROAD by Alan Whelan

TELEGRAM FROM MANDALAY by Will Cribb